...EVER WANTED
...r Love Novels: Book One

...OWL PRESS
...cityowlpress.com

Copyright ©2016 by Katrina Mills

Cover Design by Tina Moss. All stock photos licensed
appropriately.

For information on subsidiary rights, please contact the
publisher at info@cityowlpress.com.

Print Edition ISBN: 978-0-9862516-5-8
Digital Edition ISBN: 978-1-5242196-6-6

Printed in the United States of America

Mills,
Katrina

He pushed off the partition with a gigantic smile and slid into her space. At most he was a foot away from her, so close that she could feel his breath on her lips. "Nice to see you didn't lose your spunk." He tapped her on the nose with his pointer finger, a move he had done frequently when they were friends so very long ago. It used to aggravate the hell out of her because it was such a tease. You could barely call it a touch, and she used to want to be touched by him so badly.

Praise for the Works of Katrina Mills

"Katrina Mills gets an A+ with her debut novel, ALL I EVER WANTED! Teachers everywhere are going to put down their red pens and fall in love with this sexy tale. Romance does not get any better than this."

- VA School Administrator, Kelly Gwinn

"Katrina has hit her mark with this sexy story about a funny teacher, an old crush with rock solid guns for arms and an adorable Basset Hound. ALL I EVER WANTED is loaded with everything I ever needed."

- Author of TURNED INTO YOU, Cindy Dorminy

"ALL I EVER WANTED grabbed from the first sentence and had me hooked until the happily ever after. Funny, suspenseful, and sexy. Loved this book, love this author."

- VA Educator, Wenda Bransford

"A smart and sexy good time. ALL I EVER WANTED has it all from a second chance romance to quirky small town characters to one adorable pup. I can't wait for the next Summer Love novel!"

- Award Winning Author, Tina Moss

All I Eve[r]

KATRINA MILL[S]

A Summer Love Novel

CITY OWL
PRESS

This book [...]
incidents e[...]
used fictiti[...]
persons, l[...]
by the au[...]

ALL I [...]
Summe[...]

CITY [...]
www[...]

All [...]
Co[...]
rep[...]
m[...]
p[...]

With much love and appreciation to Laurie Lyon Duke,

Wenda Bransford, and Kelly Gwinn,

Your critiques and support of my manuscript when it was

merely a creative hobby inspired strength and unbreakable

determination to get my story out into the world.

You are forever angels in my eyes.

- Katrina

Prologue

Kinsley Elizabeth Bailey was going to be murdered one week before her thirty-fourth birthday. At least that's what the old gypsy woman sporting a hairy upper lip and bad body odor told her at the fairgrounds. It was mid-August 1993, when a dirty blonde, blue-eyed girl sat in a folding chair across from the scariest woman in Virginia and heard her fortune. Considering the macabre matter of the prediction, it was more like a misfortune.

Kinsley usually wasn't interested in psychic abilities, nor did she believe in palm reading or the validity of hypnosis. Occasionally, she would ask her Magic Eight Ball a question or two, but after getting several consecutive rounds of 'Better Not Tell You Now,' she labeled it all as garbage and switched its sole purpose to a functioning paperweight. She would have much rather spent her ten dollars playing *Toss the Ring* and purchasing a couple more bags of cotton candy. In fact, she was on her way to the food truck with her cousin, Nicole, when Madam Zerina popped out of her tent and jumped in front of her like the Boogey-Man. She was pretty speedy for looking so brittle.

A scarf, patterned with turquoise and gold, wrapped around her head and two angry eyebrows that could double as Woolly Bear caterpillars poked out underneath. Her skin was as thin and translucent as papyrus paper, with bright blue veins weaving close to the surface. A long maroon dress embroidered with gold stitching, depicting some sort of tribal symbols, ended mere inches above the ground. "Ju! I could tell ju were coming hours ago! I see it in my tea leaves. Ju come in my tent. Ten dollars and Madam Zerina will tell you everything ju need to know…and believe me…ju need to know this. Come!" She opened up the flap on her small white tent and motioned Kinsley inside.

Kinsley peered at her cousin, who was trying her hardest to deal with the poor decision of buying a candied apple in the dead of August. Summer in Fredericksburg was hotter than the brass hinges of hell. Nicole should have gotten a giant glass of lemonade instead of an apple whose candy coating now made the fruit appear to be hemorrhaging.

Every August, Kinsley went to the Fredericksburg Agricultural Fair with her cousin. And yes, it was as glamorous as it sounded. In temperatures hot enough to choke a goat, local farmers and businesses set up shop at the fairgrounds right off Airport Avenue. Residents arrived in droves to watch sheep shearing competitions, tractor pulls, ride the circular carnie rides that were sure to make you puke, and see who would be crowned Miss Fredericksburg.

Kinsley didn't mind being sent away so much. Her parents split up about five years earlier, and she didn't have any siblings to tend. Her Dad moved only a few neighborhoods away, but had very little to do with Kinsley or her mother. To cope with her misery of abandonment, her mother shipped her off to her Aunt Janice's for about a month during the summer for exposure to a 'normal family unit.' Nicole was around her age so it wasn't a total drag.

Two summers ago, the girls were finally deemed old enough to walk around without adult supervision. This life altering decision was just in the nick of time. Having recently turned thirteen, the girls were developing more of an interest in the boys who were cruising the fairgrounds rather than riding the Tilt-a-Whirl. But instead of attracting a hunk who could double for Jason Priestly, Kinsley got the attention of an old woman with arthritic fingers that smelled like a fart. *Typical.*

"Um… thank you ma'am, but I don't believe in fortune telling," Kinsley tried to refuse as politely as possible. No matter how loony the lady appeared, it was still scary to tell a gypsy you thought her profession was a bunch of hokum. Especially if it was in fact a real thing. She might curse her with a zit the size of Vesuvius.

"Ju don't believe?" she asked, crossing her arms in front of her chest. "Fine, I give ju a taste. A nibble, on de house." She placed her pointer fingers on the temples of her forehead with her thumbs under her jaw and closed her eyes. A low grumbling sounded in her chest, signifying intense concentration or a bad case of congestion. The two cousins glanced at one another out of the corners of their eyes, waiting for some generic debunk statement to come spitting out of Madam Zerina's mouth.

Suddenly, her eyes shot open, and she squinted at Kinsley. "You two need to stay out of dat man's beaver magazines! Young ladies do not look at de nudie pictures." Both of the girls' eyes got as wide as saucers. Kinsley was expecting her to say something about having a crush on a boy or her lucky number being seven. All those things would be plausible for any girl close to her age. But this was spot on…and horrifically embarrassing.

Nicole tried to argue. "Listen lady, I don't know what your damage is…" Poor Nicole had been trying to work in quotes from the movie *Heathers* ever since her seventeen-year-old babysitter told her she could watch it if she didn't tell her parents . She had also started wearing a lot of red. Leaning in closer to Madam Zerina, she whispered, "We would never look at girly magazines!"

If this lady had any real talent with psychic powers, she would know right away that Nicole was lying. Two days earlier, the girls had been rummaging through the garage, trying to find some of Nicole's older video games when their plans to go to the pool were shortchanged by an afternoon storm. They didn't find any Nintendo games, but they did find older copies of Playboy, Hustler, and even an annual subscription to 'Big-Boobed Babes.' Being inquisitive preteens, they spent the next three hours digging through the magazines. They didn't feel like lezbos or anything, there were men in them too. Plus, it was kind of nice to see what they might look like as adults when everything stopped changing around so much. And now, here they were in the middle of Fredericksburg Agricultural Fair being accosted by a gypsy about their curiosities.

"I know what I saw! But if ju want to argue…fine. I give one more. A big one. Then you promise to come in, pay, and let me read jur cards. Eh?" She rubbed her hands together as if she was trying to start a fire. Kinsley and Nicole glanced at each other, and then at Madam Zerina. "Okay!" she said clapping her hands together. She again put her pointer fingers on her temples and her thumbs below her jaw. She only had to close her eyes for a split second before she opened them. "Da boy, S...S...well, his name start with S! Ju like him. Ju want to make kissy faces and de knicky-knacky."

Kinsley was about to walk away. *This lady is full of it.* She didn't want to make kissy faces or knicky-knacky with anyone whose name started with an S. But then something registered and Kinsley froze. "Wait a minute. S?"

The corners of Madam Zerina's smile slithered up to her ears, revealing two missing K9 teeth. She leaned back victoriously in her chair, as pleased as if she had just predicted the winning lottery numbers. *How did she know?* Kinsley hadn't even told Nicole about kissing Bastian (aka Sebastian) and the big fat nothing that came out of it.

"So ju ready to come in and I read for you? Ten dollars is bargain." She again lifted the flap leading into the tent. Kinsley reached into her pocket and took out a ten-dollar bill.

"Kins, are you seriously going to do this?" Nicole put her hand on Kinsley's arm, trying to stop her from entering the tent.

"Yes. Please come in with me," she begged. Kinsley didn't want to go in there alone.

"Ju throw dat messy thing away before you come into my tent. People think I stuck pig, and it bleed all over de place." Nicole spotted a trashcan on the other side of Madam Zerina's tent, and the two girls followed the hunched over old woman inside. A metal folding table with an aged decorated cloth sat in the middle of the tent. Luckily, the top of the tent had its roof removed. Coupled with a fan running on low, the tent was only slightly hotter than hell itself.

After holding Kinsley's ten-dollar bill up to the light for examination, Madam Zerina pocketed the money and motioned for the two girls to sit on the opposite side of the table. She pulled out a deck of cards and started shuffling. "I have good power of my own. I can see things from past and present, but I need cards to read de future. Spirits tell me I feel great disturbance as de chosen passed my tent. Right before you walk by, I let out great big belch."

Nicole gasped. "Gross! That was your disturbance? A burp? Why don't you just give me ten dollars, Kins? I'll chug a root beer and try reading your fortune for you."

Kinsley shushed her cousin. "Shut up already. She knew about Sebastian." She turned her attention to the gypsy as the old woman laid the cards out on the table.

"Sebastian?" Nicole asked confused.

"Bastian. His real name is Sebastian…with an S. We all call him Bastian for short."

Madam Zerina squinted at Nicole. "Spirits don't always light de skies on fire to send signs. Sometimes de are smaller in magnitude." She began flipping over each card one at a time. After examining the picture, she closed her eyes and ran her hand over the card like you do to check if a burner is still hot.

Nicole knocked Kinsley's leg with her knee to get her attention. "What happened with Bastian?" Kinsley had wanted to tell her cousin about the night she harnessed every bit of bravery she could muster and kissed him. She had been in love with one of her best friends for almost two years and finally decided to do something about it three months ago. She thought she made the right choice when he reciprocated and they proceeded to have a ten-minute make-out session next to a washing machine, but after that...nothing. No phone call, no declaration that she was the one. When she saw him in school that Monday, he acted as if nothing happened. They went on being friends like before, and Kinsley sat on the sidelines humiliated and heartbroken when he started going out with another girl.

"Quiet!" Madam Zerina stared at them with one eye open. "In order for me to read clearly, I need quiet!"

Kinsley gulped.

"Okay, what ju want to know first?"

Taking a breath, Kinsley placed her hands on the table and leaned in. "Yeah, um the boy...S...Sebastian. Why didn't that go anywhere?"

"Cards do not help me see feelings or thoughts of others. Cards help only with visions of what is to come with the chosen one. That is why I get ju. Spirits need ju to know what is ahead."

"Okay then. Will Sebastian and I go out? Do you see that?" Hearing her mention Sebastian earlier was the sole reason she went into the damn tent. This old hag was going to tell her something she wanted to hear about him.

"Ju and this boy are not destined to be boyfriend and girlfriend." Kinsley's shoulders slumped a little. Even though she already knew it in the most hidden parts of her subconscious, it didn't make the news any easier to take. They were only ever going to be friends, and she wasn't sure how much longer she could keep it up. Her heart ached every time she saw him.

"Do not worry about dis boy. Ju have many exciting things to come." She pointed to the first card with an image of a woman holding a book. "Ju smart girl. Too smart to worry about the 'S' boy. Ju will go to school and be very successful." That sounded nice to Kinsley, but truth be told, her thirteen-year-old mind was still more interested in Sebastian than in going to college. That seemed so far away. She flipped over another card with the picture of a man standing on top of a boat rowing down a river. "Ju will have many travels. See many places. Enjoy life."

"Do you think she'll go to Los Angeles? I would totally come visit you if you moved to LA," Nicole interrupted.

"Quiet ju! Ju anger spirits. Important message coming next." Madam Zerina flipped over the last card in the row. The card had the silhouette of a body lying on the ground with a knife sticking out of its chest. The old gypsy woman quickly covered her mouth and flipped the card back over.

That can't be good.

"What is it?" Kinsley asked, alarmed.

Madam Zerina snatched the remaining cards from the table and started reshuffling. She shook her head 'no', that she would not be revealing the explanation of the last card.

"Tell me! Or you can give me back my ten dollars!" Sweat trickled down Kinsley's neck. Her shoulder length hair stuck to the sides of her face.

Madam Zerina peered up from the deck. "I know why spirits want me to read for ju. A warning. A sign." The color drained out of Kinsley's face.

"Come on, Kins. This woman is a few fries short of a Happy Meal." Nicole grabbed Kinsley's arm and tried to pull her up from the chair. She sat solid, unmoving.

"What's the warning?"

"Seven days' time, before ju see ju thirty-fourth year, ju will be…" She ran her finger across her throat and made the slicing sound with her mouth.

"What?" Now Kinsley thought she was going to throw up. "Murdered? Like, killed? Are you serious? How? By who?" Nicole continued to try to pull Kinsley up, but she held on vigilantly to the folding table.

"This I do not see. I see only darkness around ju. But I can tell ju this, do not listen to the sound of the cicadas. Run to the star for safety. This all the spirits let me see."

"You're nuttier than squirrel crap, lady! I'm not staying in here one more minute, Kinsley. I'm going to ride the Ferris wheel." Nicole stormed out of the tent, leaving her alone with Madam Zerina.

She stood up from her chair and wiped her sweaty palms on her daisy print shorts. "Um, thank you." Typical Kinsley, always the polite girl, even to the crazy lady who tells you you're going to be snuffed out in less than three decades.

Madam Zerina sat with a stoic expression on her face. "You have de warnings spirits need you to see. Use dem; now go after de friend before she has de snit fit."

Kinsley ran to catch up with Nicole who was practically stomping towards the line for the Ferris wheel. "Would you wait up?"

"Seriously, Kinsley, you better forget what that old lunatic said, and you better spill the beans about what happened with Bastian while we're on the ride. I can't believe you've been staying with me for three whole weeks and you didn't tell me anything!"

Kinsley kicked a plastic cup on the ground. "There isn't anything to tell."

"I'll be the judge of that." The girls handed their tickets to the ticket collector and boarded the next available cart. They sat on opposite sides. "Okay, Kins. Out with it. I know you've been in love with this guy ever since you met him in sixth grade. Now fess up. What happened? I want details." Kinsley proceeded to divulge the PG rated events that occurred between her and Bastian, including her unfortunate return to friendville. "Well, you only have to spend one more year with the jerk. Then you said he's going to a different high school, right?"

"Yep. They built a new high school. He's zoned to go there."

"Good. You need to forget this guy. It's obvious he isn't the one and not just because that lunatic told you the same thing. It's really lousy what he did. He should have at least talked to you about it! That's what a real friend would have done."

The cart climbed to the top of the wheel and stopped to let old riders off and new riders on. Kinsley sat in the swinging cart, observing the fairgrounds. It was beginning to turn dusk and the sky was painted in layers of blue, gold, and orange. This whole afternoon was classic of her luck. Bastian was literally not in the cards for her, and now she was supposed to be murdered before she turned thirty-four. Her only clue about the event was a bunch of noisy bugs and a star.

Nicole kicked her in the shin to bring her out of her listless stare. "Kins, that old lady is crazy and a fake. Using the letter 'S' was a lucky guess. Lots of guys have that letter in their names. If she would have said the same thing to me, I probably would have thought she meant Chris because he has an 'S' in his name."

"Yeah, you're probably right." At least she hoped she was. She was probably more like a magician than a real fortune teller. Using the letter 'S' was just a coincidence. But what about mentioning the dirty magazines? That part was true, but with how embarrassing that whole ordeal was, she didn't exactly want to bring it up again. Would she be murdered one week before she turned thirty-four? She had the distinct feeling her Magic Eight Ball would say 'Better Not Tell You Now.'

Chapter One

Kinsley was sick and tired of dealing with the rats of the ocean harassing her for her picnic lunch. She was also getting pretty fed up with the group of twenty-somethings sitting ten feet away and laughing it up every time she got dive-bombed. Trying to handle the situation with a modicum of grace, she determined that ignoring their riotous laughter was the best way to deal with it. However, being the headliner of their beach comedy act was getting old pretty quick, and she was two minutes away from marching over there and kicking sand into their cooler of Michelob Ultras. Of course those skinny bitches would drink low carb beer.

If one more of those seagulls dives down for my Doritos, I am gonna get the Alka-Seltzer out of my purse and have a late Fourth of July Celebration.

She placed her giant straw hat on her head to make her invisible to anymore aerial attacks. How did her easy-going, independent day trip to the beach turn into getting dive-bombed by birds and a group of hecklers modeled after the cast of Jersey Shore? Kinsley folded up her bag of chips and put them in her huge turquoise bag. After reapplying another slathering of SPF 45, she grabbed her newest Janet Evanovich book and found her marker.

That was one thing Kinsley adored about summer vacations; she got to catch up on all her leisure reading. During the school year, she was either grading papers or reading whatever "Do This Method to Be a More Effective Teacher" piece of crap her principal was making them read in a book club. She had no time to enjoy the adventures and romances of popular authors from September to June. So even though she had an audience of assholes that were taking bets on when she would get crapped on by a bird, this book was her silver lining.

Kinsley glanced out of the corner of her eye at the posse of punks next to her. The girls took great care in lathering themselves up with baby oil, *you'll regret that one in about fifteen years*, and the boys were more than happy to help with the additional coatings. Kinsley glanced down at her sunned legs poking out of her black Vera Wang one-piece and shrugged. She could probably get away with wearing a bikini. Never having any kids, decent eating habits, and Pilates four times a week kept her body surprisingly svelte for a women getting ready to turn thirty-four. Yet a little cellulite and sagging could be expected in almost any woman after the age of thirty-three— unless you were Cher. Since tan fat was better than pasty fat, and she was only slightly bronzed, she'd just as soon keep her midriff covered.

She was beginning to read a particularly steamy scene between Stephanie Plum and Ranger, when she heard Ann Wilson of Heart pelting out the song "Alone," code for her cell was ringing. Digging through her bag, she found her phone tucked into one of her flip-flops. "Hey there, Delilah. You better not be calling to cancel our dinner again tonight. Monica and Diane already confirmed they're down for Plaza Del Torro."

Delilah, Monica, and Diane were Kinsley's team teachers at Rodney Edwards Middle School. Kinsley taught science, Delilah had math, Monica for history, and Diane covered English. They spent quite a bit of time together outside of school and sometimes argued like stepsisters.

"Ugh, karaoke again?" Delilah whined. "Can't we try going to McGilligan's Pub one more time? Diane has to face her fears at some point!"

Diane's refusal to patron McGilligan's Pub on Friday evenings was a result of an unfortunate incident between her ex-husband, Ross the Rat-bastard, and his secretary, Janis. During an unannounced visit to his work three years ago, Diane discovered his secretary taking shorthand in the buff. Her first sight upon entry into his office was Janis' nipples on two perky breasts. McGilligan's pub featured a twofer on buttery nipples every Friday night, which knocked its possibility as a watering hole out of the running.

"Last time we tried to make her go, she got so upset seeing the rubber nipples they stick on top of the shot glasses that she sat in the corner the whole night crying into her White Zinfandel," Kinsley argued. "I'm not talking her off the ledge again. So get your vocalizer ready."

"Fine, but if any preschoolers start making out again, I'm out," Delilah said.

Last time the four ladies went to Plaza on karaoke night, home of the four-dollar mango margarita, the sorority of Delta Omega Kappa decided to take advantage of the cheap tequila too. The four teachers had the rare privilege of an evening filled with off-key Taylor Swift songs and a sister on sister lip lock.

"Don't worry. All the part-time lesbian pop stars went home for summer break, so I think we're safe. What's up?"

"Just checked my work email. Word on the street is we need to have an electronic presentation for this year's open house."

Kinsley rolled her eyes. "Yuck, not it!" Every September there was some additional component being placed on them for the beginning of the year dog and pony show. Regardless of how packed your presentation was, or if fifty future classmates were around, some parent always cornered you to talk about their child's bladder issues or need for creative outlet in the classroom.

"Me neither. We'll make Monica do it. She's the youngest; she's got the energy for it."

"Sounds logical to me." Kinsley relaxed into her lounger chair. She didn't want to talk about school yet. She had a couple more weeks before she had to return, and she was certain it was sacrilegious to talk about work when you were in front of the ocean, basking in the sun's rays. She could get used to living like this permanently. The only thing that yanked her out of this moment of contentment was the giant, wet, slimy pile of bird crap landing on her right thigh. "Ah, shit!" The crew of kids immediately started laughing and high-fiving. Apparently, the blond girl with a tramp stamp above her hot pink bikini bottoms won the bet because a couple of sons of bitches handed her five bucks.

"What?" Delilah asked concerned.

"I just got shit on by a seagull, sweetie. I gotta go. See you tonight." Kinsley hung up her phone and grabbed a spare towel out of her bag. She tried frantically to wipe off the bird poop, but it was a mucusy mess.

What the hell did this bird eat?

She took her beach towel down to the water and dampened it. After she had successfully wiped most of it off, she figured that was her cue to pack up and head home. Walking back up to her spot, she wrapped up the towel so the bird poop wasn't on the outside and folded her lounger chair.

Before heaving all her items across the sand to the parking lot, she peered over at where the scum-suckers had been sitting. When they saw her shoot up out of her seat to clean the bird crap, they had all taken off down to the water and dived in. She must have resembled a woman on the edge, but what they couldn't tell by her grossed out facial expression and flailing arms was that she was also very creative.

Kinsley got her Doritos bag and walked calmly over to where the fuckwads' things were lying on the sand. After opening the bag, she began sprinkling cheesy tortillas all over their towels, bags, and baby oil. Once the contents were thoroughly scattered and the flock of birds circling, she hurried back to her beach gear and sprinted towards her car. When she looked back, about fifty birds were dancing around on top of their towels, devouring the chips. Her main goal was to get them to poop all over it, but if they merely aggravated the living sin out of the crap-weasels, her mission would be a success.

Kinsley used her key fob to roll down the windows on her BMW so her face wouldn't melt off when she got in. Tossing her bag and beach chair in the trunk and sliding into her leather driver's seat set her thighs on fire. Her BMW M6 Coupe was not a typical car for a science teacher who wasn't married to a rich man or didn't have a sugar daddy, but prior to teaching she had worked as an engineer for a giant shipbuilding corporation. She got to travel all over the world and made one hell of a salary, but she traded it all for a rewarding career—depending on which day you asked her—teaching middle school. Luckily, she had smartly invested most of her income so she didn't have the financial troubles that usually coexisted with a career in education.

She turned on the engine and cranked up the A/C. Pulling off her big floppy hat, she flipped down the visor to examine her face in the mirror. The sun hadn't bleached out her color job too badly. Kinsley had the unfortunate genetic disposition of her mother and started getting gray hairs around the age of thirty. Never having a conceited nature, she let the grays take over and kept her hair chopped up to her chin. However, Monica, being a fashionista twenty-something, told her she couldn't stand her doubling as Edna Mode from *The Incredibles* anymore. Monica hauled her to a salon for a color job and an optometrist for Lasik eye surgery. Now her hair rested below her shoulders and eggplant colored tones masked her silver strands.

Despite the SPF applications, Kinsley had gotten some sun. She always tanned easily, even when using high-leveled sun block. She backed out of the parking spot and began to head down the main road that ran parallel to the beach. Luckily, she was just in time to see the Justin Bieber-Wanna-Be's trying to shoo away all the birds.

"Revenge is better than Christmas, assholes!" she yelled. It probably would have had more of an effect if she had rolled down the window so they could hear it. But it was still satisfying.

Traffic on the bridges in Hampton Roads was always torture this time of year. People visiting for vacations, locals going to and coming from work, and nitwits that didn't know how to drive clogged everything up worse than a toilet at a frat house. Kinsley sat in traffic, clicking repeatedly on her radio presets, when she heard Ann Wilson again. She grabbed her cell and saw a 540 area code. That was in Virginia, but she didn't recognize the number. She turned the volume down on the radio. "Hello?"

"Hello? Kinsley?" The voice belonged to an older female.

"Yes, speaking. Who is this?"

"Oh, Kinsley. Thank goodness. This is your Aunt Debbie." The caller waited a few moments and then clarified, "I'm the second wife of your dad's brother Jim that passed about seven years ago?" She ended her statement with a pitch that made it sound like more of a question. Kinsley didn't speak to her father's side of the family. After leaving her mother, he made the decision to divorce Kinsley too. When her mother died four years ago, he had the nerve to move back into her house because she never got around to taking his name off the deed. Her mother's mental illness was so overwhelming at times, she often didn't take care of what she needed to.

"Yes, Aunt Debbie. What can I do for you?" Kinsley couldn't think of anything she could do for that side of the family. She had written them off years ago, especially when they supported her father using a technicality to take over her mother's house.

"Sweetheart, I am calling to let you know that your father passed away yesterday." It didn't matter that she was in standstill traffic. Even if she had been doing ninety down the interstate, she wouldn't have needed to slow down or pull over. The only feeling she had regarding him, dead or alive, was indifference.

"Oh, that's a shame. How did he pass?" Stick with formalities.

"He had a heart attack mowing his lawn."

"Impossible. You have to have a heart to have a heart attack. Plus, don't you mean mowing my mother's lawn?" Her hands tightened on the steering wheel.

"Now listen here, Kinsley, I'm not calling to argue. I am calling to let you know he's not with us anymore, and the funeral will be in three days."

She sucked her teeth. "Oh, gee. That's too bad. I have to work." She didn't need to go to his funeral. He should have wanted her around when he was still alive. The only time she saw him after she turned eight was when he drove through town in his police cruiser.

"I thought you were a teacher now. Aren't you off for the summer?"

Drats.

"Yeah, but I have a summer job. I'm doing scientific research on the effects of processed foods on the digestive tracks of seagulls. It's all very scientific and I can't get away. Sorry you had to waste your time calling." She pulled the phone away from her ear to hang up, but Debbie's high-pitched hollering on the other end made her stop.

"That isn't it missy! I was going through your father's papers in his house to find out what his last wishes for arrangements were. I'm the executor of his estate. You need to come home." How dare she sound so pushy with her! Maybe if she had used that tone with her father to encourage his involvement in his daughter's life, he wouldn't have earned the Worst Dad of the Year Award over twenty consecutive times!

"Why?" She didn't care if they stuck him in a pine box and covered him in horse manure. She wasn't going to that funeral.

"He left the house to you. You need to come to Staunton for the reading and to figure out what you want to do with the house," a deliberate pause from Aunt Debbie, and then she added, "After you attend the funeral of course."

Kinsley sat motionless as if a bee were about to sting her cheek. She couldn't have heard that correctly. Why would a man she hadn't spoken to in over two decades—except when she called him a heinous son of a bitch after he legally stole her mother's house—leave her that house in his will? He was a greedy bastard.

"Hello? You still there?"

"Yes, I'm here. Are you sure you have this right, Aunt Debbie? I haven't spoken to Mitch in years. I doubt he would leave me that house."

"Mitchell, your father, left it to you. I read it with my own two eyes. Now, you may not have been able to make peace with your old man because of what he done, but he sure as heck was apparently trying to make peace with you." She could almost see Aunt Debbie's finger wagging. "You find a way to get a couple days off from them birds you claim to be working with and get your kiester up here for the services and the reading. You can stay in your father's house on account of my guest room is being used by my god son, Henry."

"You mean I can stay in my *mother's* house," she corrected.

"Well, if you want to get all persnickety, it's *your* house. Key will be in the fake rock by the holly bush next to the garage door. I'll stop by on Sunday. That gives you two days to make sure you're there and to give you Petunia."

"Petunias? He left me flowers?"

"No, Petunia is his dog. She was willed to you too. I don't care what your father done or didn't do. When a man passes, you show your respect whether you think he deserves it or not. Don't be an ingrate."

What the fuck? Seriously? He left her a dog? She couldn't take care of a dog! She barely kept the algae alive in the science tanks at school. "I don't want his dog and can't take care of one either. Can't anyone else in the family take her?"

"Since it isn't my dog to give away, I haven't asked anyone if they want her. The dog is legally yours. If you want to give her away or take her to a shelter, you're the one that needs to do it."

Getting crapped on by a seagull, and metaphorically crapped on by her dad's dead brother's wife, all in one sitting was not part of her independent beach day plans. She didn't want to go to Staunton; it was like a time capsule of bad memories. The one instant she had been back home in the past thirteen years was when her mother passed away. She had wanted to be buried in Thornrose Cemetery next to her mother, so Kinsley felt obligated to hold the services there. Other than that, her mother had always come to Newport News to visit her. She even lived with Kinsley the last month of her life because there were better hospitals in Hampton Roads.

But if she didn't go now, she would have to deal with the legality of that house sooner or later, and now there was a damn dog she had to fiddle with too. School started up in a little less than a month. Putting it off wasn't an option. No matter what, she was going to have to deal with it. "Alright, I'll be there by Sunday."

"You sure someone else will be able to track the seagulls'

droppings?" Aunt Debbie asked, sarcasm dripping like sweat.

"I'm sure they'll manage without me. I'll see you Sunday evening. Bye, Aunt Debbie." So Mitchell decided to kick the bucket after all this time. She should feel bad for him, but she couldn't help feeling nothing at all. He ran off on his wife and kid, left them both broken hearted and poor, and died a lonely man.

Still stuck in gridlock traffic, Kinsley picked up her phone and sent a group text to Delilah, Monica, and Diane.

I suddenly feel inspired…gonna be singing Garth Brooks tonight.

Chapter Two

"Wait a minute, did you just say your dad is dead?" Monica yelled across the table at Kinsley. Some poor sap at Plaza Del Toro was on stage, doing his best not to butcher Bon Jovi's "Dead or Alive," but alas, the song was brutally slaughtered.

"Yeah, I found out a few hours ago." Kinsley licked the sugar off the rim of her mango margarita before taking another big swig until the glass sat empty.

"Okay…so are you in shock or something? I'm not much of an expert on this, but don't people usually cry, or at least frown, when they find out their parent is dead?" Monica cocked her head sideways.

"Nope. No crying. No frowning. I felt my face start to spasm earlier, and I thought I was getting ready to cry, but it turned out to be a sneeze." The waiter approached the table with another mango margarita and placed it in front of Monica. The other three women sat with empty glasses, but apparently no refill was coming their way. This was typical every time they went out with Monica. Although no one in the group resembled a hyena, Monica was only twenty-four, blonde, and blessed with a big chest and an ass she was frequently told, "wouldn't quit." Men drooled over her the way a diabetic would salivate on the glass sneeze guard at an all carbohydrate buffet, thus making the other three invisible most of the time.

"Excuse me, señor. These three amigas would like another drink too, please." Delilah didn't play when it came to her discounted alcohol.

"Ah, si. Si, amiga. Uno momento." The waiter gave Monica a little smile and took off towards the bar.

Diane put her hand on top of Kinsley's. "Okay, sweetie. What's going on? I mean, I know I've never heard you talk about your dad, and he wasn't at your mom's funeral, but I've seen you get more upset when your projector in class doesn't work."

"Well, that is a very cumbersome situation when you need to project a PowerPoint and the damn thing up and quits working." Kinsley didn't want to go into the sordid details, but by the way, her three colleagues were staring at her, she knew she wasn't going to get out of this one easily. "My dad left my mother and me when I was eight years old. I didn't see him on weekends, holidays, or birthdays. He avoided me like the plague. I found out when my mother died that she never took his name off our house. Instead of doing what any decent human being would have done, he used it as legal grounds to take the house. I called him a slew of names most sailors would blush at and that was that."

"So why do you have to go back to Staunton then?" The waiter showed up with the remaining three drinks. Kinsley hoped it would be enough distraction to change the topic of conversation.

Alas, Diane was relentless. "Spill."

"For some reason, he left me the house in his inheritance. I need to go for the reading of the will and to put the house up for sale."

"He left you the house? The same one he took away from you?" asked Delilah.

"Yep, and his freaking dog too. Another thing I have to figure out what to do with."

"Why do you think he did that?" Monica chimed in.

"Hell if I know. I have to drive there on Sunday for the funeral and to talk to the lawyer." Kinsley dipped a chip in the salsa bowl and popped it in her mouth. This was not the mood she wanted to set for their evening out. It was probably one of the last nights they could go out carefree before the school year started and they were so exhausted they couldn't remember if they put on deodorant in the morning.

"Do you need one of us to go with you?" Diane placed her hand on Kinsley's shoulder.

"No, I'm not dragging anyone of you to Staunton with me. And I'm also not dragging down our night either. Now, who wants to get up there and sing 'Sweet Caroline' with me?"

Diane, Monica, and Delilah all peered back and forth at each other warily. Although she could tell they were concerned, Kinsley refused to carry on this conversation any further. In her mind, she buried her father a long time ago. His departure from this world now was not enough to spoil a four-dollar margarita that could probably be used to power a small dirt bike.

Delilah smacked the table. "Ah, hell. I'll do it. Come on, Neil Diamond."

***

Sunday afternoon, Kinsley cruised down Interstate 64 listening to Madonna's *Like a Prayer* album. Every time she drove home to Staunton, she listened to nostalgic music from her childhood. "Like a Prayer" released during elementary school and was the catalyst in her trying to dye her hair platinum blonde in eighth grade. It ended up looking like she fell into a tub of Clorox. This should have been enough to make her pause in her quest to imitate the Queen of Pop, but not before she got into a yelling match with her mother about wanting to purchase a black lace leotard to wear underneath a business suit jacket.

Ah memories. She also distinctly remembered listening to "Like a Prayer" on repeat in her room while drooling over the yearbook picture of Bastian. They had fallen out of being friends by the end of middle school. His blond hair, blue eyes, and beautiful face made him the object of desire for many girls. Plus, he was popular and had a different social circle. Kinsley was pretty then, plenty of boys paid attention, but she was far from winning any "most liked" contests. Not a pariah, but many blank spots resided in her yearbook where people could have signed if they had wanted.

Bastian ended up zoned for the new high school that opened up her freshmen year. Even if they had been in the same homeroom with adjacent lockers, she doubted they would have stayed friends. During her junior year, she had heard a familiar voice calling her name at a field party from the bed of a crappy pickup truck. Hopping down from the Ford, Bastian walked over and hugged her. Not much of a conversation was exchanged between them. At that point they hadn't spoken for over a year, so they didn't know anything about each other anymore. When his attention refocused to the cute brunette sitting with him in the truck, she told him to have a good night and went off with her Miller Lite. It was the last time she saw or spoke to him. She heard he went into the military right out of high school, fairly certain it was the Army.

Shaking distant memories from her brain, she turned her attention to the road once again. She was on her favorite part of the drive, climbing and descending the mountainside of Shenandoah National Park. The miniature appearance of the farms below always made her think of the Mr. Rodgers show when you would go flying over the fake neighborhood. Boarders of fields, growing crops or housing animals, provided texture to the landscape below. The road would slowly curve and wind, providing a calming effect during the drive with the exception of randomly passing the signs telling you to watch out for falling rocks.

Kinsley would have rather been in a rockslide than have to go home to deal with her father's estate. The word stunned didn't quite cover her feelings about being willed the house...and his dog. Maybe he had dementia his last few years. Even prior to his disappearing act from her life, he wasn't around that much. As Chief of Police, he was gone most of the time doing paperwork at the station or on calls in town. He often left before she woke in the morning and returned right at her bedtime. Tucking her in and kissing her on the forehead was the extent of their father/daughter relationship.

While seven-year-old Kinsley waited for sleep to come, she would lie in bed and listen to her parents argue. The details of each fight weren't always clear, but the frustration within the yelling was unmistakable. Then, her mother would start crying, and Mitch would make his exit to the garage to tend to his collection of antique guns and rifles. His absence made Kinsley's reliance and attachment to her mother develop beyond normal parameters. That was probably the reasoning behind why she put up with her mother without question.

Kinsley remembered the severe highs and lows her mother experienced. She would cycle through periods of extreme happiness and then despair so gut-wrenchingly horrific that she wouldn't get out of bed for days. One argument between her parents that she could remember vividly was when her father came home to find she had emptied their checking account because of a hare-brained idea to raise minks to sell for fur. The garage was filled with cages, food, and supplies, while unpaid bills stayed in the basket above the fridge. In order to make ends meet during the months it took her mother to recoup the money she had wasted, he had to sell seven of his antique rifles.

Despite the endless rotation of money spending and

debilitating spouts of depression, he always came back. For a while, Kinsley held onto the delusion that *she* was the reason he kept returning. Even though he was somewhat distant and not as involved as her friends' fathers, he still came home and tucked her in. But that all ended when she was eight.

She remembered getting off the bus from school and walking into the house to find her mother sobbing on the couch. At first, she thought it was simply mom doing what she did and crying about something insignificant. Through the wails, however, her mother confessed that her father had left and wasn't coming home. Kinsley didn't believe it until she found his side of the closet barren and the firearms in the garage gone. It didn't matter, he'd be back to tuck her in…he always came home for that. That night, she fought sleep waiting for him to walk into her bedroom, but lost her battle around eleven o'clock.

The next day at school, Brian Watts told Kinsley at lunch that his mom and dad didn't live in the same house anymore either, but he went to his dad's apartment on the weekends. That afternoon, while her mother lay crying in bed, she anxiously packed a bag. It was only two days until the weekend, so she needed to be ready when he came to pick her up. Friday afternoon, she sat on the porch with her Strawberry Shortcake suitcase until eight o'clock. He never showed up and never called to reschedule.

After five solid days of her mother refusing to get up or shower, Kinsley went into her bedroom crying because she couldn't find anything to eat. The milk had run out and cereal was the only thing she knew how to make without using the stove. The peanut butter and jelly had been used up two days earlier. Seeing her daughter upset, hungry, and sobbing was enough to pull Mrs. Bailey out of her self-indulgent spiral. She got herself out of the bed, made her daughter some soup and a grilled cheese, and took a shower. After drying off and putting on a robe, her mother sat her down and promised that she would not let her father leaving keep her from taking care of her daughter.

She held her oath as best as she could. Kinsley still had to deal with the cable or phone being cut off now and again due to unplanned shopping sprees at Sears, but the lights and heat were always kept on and Kinsley never wanted for food. However, she soon realized the tradeoff for her mother holding it together was becoming her best friend and sounding board. She would talk Kinsley's ears off about her failed marriage and verbally bash her father. All things a child of a divorce should never have to hear.

One day when Kinsley was ten, she went to town with her friend Erin to Ringwald's Ice Cream Shop, which was conveniently located next to Staunton PD headquarters. Erin's mother had told them to eat their ice cream and wait for her at the counter as she went next door to pick up a few groceries. With a little convincing, Erin agreed to walk with her over to the police department to see if her dad was there. The two ten-year-olds went to the front desk where a woman in uniform was answering phones.

"Excuse me, I'm Kinsley Bailey. My dad is Chief Bailey. Can you please let him know I'm here and see if I can go to his office?" The woman behind the desk smiled, picked up the phone, and punched in three numbers.

"Yes, Chief Bailey. I have your daughter in the lobby. Do you want me to buzz her in so that—" She stopped speaking. Her father was saying something on the other end. "Okay, sir. I'll let her know." She hung up the phone, frowning. "He says he can't see you now sweetie."

"But I haven't seen him in—"

"Honey, he said he is very busy and can't see you now. So you two run along, and I'm sure he'll talk to you soon." Little did she know that her father hadn't spoken to her in over a year.

Soon was never going to happen. Kinsley and Erin walked back to Ringwald's, and she quietly cried into her hot fudge sundae.

At the divorce proceedings, her father relinquished his rights to see her, but agreed to pay monthly child and spousal support. It was going to be her and her mother, just the two of them. She coped with her mother's mood swings by diving further into her academic studies while locked in her bedroom. Rather than using the unhealthy habits some kids of divorce clung to in order to ease the pain, she was going to use her grades to get the hell away from Staunton and the memories it held.

A few months after the divorce was finalized, her mother got a job as a receptionist at a dentist office. Regularly working helped tame the emotional demons that lay within her, which were later diagnosed as bipolar disorder. Her mother had her issues, but despite them, she remained her parent. All through college and into her twenties Kinsley occasionally got angry thinking about how quickly she had to fend for herself when the manic episodes set in, but she let go and forgave when her mother died of cervical cancer four years ago. It was stage four by the time it was diagnosed, and she was gone within a month. Her mother's body was hardly cold and in the ground when Mitchell started moving his things in the house. Now, for some unforeseen reason, he left it to her. The little girl he refused to call on Christmas or even give a nod of recognition from his police cruiser as he drove past. Something smelled funny about this, and it wasn't the dead skunk she just ran over.

Kinsley made the left hand turn onto Eagle Rock Lane. Her mother's house sat on the outskirts of the town, so the yards remained large and farm pastures surrounded the few residential roads. A total of eight houses lined her street and her mother's—being the sole log cabin—stuck out like a sore thumb. The homes situated on the right all sat in front of Middle River. Except in times of extreme flooding, the water level rarely got higher than your knees, and it spanned a whopping seven yards from edge to edge.

She turned into the asphalt driveway and parked in front of the garage. As the car engine idled, she sat taking in the house. It wasn't fancy like the log cabins you would see on "Mountain Getaway" websites. No wrap around porches or expansive bay windows, just a simple two-story, three-bedroom log home. It was exactly like she remembered it four years ago when she said she would rather see it burned to the ground than have that selfish bastard living in it again.

She inhaled deeply, trying to calm herself and absorb the absurdity that a man she hadn't spoken with in over twenty years left her this house. Instead of composing her nerves, she got a giant whiff of dead skunk spray and decided it was time to get out of the car. She would need to wash it in tomato juice or something.

Kinsley opened the door of her beamer and stood, smoothing out her knee length purple summer dress. She headed towards the garage door to locate the fake rock that was supposed to contain the key. Between two holly bushes and next to a cement figurine of a frog, she found the plastic stone and slid out the bottom compartment. The key dropped right into her hand. Placing the rock in its original position, she slowly walked up the sidewalk to the entrance.

Opening the front door was like traveling back in time and finding your home in an alternate universe. The layout was the same, but all the furnishings had changed. Closing the door behind her, she took her time inspecting the house. Master bedroom and bathroom were off to the left of the entryway and stairs to the second floor were on the right. Moving forward into the living room, she found that Mitch had replaced the drywall with wood paneling and added a freestanding iron fireplace. He had also built bookshelves into the living room wall behind the couch, stuffed with rows of gun enthusiast literature. Nice to see there was one thing he hadn't abandoned during his lifetime.

To the right of the living room sat a small kitchen with new granite countertops and matching Frigidaire appliances. His stainless steel fridge had six magnets on it, all from some place called Five Points Firearms. He had probably been one of their best customers. A sliding glass door off to the left of the kitchen laid an exit to a very plain, uninteresting porch with a hanging bench swing. She could see two pink ceramic dog bowls, one labeled Petunia, on the floor next to the door. Turning around to scan the entire lower level layout, she realized there were no photographs of him or his family anywhere. Only portraits of deer or winter farm landscapes that was synonymous with Staunton.

Before heading upstairs to check out what had changed on the second level, she veered left to the garage and basement doors. The garage door was jammed a bit at first and required one hell of a shove, but she got it open after a few pushes and a couple of swear words. Flicking on the light reaffirmed that Mitchell's love of firearms had not changed. In fact, it appeared as though his collection had grown quite extensively. The wall opposite her was blanketed with mounted guns—most of them restored antiques. What the hell was she going to do with all of these? The most likely solution was to sell them, but to who? Maybe she could call the place on all those magnets on the refrigerator. They should at least be able to point her in the right direction.

After exiting the garage, she decided to skip the basement. She remembered it being dark and dusty down there, so it could wait until later when she had on sneakers instead of flip-flops. Spiders and crawly doo-hickies hung out in dark and dusty places. The stairs creaked under her weight as she climbed to the second level. A long narrow hallway of cheap carpeting lined the floors leading to two smaller bedrooms and one more bathroom. Freezing at the sight of her bedroom door, she felt the weight like an elephant had decided to use her ribcage for a stepping stool. Despite her lack of air, she headed down the hall to her old bedroom.

After she graduated college and broke the news that she would not be moving back home, but instead was joining the Peace Corp to help engineer water cleaning systems in Africa, her mother immediately converted it into a guest room. Despite her mother's threat to send all her belongings to local Staunton landfill for her "ridiculous career decision," several of Kinsley's personal effects remained in the new guestroom...or at least they had up until Mitch took over the house. Opening the bedroom door revealed her lamp and nightstand had not been moved, but the bookcase with all the textbooks she couldn't sell back to the college bookstore and all her yearbooks were gone. What had that asshole done with all of her stuff?

Her fuming was cut short by the sound of three loud knocks pounding on the door. Looking at her silver Movado watch, she realized it was already six in the evening. *Likely Aunt Debbie.* She hurried downstairs and reached for the doorknob, finding her aunt on the front stoop looking as though she was thoroughly being put out. Her hair was stark white now, cut short, and curled like the little old ladies who visited the salon every week for a wash and style. She wore a red short-sleeved t-shirt with an American flag bedazzled on the front in red, blue, and silver gems. Her jean shorts ended right above her knees and, by the looks of the material, were the kind of bottoms that had the elastic accordion waistbands.

"Kinsley? Is that you?"

"Yes, Aunt Debbie. It's me." Glancing at her aunt's feet, she saw what resembled a giant sack of brown and black skin with eyes wagging its tail. Petunia was a basset hound.

"Oh, my lord, child. You look fantastic! Glad you quit doing that whole beatnik thing you were pulling the last time I saw you." If Kinsley had to select one word to describe her former sense of style, beatnik would have been her choice too. Along with growing out and coloring her hair, Monica helped her expand her wardrobe to include every color on the color wheel in lieu of the blacks and grays she had grown accustomed to buying.

"Thank you. I assume this is Petunia." She stepped to the side to let her aunt in. Petunia shuffled into the house on her big fat padded feet while Aunt Debbie followed in similar step behind her.

"Sure is. Your daddy got her from the local animal shelter about a year ago. She's a good dog, won't run off out of the yard, but hold onto your food! She won't let nothing get in the way of her and whatever it is that you're eating. Other than that, she sleeps most the time." Aunt Debbie reached down to unhook the leash from Petunia's collar and then plodded over to the navy blue and beige lazy boy to take a load off. "Say, do you think one of them pigeons you been working with crawled up into your fancy car engine and died? It stinks to high heaven!"

"It's seagulls, not pigeons. And no, I accidentally ran over a dead skunk on the way here." Since her aunt apparently decided to stay a spell, Kinsley sank into the oversized beige couch across from her.

"There's a car wash over by the Kroger down the road. You remember where the IGA used to be? Well, it's now a Kroger. You'll most likely need to stop by there tonight anyways on account of the fridge looked pretty empty when I was here the other day."

"Thanks. I'll do that." An awkward silence lay between them for a few moments before Debbie decided to get down to the nitty-gritty. "Okay, here's the deal. Viewing and last words is tomorrow at Wilbur and Wilcox's Funeral Home at two in the afternoon. Light refreshments will be hosted at the My Holy

Redeemer Church, which is a rock throw down the street from the funeral parlor. Your daddy asked to be cremated, so there isn't going to be a graveside service."

"When is the reading of the will?"

"Is that your only thought?" Debbie shook her head in obvious disappointment. "When's the reading?"

"Debbie, I don't want to argue about this. You need to understand that I have not known this man for over twenty years. He left when I was eight and refused to have anything to do with me, except for the check he was legally bound to write once a month. Then, he stole, yes I said stole, my mother's house and decided I need to have it when he dies? I'm sorry you think I should feel more for that man, but I don't. I'm not angry, I simply don't care."

Kinsley ran a hand through her hair as Debbie continued to stare. She took a breath, and continued, "As my life is almost four hours away and now I have this house, its contents, and a dog to figure out what to do with, I need to know when I can start taking care of things. I'll be at that funeral tomorrow, but it won't be in the capacity you think it should be. I do, however, want to thank you for making all the arrangements. That would have been very difficult for me to do living so far away."

From the scowl on Debbie's face, she clearly didn't agree with Kinsley's feelings towards her father, but instead of continuing to bicker, her forehead slowly released its harshness. "I don't mind doing it at all. I have experience with arranging funerals when your Uncle Jim passed. I remember how overwhelming it was, so I can't imagine having to do it long distance. Luckily, I had your father there to help me with organizing everything. I truly appreciated it, especially since he and Jim never really got along as brothers should. But no matter how sour the relationship was, family is family, blood is blood, and he came round to help me then, like you are now."

Kinsley didn't especially like being grouped in the same

category as her father, but it wasn't worth asking her to retract. Petunia galloped over to Kinsley and stood beside the couch. She wriggled her wrinkly big butt, bowed down, and leapt up like an overweight flying squirrel. She walked over the couch cushions to lay her head and long floppy ears on Kinsley's lap. The drool seeping out the corners of her mouth made dark blotches on Kinsley's dress.

"So last time you were here four years ago, I heard you had stopped building ships and started teaching. I wanted to ask you about it then, but you were meaner than a damn rattlesnake, and it didn't seem like the proper time to ask what was new."

Kinsley tried lifting Petunia's giant head off her lap but was unsuccessful. The dog was already snoring. "Yes, that's right. I started teaching about six years ago. The hustle and bustle of the corporate world wasn't for me. I was bored. That's one thing I never am in teaching, bored. There's always something to grade, some kid to accost for their inappropriate clothes, or a new lesson to make. I stay busy and I like the kids."

"Seems a shame to waste your degree in chemistry and engineering to teach a bunch of preschoolers."

"I don't teach preschool. I teach sixth grade science, so I still use my degrees, just not on multi-million dollar ships."

"No money in preaching and no money in teaching. But I guess you don't need to worry about all that now since he left you the house and all them firearms in the garage. He's had a lot of them professionally restored, you know. I'm sure they're worth a pretty penny." Debbie crossed one knee over the other and began rocking. Kinsley noticed a very distinctive pantyhose line going across her toes in the opening of her sandals. Only in Staunton would you find a woman wearing pantyhose with shorts and sandals.

"I don't need the money. I invested well when I was making a better salary, and I'm living quite comfortably between that and my monthly paychecks from teaching. Do you know if he had the guns done at that Five Points Firearms place? The magnets are all over the fridge. I need to figure out how to get rid of them all, and I don't know where to even start."

"Yes, ma'am. Tommy Rollins and his cousin run it. They sell guns, refurbish antique ones, and they even have a shooting range! I took a class there last spring because some damn turkey buzzards kept roosting in my maple and crapping on my Buick. After six courses, I took those suckers out like shooting at one of them ducks in the carnival games."

Kinsley glanced down at her left hand and realized she had begun petting Petunia's head. She would probably have found rubbing the dog's furry folds more relaxing if she didn't have a puddle of spittle accumulating on her thigh. Damn this dog drooled a lot. "You know you could have just whacked your tree with a shovel a couple of times. The loud noise and vibration would have scared them off."

"I suppose a person who studies bird poop for scientific purposes would say that, but I chose a pistol instead. They're lucky I didn't stick their little bodies on pikes around the tree to show all their little friends what could happen if you crap on my Lesabre." Even Kinsley had to laugh at that one. "Well, I best be getting back home. My godson will be expecting supper. You need directions to the funeral home for tomorrow?"

"Nope, my car has GPS."

"Great, and do us all a favor, huh? Take it through the car wash before you show up. That stench being near a funeral parlor will have folks talking." Debbie stood up while Kinsley tried her best to extract herself from the massive pile of skin that was using her lap for a pillow. "Don't get up, I'll see myself out." Debbie leaned down to Kinsley and wrapped her arms around her in a hug that she was not expecting. "Look, sweetie, I know you aren't happy to be here, but I sure am glad you came." Physical affection with a woman she barely knew was not in Kinsley's comfort zone. So she did the only thing she could do, the infamous "three pats on the back to let her know the hug was over" move.

Debbie released Kinsley, patted the sleeping dog on the head, and let herself out. At the sound of the door closing, Petunia arose from her slumber and decided to lift up her massive cranium to look around. Kinsley seized the opportunity to leap free from the hound dog captivity. A giant wet stain covered the front part of her dress, giving the appearance that she hadn't gotten to the bathroom in time. Before going out to her car to get her suitcase, she raided the kitchen to see what she would need and to check for dog food. Petunia sat dutifully at her side, hoping to get some sort of treat. "Sorry, girl. Just taking inventory."

Debbie was right. She was going to need to go to the store tonight. The only thing the man had was Campbell's Vegetarian Soup and Wafer Crackers, not an ideal meal for a warm August evening. She walked out to her beamer, retrieved her suitcase while holding her breath, and headed into the house to change. Setting up shop in her old room was the only option she felt comfortable with. She climbed the stairs to the second level bathroom and changed into gym shorts and a tank top. After double-checking that Petunia had a full bowl of water, she grabbed her wallet and keys, and headed out to her beamer. Eau de Skunk practically punched her in the nostrils, making a trip to the carwash priority number one.

Chapter Three

Unpacking the groceries proved difficult with a seventy pound basset hound weaving in and out of her legs. Kinsley purchased tuna fish, bread, cheese, olives, yogurt, red wine, and coffee creamer for herself. Never having owned a dog before, she wasn't sure what exactly to get Petunia so she bought three different twenty-pound bags of dog food, five varieties of canned food, a box of milk bones, a bag of pig ears, and six rolls of super absorbent paper towels to clean up all the drool. Petunia moved with the quickness of a sloth most times, but when she smelled the pig ears, she jumped higher than a gazelle to snatch it out of Kinsley's hand.

She poured a glass of red wine and made a tuna sandwich. Scrubbing a car with "Skunk B Gone" at the car wash caused a person to work up an appetite. She ate at the kitchen counter quickly while Petunia was distracted and devouring her pig ear. Tuna didn't go well with red, but waiting sixty minutes to refrigerate a white wasn't something she was willing to suffer. She needed a drink *fast*. Looking at all the furnishings Mitch left behind made Kinsley begin to ponder what in the hell she was going to do with all of it. She recalled seeing commercials for trucks that would come and clean out your house for you, donate the usable things, and trash the others. That was going to be her plan of action, but first she would need to take care of all the guns. She pulled one of the Five Point magnets off the fridge. The funeral wasn't until two o'clock. She could probably stop by there tomorrow morning and see if they could help her with selling the collection.

After cleaning up her dishes, she started upstairs to take a shower. Petunia sat on the platform at the base of the stairs like a sad Precious Moments puppy, whimpering. "Come on," Kinsley tried coaxing her. Her fat little feet padded up and down in the same spot as if she were marching in place. "You can do it. Come on." Kinsley made a pathetic attempt at a whistle, but it mostly came out as spit. "Petunia, come here!" Raising her voice did not get the response she was hoping. Instead of following orders, the dog's whimpers turned into pitiful howling.

"Oh for God's sakes!" Kinsley stomped down the stairs, hoisted the bag of breathing wrinkles into her arms, and carried her up to the second floor. Thank goodness Pilates built strength and flexibility. She placed Petunia down on her fat feet and raced to the spare bedroom. Kinsley grabbed her shampoo, conditioner, soap, razor, and shaving cream and took a long hot shower. Mitchell had installed a new sink and tub in the upstairs bathroom that made the space feel larger and more user friendly. Knocking out the linen closet to install a full sized tub instead of a standing shower made bathing a lot easier too. The former standup used to be the size of a BDSM closet in a cramped Manhattan apartment.

Kinsley dried off and slipped into a white night shirt. Returning to the old bedroom, she discovered Petunia had decided she would also be sleeping in the same bed. "Alright, as long as you stay down by my feet." She tugged the dog towards the end of the bed and slipped between the covers. Pulling out her Stephanie Plum book that she hadn't been able to finish at the beach, she read until about midnight when her eyes couldn't stay open anymore. Petunia had fallen asleep almost two hours ago and was breathing so hard she could hear the dog's lips flapping. Reaching over, she turned off the lamp and listened to the crickets chirping their summer symphonies and Petunia sawing logs. Letting her lids grow heavier, she drifted off to sleep peacefully, not at all the way a daughter mourning the death of her father would have done.

***

That night, Kinsley had a nightmare she was being smothered by a giant pillow. Gasping for air and flailing her arms, the weight of the pillow overwhelmed her. Tossing and turning, trying to get free, proved ineffective. She was being suffocated in her sleep. This was it. Mitchell's revenge! He left her this house so his ghost could take her out with a Serta pillow. At the moment she was about to embrace death, a giant wet slug crawled across her face, jarring her from sleep. Opening one eye, she found Petunia licking her nose and breathing heavily. Apparently in dog language, *end of the bed* translates to *on top of my face*.

Seeing that she was successful in waking Kinsley, Petunia sat on her chest and wagged her tail. "What? What do you want?" Petunia let out a soft whimper. *She must need to go outside.* "Alright, fine. Let's go."

Petunia hopped off the bed and stood at the top of the stairs. "Go on. Go down." Kinsley motioned at the staircase. The dog began to whimper and march her feet again. "Are you kidding me? You're scared of going down too?" A hefty bark answered Kinsley's question. "Damn it." She bent at the waist and heaved Petunia into her arms. "I'm not doing this every morning I'm here, just to let you know. And I doubt they'll be carrying your butt around at the shelter, so I wouldn't get too used to it."

At the base of the steps, Kinsley put Petunia on the floor

and the dog bounded towards the back porch. She slid the glass door open, and like a brown bolt of lightning, Petunia ran off the porch onto the grass and squatted to wiz next to a tree. Kinsley began the process of making coffee to wake herself up. It was already nine and she wanted to find a realty company after visiting Five Points. She filled Petunia's pink dog bowl with one of the dry dog foods she had purchased at the market the day before. The dog apparently had no issues with the brand and snarfed it down.

While Petunia satisfied her appetite, Kinsley returned to the upstairs bedroom to survey the clothes she packed for her stay. Showing up to the services all sweaty from walking around town on a summer day probably wouldn't go over well at the Wilcox and Wilbur funeral home; well, unless you just got off your tractor to attend the services. She left her black wide strapped dress on the hanger and chose a floor length light blue maxi dress instead. She was sure she'd be home in time to take another shower and change for the funeral. She twisted her hair up and held it in place with a few bobby pins. After applying a little anti-aging make-up, she brushed her teeth, and let Petunia out to do her business one last time. "Don't eat anything you aren't supposed to while I'm gone," she ordered, pointing her finger at the dog. Petunia yawned, circled around three times, and flopped down on the Wipe Your Paws mat in front of the sliding glass door.

Kinsley grabbed a magnet off the fridge for Five Points, her bamboo purse, and locked up the house. She plugged the address written on the store's magnet into her GPS and followed the robotic verbal prompts into the heart of Staunton. The main town hadn't changed much in twenty years. Many of the older feed factories and tractor supply stores had been converted into antique shops or new restaurants, but the outward appearance remained the same. Tall brick buildings with big bay windows to display merchandise lined up along

Main Street. Very few of the stores remained from her childhood, but the buildings were still there and appeared almost identical.

The GPS informed her that her destination was further down the road, past the main hub of the city. Crosswalks and attached storefronts turned into solitary buildings as she reached the outskirts of town. Right as the voice came over the speakers alerting her that the destination was in thirty feet, she saw the giant white sign for the funeral home on the left and a hand carved wooden sign reading, "Five Points Firearms," on the right.

The white wooden building had two large windows displaying various sorts of rifles and pistols behind thick glass. American and POW flags were hung on poles at both sides of the entrance. The large glass door leading into the store was screen printed with the Five Points logo: a five pointed star with the letters F & P. The rear of the building changed from white wooden siding to industrial metal walls. Kinsley thought the gun range Debbie was so enthusiastic about must be housed there.

Kinsley strolled up to the entrance and was about to push the doorbell to be let in, but a man wearing green coveralls came walking out right as she approached and held the door open for her. Grey tile floor spanned the entire shop, which had glass gun cases along the perimeter of each wall. Firearms were displayed on every wall and spinning racks of gun accessories speckled the floor. A steel door labeled, "Gun Repair Shop: Employees Only," was behind the counter holding the cash register.

A man with brown hair, wearing a tight black t-shirt with the store's logo on the pocket, glanced up from his paperwork by the register. He appeared to be about Kinsley's age and a little rough around the edges. Most gun enthusiasts probably looked that way, or at least she imagined it to be the case. "Good morning, ma'am. How can I help you today?"

Kinsley headed over to where he stood and put her purse on the counter. "Hi. Good morning. Very recently, I've come to inherit quite a bit of antique rifles and shot guns. I'm not into guns personally, and I don't know many people who would be interested in this extensive a collection. I found your magnet on my father's refrigerator, and my aunt said that your company did some of the restorations for him. I was wondering if you would be interested in the collection or could help me with locating a buyer. I would be willing to pay a finder's fee."

The man stuck his click pen in his mouth and chewed for a second. "Where'd you say you got these guns from?"

"Inheritance. My father passed away a few days ago."

"I'm sorry to hear about your loss. Well, let me go get my cousin from the workshop. He's the restoration specialist and has helped with quite a few buyers and sellers on antiques. My name's Tommy Rollins. I'm the owner of Five Points." He reached over the counter to shake her hand.

"I'm Kinsley Bailey. Pleasure to meet you."

He put his pointer finger up in the air. "Give me one second." Turning around, he punched a code into the steel door. High tech security must be required for a gun shop. She had noticed the cage pull downs above the windows when she walked in and the doorbell must be used to monitor who was coming in and going out. Tommy yelled into a large warehouse style room. "Hey, Bass! A lady up here needs to speak with you about a collection of antique guns she just inherited."

Great. Only in Staunton would I have to talk to a guy named after a fish.

A man about six feet tall came through the doorway after Tommy. He also wore a tight black t-shirt with the Five Points logo on the pocket, but it fit him much better. Gun repair must work your upper arm strength. She wondered if he ever told that lame joke about giving a woman tickets to the gun show and flexed. A sleeve of black tattoos, ranging from naked women to weapons, snaked its way from his right wrist all the way up his arm, disappearing under his shirt sleeve. His hair was dirty blond and short, but not like the military haircut the owner had. His face was beginning to show scruff growing in and his eyes were a piercing blue…a very familiar piercing blue.

Holy shit.

"Hi. I'm Bass." He stretched over the counter and shook her hand. His smile was entirely as bright and magnetic as she remembered. His face was older, obviously, but she could spot that smile anywhere. She had spent hours staring at it in her yearbook or sneaking glimpses in math class when she should have been finding lowest common denominators.

"Hi…nice to meet you." She hesitated to see if any flash of recognition came across his face. There wasn't any, only a smile he most likely reserved for his potential customers and women he wanted to swoon. As the recognition was one-sided, she chose to say nothing. "Yes, as your co-worker said I've recently come into quite a large collection of various guns. I was hoping either the shop would be interested in purchasing them or could put me in contact with a buyer."

He rubbed his hand on his chin. "How big of a collection are we talking?"

"I would guess around sixty. Maybe more."

He whistled. "That is a pretty large collection to expect to unload on one interested party, even for a store. I would definitely have to see what we're working with in person and do some research."

Tommy chimed in, "She said you did some of the work for the person that she inherited the guns from. Who was that, Miss?"

"Mitchell Bailey." Her eyes darted back and forth between the two men while she chewed on the side of her mouth. Bastian's brows scrunched together and his head tilted a bit to the left. After a moment, the tension on his forehead released, an expression of surprise replaced the confusion.

He let go of his chin, placed both hands on the counter, and leaned in a little closer as if he were examining her face. "Kinsley? Kinsley Bailey?"

"Yep, that's me. How are you Bastian?"

"Well, right now I'm surprised. How the hell have you been? I mean, with the exception of your father passing. Sorry to hear about that."

"Don't apologize. You might remember I didn't speak to him when you and I were friends. That never changed." Kinsley had a death grip on her bamboo pocket book handles. If she didn't squeeze the hell out of something, she was going to run out of the store, and she needed this guy to help her get rid of these guns.

"You're right. Man that was a long time ago. How long ago do you—"

"Twenty years," she interrupted, "you know, give or take a year."

He shook his head. "Damn. Well it is really good to see you, even under the circumstances. You look great! Sorry I didn't recognize you at first. Your hair was blond the last time I saw you. I like it that color too though. "

"You seem like you're doing well, too." Staring him in the face was like slipping into a vortex that she did not want to get trapped in again, so she kept her focus glued to the counter. His hands were still on top. She noticed there was no ring on any finger. But why would she care about that?

She didn't.

"Yeah. I did a few restorations for your dad over the years. I never saw his entire collection, only what he brought in to get fixed. So I would still need to come and check things out to get an idea of what we might want to purchase for the shop and brainstorm potential buyers. What are you doing later on today?"

"I have my father's funeral at two."

He nodded, giving her a sympathetic look. She didn't need his pity. Lord knows she didn't even have any for her father. "When would be a good time for you?"

"Tomorrow morning I have to meet with his lawyer to finalize a few things, but how about in the afternoon? Say one o'clock?"

"I can do that." He nodded.

"Do you need the address?" She released her sweaty hands from her purse handles and began digging for a pen.

"Nope, we have old billing statements in the computer. I can get it off that. What's your number in case something comes up on my end or yours and we need to reschedule?"

She grabbed the store's business card, wrote her name and cell phone number on the back, and handed it to him.

"Seven, five, seven?" he asked after seeing her number.

"Yeah, I live in Hampton Roads. Just here for the funeral and to take care of some loose ends. I hope to get home by the end of this week. Next week at the absolute latest."

He put the card in the back pocket of his jeans. "Alright, I'll see what I can do to help you get rid of those weapons and get you outta here quick as possible. I'll be by tomorrow at one." He placed his hands on the edge of the counter and stared at her as if he was waiting for the moment she would vanish and the whole encounter was a figment of his imagination. Her skin was beginning to prickle and sting at the intensity of his gaze. She was seconds away from telling him to forget the whole deal. Luckily, he spoke again before she deemed an emergency escape necessary. "Damn, Kinsley. It was great to see you."

"You too, Bastian. I'll see you tomorrow. Thank you for your help." She nodded at both men, snatched her purse off the glass case, and tried her best to walk casually out the front door. She applied her hand to the bar, pushed, and shoved, but it wouldn't budge. A tan arm featuring a 40's style pin up in an army bikini reached over her shoulder. When she turned her face, there was Bastian with a smug, amused expression. Obviously tickled by her frustration.

"Here, let me get that for you. It locks automatically every time the door closes." He pointed to the black and neon green sign next to the lock reminding you to undo the deadbolt before exiting. If it were any closer, it would have smacked her in the face.

"Um, yeah. Thanks. See you tomorrow." She unlocked her BMW with her key chain. Bastian stood with the door propped open, watching her.

"Nice car. This year's model?"

"Last year's." She was about to sit down in the driver's seat when she remembered she needed to visit a couple of realty companies to help sell her mother's house. Realizing that she could either start wandering around town in a crapshoot attempt to find a decent realtor or simply ask the man in front of her for some suggestions, she stood back out of her car. "Hey, Bastian. Quick question before you go in. I need to find a reputable realty company in town to handle the sale of my mother's house. Word of mouth is always better than any website. Any suggestions?"

"I thought you said it was your dad that passed."

She smiled slightly. "Long story."

"Frank Goldman runs Blue Ridge Realty. Do you remember him? He went to school with us. I got my rental house through his office. He seems to run a decent, fair business. You want me to get you the address?" he asked pointing into the shop.

"No, thanks. I have a GPS in the car. Blue Ridge Realty?" He nodded. "Okay, thanks again." She sat down in the car and turned over the engine. Glancing up from the steering column, she saw Bastian still watching her. His black company t-shirt was tucked into a pair of faded jeans that fit him all too well. Trying to avert her eyes from the lower half of his body, she directed her vision upwards as he was waved goodbye. Turning over her shoulder to back out of the parking space she muttered to herself, "You've gotta be fucking kidding me."

Before pulling onto the main road, she typed Blue Ridge Realty into her GPS and headed down Main Street utterly amazed at how this week's events were unfolding and nervous at what else might be in store.

Chapter Four

Bass walked through the shop and headed to the steel door behind the counter to finish working on his latest order. Tommy stood at the register filling out an attendance sheet for that evening's shooting class. His cousin wasted no time. "So, you know her from where?"

Of course Tommy would have questions about her.

"From a long time ago," he dodged. He peeked over his cousin's shoulder at the registration list. "How's tonight's class looking?"

"Full house. Attendance has picked up a bit since all those break-ins and the return of the turkey buzzards. Oh and Mr. Stevens from the high school called. He needs you to give him a ring back about pulling that ROTC float in the parade this Saturday. How'd you get suckered into that one again?"

"Hell if I know." Bastian wasn't particularly thrilled about the idea of driving two miles in first gear with twenty pimply kids following him in their uniforms. Last month he was a guest speaker for the club, presenting on the pros and cons of entering the military directly out of high school. Somehow between the Roll Call and the Motion to Adjourn, he discovered he and his Wrangler were signed up to tug the float in this Saturday's Founder's Day Parade. He could have backed out, but guilt kept him from doing so when he found out their sponsor, Mr. Stevens, drove a Ford Fiesta. That car couldn't drag a dead cat behind it. "I'm gonna go in the workshop and wrap up that Remington Rolling Block. You need anything while I'm up here?"

"Yeah, answer one quick question for me...was she wearing a ring?" Tommy's inquisitiveness, coupled with a smile that could be a close second to The Joker's, pissed Bastian off. His cousin had a long running, though slightly unstable, relationship with Darlene Mott who ran *The Best Little Hair House* down the road. Why would he want to know if Kinsley was available?

"What's it to you?"

Tommy shrugged. "I was just curious if she was single."

"Why? You interested?" Who could blame him? That blue dress brought out the grayish silver color of her eyes and the light mocha color of her skin made it look like she had recently returned from a vacation near the equator. She was stunning.

"You offering to set it up?" Tommy put his pen down and faced Bass.

"I'm not offering anything, you jackass. But no, I didn't see any ring." Tommy smiled at him, nodding like he solved who killed Scarlet in the library with the candlestick. "What's that smug look for?"

"So you were checking yourself to see if the cow had been bought and paid for. Good, that's a step in the right direction." Tommy picked up his pen and continued working on the shooting class roster.

"Oh shut up, Tommy. It was merely an observation." Bass pushed off the counter and walked towards the gun shop door.

"Sure man, if you say so." Tommy laughed a little.

Ignoring his cousin, Bass punched in the numbers on the security code and headed to the workroom. The back of the gun shop, before you moved into the shooting range, was set up like a large warehouse. Four counters with attached vice grips for holding the guns in place ran along the sides of the walls. Lord knows why Tommy wanted four counters; Bass was the only one that did any of the repair and refurbishing work. Peg boards with every kind of tool you could imagine lined the walls behind each counter.

Bass sat on the metal stool and put his safety goggles on. Jesus, it had been a long time since he had seen her. Even before he went into the military and she moved away, they hadn't seen each other much. It was a shame they had fallen out of touch so quickly when they went to different high schools. About a month after he discharged from the Army and moved back to help Tommy expand his business, Mitchell Bailey stopped by trying to get the forearm of a W C Scott Hammer repaired. Chit chat led to Mitchell telling him Kinsley had gone into the Peace Corps before working for some sort of ship builder. He wasn't surprised by that, she always was smart. But Mitchell said she wouldn't be coming to see him anytime soon, so Bass just figured he wouldn't be seeing her again either.

His train of thought shifted to the summers they spent together in middle school. Her best friend, Erin, lived a few houses down from Bass and her in-ground, heated swimming pool made her house the prime destination for kids in the neighborhood who were too young to drive. Kinsley was always at her house in the summertime for days on end. Bass, his best friend Jimmy, Erin, and Kinsley would go swimming almost every day while the parents were at work.

Bass remembered his favorite part of the pool parties were when they'd play chicken. One of the girls would have to sit on his or Jimmy's shoulders while trying to knock the other one into the water. It didn't matter that they were all just friends, he was thrilled—and usually hiding a hard on—whenever one of those girls' crotches sat on the back of his neck. He smiled at the thought of the simpler, younger days. No problems, no worries, only good times.

Thinking about Tommy's earlier question, he hadn't seen a ring on her hand, and he was fairly certain that tan of hers would show a clear white line if she had recently worn one. He found it hard to believe a woman as attractive as her was still single. Maybe she was divorced, like him. Or maybe she was a nutter and no man would marry her.

Pushing the questions out of his head, he turned his attention to the W C Scott lying on his workbench. Besides, he was going to her house tomorrow. He would find out about her relationship status then. He was fairly confident in his abilities to sway conversations with women in his desired direction, even if he found this particular woman more desirable than he'd like to admit.

***

Kinsley had hoped she would have a chance to take a shower before the viewing, but she was running short on time due to that creepy little sleaze ball at the realty company. She had gone to Blue Mountain Realty per Bastian's suggestion but should have turned and walked out when Frank Goldman made it a point to give her a full body scan as he shook her hand. When she told him her name and he made the connection of them previously going to school together, a convict in solitary confinement would've had higher chances of escaping than her. After his endless tirade about how successful he had become since they had last seen each other and his recent single status, Kinsley agreed to take his business card and give him a call later once she had time to think about it.

She barreled into the house, almost tripping over Petunia who was trying dutifully to greet her at the front door. She let Petunia outside to tinkle and ran upstairs to put on her black dress, pantyhose, and black heels. She repaired the loose ends on her hair twist, freshened her makeup, and let Petunia back in. Grabbing a bottle of water and a hunk of cheese and olives (that sucker made her miss lunch), she took off out the front door. At least she knew exactly how to get to the funeral home since it was across the street from Five Points.

When the engine purred to life, her radio started replaying the *Like a Prayer* album. She shut it off immediately. Thinking about running into Bastian again after all these years or focusing on the fact that he would be at her house tomorrow was not an option. Obviously there weren't any residual feelings for him, but the saying was true, you never forget your first love. She knew it sounded a bit ridiculous claiming to be truly in love in middle school, but how else could she justify that she thought fondly of him from time to time?

The only other circumstance she had to compare it to was her relationship with Patrick. They met in the Peace Corps while digging a well for a village in Morocco. Patrick had left his sunscreen in camp and was turning pinker than a freshly smacked behind. Kinsley offered him her 50 SPF, and they were inseparable the rest of their time in Africa. They had so much in common regarding interests and hobbies, and they could both qualify for Mensa, if they felt it necessary to apply.

Prior to joining the Peace Corps, Patrick attended George Mason University. He was a double major, like Kinsley, but in History and Liberal Arts instead of Chemistry and Engineering. He was deep, soulful, and wanted to help the world one impoverished community at a time. They would have intense, meaningful conversations for what seemed like twenty minutes only to discover three hours had passed. She thought she had found her soul mate, and across the ocean digging in the dirt no less!

When they returned to the States after two years abroad, they decided to take the next logical step and move in together. Wanting to begin a normal relationship, they both determined that finding permanent jobs would allow them to explore the possibility of a long-term commitment. She went on to work for

Northrop Grumman as an Engineer Technician on aircraft carriers, but Patrick had much more difficulty finding a job. Although he graduated college Suma Cum Laude, his degree choices required graduate course work in order to be employed in that field. With student loans on the verge of delinquency, going to graduate school wasn't an option.

After two months of not working, Patrick settled for an assistant manager position at a golf resort. He hated his job and barely cleared twenty grand a year. When Kinsley's income hit quadruple his, his resentment was a constant presence. In order to make her feel bad about her rising success, he applied to manage a ski resort all the way out in Colorado and accepted the position without even discussing it with her first. She begged him to stay, knowing what would happen if they had that much distance between them. He fessed up that he would no longer be sticking around to watch her climb the corporate ladder while he was pouring drinks for drunken golfers. Three days later, his drawers in the dresser had been emptied and a forwarding address to send his half of the security deposit sat next to her jewelry box.

Instead of letting her devastation take hold, she accepted assignments at work that required travel and spent his half of the security deposit on new luggage. She needed to get over Patrick and there was nothing like adventure to help you stop thinking about heartbreak. And that was how she spent the next three years of her life: traveling, schmoozing, and making an obscene salary with her knowledge of engineering and creative visualization. Yet staying in one place for no more than two months at a time does eventually get to a person and she decided to plant some roots, although she was the only one in the garden. Kinsley resigned from her high-paying corporate job and interviewed for a middle school science position. She wanted to pass on her love and desire for science, math, and knowledge onto children, even if they weren't her own.

Her BMW crept through the last part of Main Street up to the funeral home, which was apparently the happening place to be in Staunton. The parking lot was surprisingly full for a man that had no soul. She parked her car, turned off her cell phone, and began her procession into the funeral parlor, trying not to get her heels stuck in the gravel. Turning the corner to the front entryway, she saw her Aunt Debbie with another lady who probably wore pantyhose with shorts too.

"Kinsley, I'm so glad you came." Debbie wrapped her arms around her in a giant hug. "Good Lord, girl. You need to start eating more! I could snap your collarbone like a chicken wing." Coming from a woman who was squishier than a can of play dough, Kinsley figured her frame was just fine.

"Is this little Kinsley Bailey?" asked the woman standing next to Debbie.

Kinsley reached out her arm for a handshake. "Yes, ma'am. And you are?"

"I'm Ida Robinson. Your father and I were…friends a few years back."

Eww.

"Oh, uh…how nice." Kinsley pulled her hand away and discreetly wiped it on the side of her dress. "Say, Ida. Since you were, um, friends with Mitchell, you wouldn't by chance be interested in adopting his dog, Petunia, would you?"

"Oh, heavens no." She waived her off dismissively. "My pussy wouldn't allow it."

Kinsley's eyes widened. "Excuse me?"

"Chester, my orange tabby. He hates dogs." She giggled a little to herself. "So, will you be joining us at My Holy Redeemer's after the service? I made my famous Tic Tac pie."

Kinsley's brows shot up. "Tic Tac pie?" Ida nodded enthusiastically. "Sure! Sounds delish. Um, should we go in now?" Kinsley pointed to the entrance of the funeral home and let the two ladies walk ahead of her.

"Please, Lord, make this as quick and painless as possible," she muttered under her breath.

Apparently, the good Lord decided he wasn't in a hurry to eat Ida Robinson's Tic Tac Pie either. During the open viewing, Kinsley couldn't turn around without some old coot running up and hugging her or patting her on the shoulder. Did all these people have amnesia? Her father had nothing to do with her. Did they not remember his total abandonment of his family? The straw that broke the camel's back was when a man with more hair on his knuckles than on the top of his head copped a feel while pushing her toward the memorial collage eternalizing Mitchell's great commitment to the police force. Kinsley decided the best, most mature approach to the problem was to take the funeral program into the bathroom and hide until the services started.

She found an empty stall in the ladies room, locked the door, and after carefully placing half the roll of toilet paper on the seat, sat down. She took a deep breath, which turned out to be a bad idea since Ida Robinson had left looking ten pounds lighter, and flipped through the funeral program. The front page had Mitchell Wallis Bailey scripted across the top in Sanskrit. Below his name, the "Date of Entry into Eternal Life," and the date of the service appeared printed in similar font. Scrolling through the hymns and guest speakers on the inside cover divulged a horrific realization. She was supposed to speak right after Banjo, the K-9 drug-sniffing dog, assisted in the removal of the Staunton PD flag.

"Oh, Damn it all to hell!" she wailed, putting her head in her hands.

"Sounds like someone else had a cup of that black tar coffee they're serving out there too!" said a voice from the next stall over.

Oh, Sweet Jesus! Kinsley shot off the toilet and escaped the pending explosion as quickly as possible.

Despite Aunt Debbie's pleading, Kinsley sat on a bench in the back of the viewing room while neighbors, friends, and former co-workers from the police force went on about what a noble man Mitchell Bailey was for over an hour. When Banjo the German Sheppard padded up the walkway to help two officers remove the flag, her heart beat faster than a Jack Russell's on a run. Scanning all the doors for a last minute escape, she noticed the only door that was slightly ajar was up in the front by the casket.

The two policemen escorted Banjo out of the viewing room, and Aunt Debbie walked up beside the coffin. After wiping her nose with a giant wad of used Kleenex, she said, "And for our last testimony to how greatly Mitchell will be missed on this earth, his daughter Kinsley Bailey would like to say a few words."

Every head on top of every set of shoulders turned around to stare at Kinsley. She swallowed slowly, grabbed her purse like a shield, and stood up to make her way down the aisle towards Mitchell's casket. She had avoided seeing post-mortem Mitch this entire time, but now there was no way around it.

Peering into the casket, she saw he was extremely pale, as most corpses tend to be, with maybe a touch too much rouge. He was being buried in his uniform, a blue grey polyester getup. Although he was whiter, more wrinkled, and seemed to be wearing peach colored lip gloss, he still looked the same as the last time she saw him. Hardened to the world and uncaring to those he should have held closest. This could be her chance. Her opportunity to air out all the dirty laundry about what kind of person her father truly was: a leaver, a sorry excuse for a man, and a thief. But when she turned to face the crowd—all the bad perm jobs, Betty White hair-dos, and old men with water in their eyes—she couldn't do it. She knew who he really was, but these people thought he was something different. Something good. She wasn't going to take that away from them while they were obviously grieving.

"I don't have too much to say about Mitchell Bailey. The years I remember most don't include him that much, I am sorry to say. However, I can tell by how packed this room is and by the looks on all your faces that you all did know him…a lot better than me. I can see how much he'll be missed and how devoted he was to this town and all the people in it." She did it! She was pulling it off without sarcasm or rolling her eyes. She made an eloquent speech about a man she didn't know personally, but knew well enough to hate. "So I wish Mitchell…um, my father…a peaceful walk into the hereafter and I am sure we will all be seeing him again soon." The nightmare was almost over. "Some of us sooner than others."

Oh, shit. Did I just say that out loud?

With an audience of appalled, wrinkled faces staring at her in shock, she was pretty sure that comment wasn't a flittering a thought in her head. A needle being dropped on the four-inch thick plush green carpet could have been heard. She needed to think quick; otherwise, there might be an uprising. What the hell was she going to do? She just told a bunch of old people in a funeral home they were going to die soon. Her mind was drawing a blank. Somewhere someone coughed. And then a single idea popped into her head.

"I am weak, but Thou art strong….Jesus, keep me from all wrong."

She was singing.

By God I'm standing in front of all these old people and a corpse…and singing!

"I'll be satisfied as long…"

Yep, still up here…singing.

"As I walk, let me walk close to Thee…Just a closer walk with Thee."

Couldn't Jesus make an appearance to get her out of this hell? She had about as much singing ability as a dying cat, but here she was.

No music.

No dignity.

Just singing.

The groves in the bamboo handles on her purse dug into her sweaty hands from her death grip. She really was going to need to buy a new pocket book with softer handles if she kept getting into situations like this.

Thankfully, a handful of old ladies in the audience, prompted by her Aunt Debbie, stood and began to sing along. "Grant it, Jesus, is my plea…" Slowly one by one, the entire room stood and joined in. Together, they all sang from the last "closer walk with thee" all the way to "resting on the kingdom shore." As soon as the word "shore" finished, she made a hasty exit from the room via the open door beside the casket. Behind her, she could hear her Aunt Debbie speaking to the crowd, "The ladies of My Holy Redeemer Church have prepared a wonderful luncheon for us. Feel free to drive or leave your cars parked here, since it is only two buildings down."

Kinsley hid in the one place she could get some privacy and think…the bathroom stall. The idea of free food prepared by Christian women prompted canes and walkers to make a mass exodus from the funeral parlor to the parking lot. What was her Aunt thinking? Over half the cars in the parking lot had handicapped license plates. They weren't going to walk over to the church. She waited silently as the sound of footsteps and voices became fainter. There was no way she could go to the Holy Redeemer church after that scene; she was too humiliated. They probably wouldn't care one way or another if she didn't show up, one less person to share the Tic Tac Pie.

Peeking out of the ladies restroom, she discovered an empty hallway. Quietly and quickly, she walked through the front door and headed in the direction of her car. One of her heels became wedged between two pieces of gravel and stuck in the dirt, taking her shoe ransom. "Forget it. Casualty of war," she huffed. Hobbling around the side of the funeral parlor, she was ready to unlock her car and get the hell out of there, but found Aunt Debbie leaning against her driver side.

"Looks like you lost a shoe," she said with her arms crossed. Kinsley tried to fake surprise, but didn't pull it off too convincingly.

"Oh imagine that. Must have fallen off somewhere back there. You go ahead to the church and I'll catch up in a bit." Kinsley turned and limped towards the entrance of the building, hoping she had persuaded her aunt to leave so she could make her get away. By the sound of gravel shuffling behind her, she was fairly certain she was being followed.

"There's no reason to be all embarrassed. I think you covered it all up real well." Debbie caught up with her pretty quickly since Kinsley was at a disadvantage having to walk on gravel sharper than nails with one bare foot. "I thought that song you sang was real lovely."

"Oh please, Aunt Debbie. I was a damn fool up there." Her shoe was barely a few feet away and unable to stand the jabbing and stabbing anymore, she hopped on one foot the rest of the distance.

"Well, I thought it was real endearing." Debbie knelt down to grab her shoe.

Kinsley tried to stop her. "Oh, Debbie, you don't have to—"

"Are you gonna do it yourself on one foot and in a dress?"

Kinsley bit the side of her mouth. She did take Pilates, so she probably could do it if she were in yoga pants and on a soft mat, but being in a dress on rocky terrain was a different story.

"That's what I thought." Right before she slipped the shoe onto Kinsley's foot, she hesitated and stood. "You *are* coming to the church, aren't you?"

"Aunt Debbie, I really don't feel comfort—"

"Now then, it really isn't about you, is it? Did the program have your name on it?" she asked, pointing the shoe in her face.

"No, ma'am."

"That's right. It had Mitchell's name on it and in lovely font too. And since he made it a point to leave you that house and Petunia that means he wanted you here. So you come on now and stop being foolish. Netty Wilkins makes the best fried chicken below the Mason Dixon Line. Come get you a drumstick and visit for a little bit. No pressure about the Tic Tac Pie. I don't know what the heck Ida was thinking when she came up with that one." She slipped the shoe on Kinsley's foot. "You coming then?"

"How can I say no to the best fried chicken this side of the former slave owning half of our nation?"

Debbie rolled her eyes and grabbed Kinsley's arm. "Follow me." As they crunched along the gravel, Debbie motioned in the direction of Five Points. "Did you get over there today? To ask about all those guns?"

"Yes, Bastian is coming to the house tomorrow at one to inventory the collection. The store will hopefully buy some, and he'll help me find buyers for the rest."

"Mmm mmm mmm, I love me some of that Bass. He's the one who taught me to shoot to get rid of all those buzzards. That's one fine looking man."

"Really? Didn't notice." Kinsley took her cell phone from her purse and turned it on. She was pretending to check text messages to avoid the conversation about Bass.

"You didn't notice? Your lady bits not working properly or something? That man is chased after by more women in this town than iced tea at a Fourth of July picnic. I think he's about your age too."

Some things never changed. Bastian had women lining up for him and not a single soul had called Kinsley on her cell. "With all the women going after him, I'm sure his dating calendar is too full to add me in it."

"You'd think it, but no. He doesn't date anybody."

"Gay?" *Please, God, let him be gay.* That would make her feel so much better about their little incident over twenty years ago.

"Heavens, no! He moved back here after being on deployment about two years ago. His cousin Tommy said when he got home he found the house empty and a Dear John letter. She took the kid too. My guess is he doesn't much feel like dating."

Divorced and with a kid? She didn't comment on either. "Well, just cause he isn't dating doesn't mean he isn't doing other things with all those women."

"Why do you always have such a sour puss attitude? Maybe you need to do some of those 'other things' yourself and lighten up a little."

Kinsley's head jerked towards her aunt ready to argue, but no witty comebacks or explanations came to mind. It was true. She hadn't had some of those "other things" for over a year. And the last time didn't account for much since the man's thing was the size of a mini-gherkin. Thankfully, they arrived at the My Holy Redeemer Church so the current conversation could come to a close.

In the basement community room of the church, tables upon tables of sandwiches, chicken, salads mostly made up of mayonnaise, and desserts stretched from one wall to the other. The guests wasted no time digging into the food and socializing at long, cafeteria style tables. Kinsley grabbed a plate of food, avoiding the Tic Tac pie, and sat with her aunt next to a man named Merve. Either Merve didn't have the batteries in his hearing aid checked or the hair in his ear canals muffled voices, but Kinsley spent the majority of the conversation repeating every other sentence. On the bright side of things, Merve wasn't able to hear her comment at the funeral home regarding everyone dying soon.

Surprisingly enough, the luncheon went quickly and as soon as Kinsley noticed other people leaving, she took advantage and headed out herself. As she walked towards the funeral parlor to her car, she couldn't resist the temptation to glance in the direction of Five Points. What her aunt had told her was pretty interesting. Bastian had been married and walked out on, and he also had a kid somewhere. She wasn't too surprised. Most people her age were either still married with kids or had the baggage from previously wedded hell.

.Away from the stress and in the sanctuary of her car, she let out a sigh and laid her forehead on the steering wheel, which was not the best decision in the dead of summer with an all-black interior. She made it out alive from the worst part of this whole ordeal. Now, all she had left to do was meet with the lawyer, get a realtor to represent the house, and take that bag of fleas to the shelter. Oh, and meet with Bastian again about the guns. But that was no biggie. Easy Peasy. It was business, that was all. Maybe the shelter was still open. It was only four-thirty. She could run home, grab the pooch, and GPS it to the nearest Humane Society. Then again, maybe Bastian would want to adopt her. She'd be rescuing an animal if he did end up keeping her, and for understandable reasons, Kinsley had an aversion to abandoning living beings. It was better to hold off…just in case.

Chapter Five

After changing out of her funeral attire and fueled by the bravery of a glass of red wine, Kinsley decided it was time to check out the basement. She slipped on some sneakers to protect her feet from anything creepy crawly and headed down the rickety stairs. She always hated that damn basement. It wasn't even partially finished, so the cement blocks and exposed pipes made the ambiance eerie.

Flipping on the light switch to illuminate the rest of the basement, Kinsley found a semi-new washer and dryer set. Other than that it was pretty empty; only a few tool workbenches and a ladder sat out in the open. Although the whole area was spotlessly clean with no sign of arachnid, she figured she better not press her luck. Turning to climb the stairs to the main level of the house, several boxes tucked underneath the stairs caught her attention. Moving closer to read the handwritten labels, her throat nearly closed when she realized the black marker read "Kinsley's Things" on three of the boxes.

"Holy Shit. I thought he threw it all away." Lifting the flaps on the top box, a wave of emotions hit her at the sight of her old yearbooks. Pushing the questions of why Mitchell would store her belongings out of her mind, she pulled out the yearbooks one by one, stacking them in her arms.

"Booow," came a call from the top of the stairs.

"Hold on, Petunia, I'm coming," she yelled. That dog needed to learn how to go up and down stairs.

"Booow…. Booow…. Booow."

"Alright, damn it, I'm coming up now!" With five yearbooks in her arms, Kinsley flicked the light switch with her elbow and headed up. Petunia was marching in place and wagging her tail. "You need to learn how to handle stairs. Oh, but wait. The shelter probably doesn't have stairs, so you don't need to worry about it. What do you think of that?"

Petunia let out a low growl and shuffled over to her food bowl. "Ah, so that was the emergency, huh? You're out of kibble. Tell you what, I'll mix up some canned food with the dry food for you, kind of like a free man's last meal before going to the big house…unless Bass decides to spare you of your fate. Would you like that?"

Kinsley lifted Petunia's bowl off the laminate floor and mixed a can advertising chicken chunks and gravy with a cup of dry dog food. The dish hadn't yet hit the floor before Petunia pounced on it like a kid on candy. Kinsley poured herself another glass of red and plopped down on the recliner armed with the yearbooks she had managed to grab before Petunia's temper tantrum. Gently rocking in the chair, she found three high school yearbooks and two from junior high. She flipped through the pages from her senior year, reminiscing over her team pictures on the dance squad, the environmental club, and honors society. Looking at the pictures of all her classmates, only a handful of which she was still in contact with, made her smile. The girls in the photos were trying desperately to wear the famous Rachel haircut and the infamous jean vests with long flowered skirts.

Kinsley put her senior yearbook down and decided to grab one from middle school. The white leather bound book was from seventh grade. Feathered bangs and overalls held on by one strap were even more entertaining than the pictures from high school. Lifting her wine glass to take another sip, she paused at the next familiar photo that greeted her. There was Bastian's picture. Spiky blond hair and that boyish smile that used to make her heart ache for hours on end. Mother Nature's cruel joke of allowing men to become better with age applied times ten to Bastian Harris, so what Debbie had said about him being the hot ticket in town was most likely true. She took a long, slow sip of the mellow tasting wine. Resting her head on the chair, she thought about the night she went for it and kissed him.

She had been at her friend Erin's house for the weekend. That May in the mountains was warmer than usual, so her parents went ahead and got the pool ready early. It was a Saturday and Erin's parents had some work-related cookout to go to that evening. They asked if the girls wanted to tag along, but Erin and Kinsley recognized the opportunity of being parent free when they saw one. The minute their headlights disappeared, Erin got on the phone with Bastian to see if he and Jimmy wanted to come over and go swimming.

Erin was allowed to have boys over while her parents were home, but the girls liked the times Erin's parents weren't around best. They could play what music they wanted, cuss every now and again, and be a bunch of goofballs without her mother spying out the window blinds the whole time like Nancy Drew. Erin's parents hadn't been gone for more than ten minutes when Jimmy and Bastian came knocking on the door wearing swim trunks and with towels in hand. The girls had already changed into their bathing suits and the four of them headed to the patio. Along with being heated, the pool also had underwater lights, so they decided to leave the porch lights off and see only by the dimly lit water.

They swam around, played Marco Polo and chicken, which was one of Kinsley's favorites, especially when she got to be on

Bastian's shoulders. Even though the water was warm from the heaters, the night was still cooler. When she had gotten on top of Bastian's shoulders, he joked about how bumpy her legs were and how her hair was going to grow faster, and he called her Chewbacca. Kinsley secured her legs around his chest and hurled herself backwards, taking him underwater to teach him a lesson. They started kicking, splashing, and essentially trying to drown each other—typical middle school pool behavior.

After things had settled down, she decided to get out and get a drink from inside. She hopped out of the pool, wrapped herself with a giant towel, and slipped through the sliding glass door. If she thought she was cold before, inside was worse. The air conditioning blasted through the room, and Kinsley shivered as she grabbed a Sprite out of the fridge. Hearing the door slide open behind her and seeing Bastian come towards her with his towel around his neck, glistening with water droplets and delectableness, made the knot that regularly resided in her chest at his presence grow larger than usual.

"You want a drink?" she asked holding out a can of soda.

"Yeah, please." He took the can from her and popped the top. As she sipped her drink, she must have still been shivering because Bastian eyed her. "You cold?"

"Yeah, aren't you?" He put his drink down on the counter and took the towel from around his neck, wrapping it around Kinsley's shoulders. He began to run his hands up and down her arms quickly. They never had the touchy feely sort of friendship, so his hands on her arms created a buzz in the pit of her stomach. It didn't matter that the fuzzy cotton towel created a barrier between his fingertips and her forearms; the heat she felt was as strong as if he were caressing her skin. She tried to collect her thoughts.

"Nah, it's not that bad." Kinsley put her drink down to further wrap the towel around herself. As much as she wanted the friendly affection to continue, she needed to step back for a moment before she did something she would regret.

"Better?" he asked giving her that smile. The boy she spoke to on a daily basis as a friend, and fantasized about hourly as being more than a friend, had now given her his towel and rubbed her arms. She knew it was most likely a simple act of a good friend, but the water droplets on his nose and the gentle curve of his mouth drew her in like a tractor beam. It was now or never, and if she never did it, she would always wonder what could have happened if she wouldn't have been a chicken and gone for it.

After taking a deep breath, Kinsley leaned forward and kissed him. Her lips were still trembling from the cold, and her wet hair felt like icicles against her cheeks. She was stiff, thin lipped, and ready for rejection. His lips were much warmer than hers, but stayed rigid, probably from the shock of her kissing him. Kinsley had never told Bastian about her feelings for him. She had always been afraid it would ruin their friendship, and he would run screaming for the hills to escape the awkward predicament.

Although he constantly had girls—even from the upper grades—following him around and trying to get his attention, he always seemed more comfortable with her. They got along and understood each other's sense of humor. She knew all his groupies hated how much time he spent with her and that power kind of made her feel awesome. But she wasn't taking this leap for the envy, she was doing this because she had been secretly in love with him for two years and if she never tried, she would always wish she had.

Internally she made the resolve that if he didn't move in the next three seconds, either to deepen the kiss or to ask her what the hell she was doing, she would be the one to pull away and then apologize frantically. She mentally started counting, one...two... ready to move away and begin a string of excuses. Just as her heart began to break in half at the realization that he wanted no part of her advancement, he lifted his right hand and cupped underneath her chin. He stepped forward, tilted his head, and kissed her. They stood there for a moment, softly kissing in front of the tan Frigidaire.

A resounding scream that declared Jimmy a jerk echoed from outside and made them pull apart. The loud splash that followed led her to believe Jimmy had thrown Erin into the pool for the tenth time that night. The continuous sounds of laughter and splashing confirmed they would not be getting interrupted, and Kinsley released the breath she had been holding. She had waited for that moment for over 400 days and finally sacked up to go for it. Bastian turned around to face her, and she braced herself for possible rejection. Without saying a word, he grabbed her hand and led her into the laundry room off to the right of the small kitchenette in the basement. Once inside, he closed the door behind him and proceeded to continue the make-out session Kinsley had initiated.

Her heart pounded with the fury of a military marching band drummer as his soft lips and moist tongue invaded her mouth. He must have secretly felt the same way she did. Even after the interruption, *he* led her into the adjoining room to continue kissing *her*. This was it. This was real. She liked him and he liked her…and he was a fantastic kisser…not that she had too much experience in that department. After several minutes of euphoric bliss, they pulled away from each other, breathing very heavily.

"We better go outside or they're going to think something is up," he said inches away from her face. Her voice betrayed her in a mere squeak and all she could do was nod in agreement. The fantasy she must have played over and over in her head more than the *Like a Prayer* album had come true. It was real. It wasn't in her head anymore. It. Was. Real.

Bastian stepped away and opened the door leading into the kitchenette. The light was almost blinding after being in a blacked out room for so long. Kinsley rewrapped her towel around her and followed him through the basement to the patio. He grabbed his towel from the floor—she must have dropped it when he returned her kiss—and wrapped it around his waist. Thank goodness it was dark outside; otherwise, Jimmy and Erin would have definitely known something had gone on in the kitchen other than drinking soda. She couldn't keep the smile off her face and knew she looked like an idiot.

After about twenty more minutes of swimming, Erin started to worry about her parents coming home and finding the boys there, so she told them they better get going. Kinsley waited on pins and needles to see what Bastian would do when he said goodbye. Would he kiss her again? Would he do anything differently than the other fifty times he and Jimmy left the pool to go home? She got out of the pool in case he wanted to. To her disappointment, Bastian slipped on his flip-flops, grabbed his soda can, waved goodbye, and headed down the driveway into the darkness.

Kinsley refused to worry. Maybe he didn't want to do anything in front of Erin and Jimmy. They probably would be pretty shocked. As far as either of them knew, they were simply hanging out downstairs and not making out against the washing machine. As soon as the boys were down the road and out of earshot, Kinsley spilled the beans to Erin.

"You guys did what in my laundry room?" *Okay.* Not exactly the reaction she was hoping for.

Kinsley explained it all, detail by glorious detail, and waited for Erin to give her a giant hug or at least a high five. Erin knew how much she liked Bastian, quite often she would tell her she needed to shut up about it. No hug or hand gesture of excitement ever came. "Just don't get your hopes up Kinsley. Not saying anything about you. You're wonderful, and he is an idiot if he doesn't like you, but he's a boy. A boy has a pretty girl kiss them, no matter if they are the biggest bitch in the world, and they're gonna kiss 'em back. Case in point, most of the dunderheads he goes out with."

Despite her friend's warning, Kinsley floated on top of cloud nine for the rest of the night. She fought the urge to talk about Bastian every chance she got. On Sunday when she went home, she waited all day for the phone to ring. Surely Bastian would call her and want to talk, maybe not about kissing, but at least to hear her voice. By eight o'clock that night, when she still hadn't heard from him, Kinsley broke the cardinal rule and called his house. His mother said he was outside helping his dad in the garage, and she would tell him to give her a call later. Her phone remained silent for the rest of the night.

Monday morning at school, she stood patiently by his locker. She missed him all day Sunday and anxiously waited to see how they were going to move forward together. He turned the corner of the hallway and paused when he saw her. She must have looked like a fool waiting for him like another one of his groupies. He resumed his movement through the hallway and slowly walked up to her. "Hey, Kinsley."

"Hey, Bastian. What did you do the rest of the weekend?" She stood like a grinning fool, holding her trapper keeper in front of her chest.

"My dad made me clean out the garage. You?" He opened his locker to switch out his books for the first two periods.

"Nothing much."

He nodded, finished getting his supplies from his locker, and turned towards her. "You ready for the math test today?" Without waiting for her response, he began walking down the hall. She spun quickly to walk with him as they usually did, but something was definitely off. He seemed to be keeping distance between them, which was not an easy task in a crowded hallway during class changes. His tone was the same and he didn't act like he needed to get away from her as fast as possible, but he wouldn't get too close either. They went to class and proceeded to take their math test. Kinsley was fairly certain she failed since she kept drawing hearts in the margin instead of showing what X equaled. When the bell rang to switch to English, she hopped up out of her seat and turned to see him already leaving the classroom with Robbie Wallace.

By the end of the school day, when he hadn't done anything to acknowledge what happened, Kinsley went into the girls' bathroom and cried. Apparently, women's restrooms had been a safe haven for her since childhood. Refusing to talk to her would have at least been something, but acting like he had amnesia about it felt far worse. It meant so little to him. Like Erin had warned her, he chose to block it out and proceed as usual.

Kinsley waited all week to see if his actions would change, but they didn't. He continued to be mister charismatic and friend to everyone, including her. After several weeks of this cruelty, she resolved that if by the last day of school they had not discussed what had happened, she would muster up the courage to start the conversation. However, she was pretty sure if she had to be the one to initiate the topic that she would disprove the theory that no one had ever actually died of embarrassment. Her fingers remained crossed throughout the remainder of the month in hopes that her day of redemption would arrive. The cramping in her knuckles became worrisome until the last week of school when something finally happened, but not what she had hoped. As she pushed the door to the girls' locker room to dress for gym, she spotted him walking down the hallway with Melissa Childress...and they were holding hands.

"What an asshole." Kinsley stacked the yearbooks on top of the coffee table in front of her father's recliner. She went into the kitchen and made herself yet another tuna fish sandwich with Petunia at her heals. Remembering her aunt's story about Bastian's somewhat recent divorce, she mused that Bastian had met his match in some lucky woman.

After cleaning up her mess and giving Petunia the left over tuna, she went upstairs to take a shower. While the hot water sprayed down on her, the thoughts of Bastian were replaced by the next day's meeting with the lawyer. Her appointment at the office of Raklin, Brian, and Hoffman was tomorrow at ten-thirty. No matter how many people showed up at the reading, it couldn't be any worse than what she had to endure at the viewing. With any luck, she would get everything finalized and could set things in motion to get the hell out of Staunton and home again. In Hampton Roads, turkey buzzards weren't a problem and neither were blue-eyed, blond haired memories.

Chapter Six

Kinsley arrived at the lawyer's office almost twenty minutes late. Petunia decided after she did her business in the backyard that it was warm enough to take a dip in the river behind the house. Kinsley was dressed and ready to go when she found the mutt outside trying to catch some sort of small silver fish while it swam upstream. Refusing to come when called, she eventually had to wade in after her and pull her in by her collar. The water level of the river was so low that it wouldn't have been an issue if she were dealing with a Great Dane or a Rottweiler. But Petunia shook the excess water held within her ten pounds of skin folds all over Kinsley's Vera Wang dress and left muddy paw prints around the kitchen and living room floor. After cleaning the mess and getting changed into a pair of jeans and sleeveless white blouse, she drove her BMW like it was stolen to the reading.

When the secretary showed her into Mr. Brian's office, she found her Aunt Debbie and an older gentleman she had seen at the viewing sitting in the puffy leather chairs. Mr. Brian sat behind a large mahogany desk with a disapproving scowl on his face.

"Sorry everyone, Petunia decided to... Oh never mind. I apologize for being late." She sat down in an available chair, causing a giant whoosh of air to expel from sinking into the thick leather.

"Mrs. Bailey, thank you for joining us." Mr. Brian folded his hands on the top of his desk as if he were praying. "No worries, we waited for your arrival to begin." His judgmental brow said the sentiment wasn't exactly genuine. Mr. Brian was an older man, probably in his early sixties. Silver hair swept over his balding dome in a pitiful attempt at a comb over. His dark grey suit and navy blue tie looked like they had been starched enough to stand up on their own. "Please be advised I have another engagement in roughly thirty minutes, so we will get down to business. I know your aunt, being the executor of the estate, has already given you some information regarding your inheritance. However, we do need to go over the details in order to get everything finalized."

"Yes, of course. And it's Miss, not Mrs." Kinsley felt like she was a kid in the principal's office getting an ultimatum for skipping class. The fact that she had sunk so far into the chair that her knees were practically bent up to her boobs didn't help either.

"Please note that I prefer to record these sessions in case any discrepancies arise. Does anyone object?" All three nodded their agreement. Mr. Brian pushed the red button on a recorder. "Today's date is July 28th, 2015. This is the reading of the last will and testament of Mitchell Robert Bailey. Included in the audience is Kinsley Bailey, daughter of Mitchell Bailey, in addition to Debra Bailey, sister-in-law to Mitchell Bailey, and Gregory Whitman, Chief of Police for the city of Staunton, Virginia. All those mentioned are beneficiaries or representatives thereof included in Mitchell Bailey's will and therefore their presence was requested. The reading begins as follows.

"I, Mitchell Robert Bailey, resident of the city of Staunton in the state of Virginia being of sound mind and disposing memory and not acting under duress or undue influence, and fully understanding the nature and extent of all my property and of this disposition thereof, do hereby make, publish, and declare this document to be my Last Will and Testament, and do hereby revoke any and all other wills and codicils heretofore made by me."

Say what? Kinsley was an intelligent person, but even she got lost in the legal mumbo jumbo. The first part of the will revolved around settling debts accrued in life and for funeral expenses to be handled by her aunt. Beyond the viewing and cremation costs, there were none. The confusion continued to include any taxes or leans owed upon his property, which Aunt Debbie was still appointed to take care of.

"I bequeath the Staunton Police Department, to be represented by Chief Gregory Whitman, an allotment of twenty-five thousand dollars to be restricted in continual funding of the Cops are Pops program."

Kinsley raised her hand to get Mr. Brian to pause. "Excuse me, what is Cops are Pops?"

"It's a program your father started about four years ago to support fathers on the force who become injured in the line of duty. It helps families keep food in the house, pays for a cleaning service to tidy the home up once a week, and a weekend trip to Busch Gardens for the kids after the father has recovered. It is a wonderful program," explained Chief Whittman.

Kinsley's jaw about dropped to the floor. That rat turd couldn't even bother to pick her up for a lousy weekend visit, and he starts a program that helps injured cops get better and return to their kids faster? *What the hell?* She felt like she had entered the twilight zone.

"I bequeath Debra Bailey twenty-five acres of farm land residing at 723 Jessup Lane under the guidelines that it still be used to supply affordable rent to farmers in need and all remaining monies after debts and funeral charges have been settled."

Aunt Debbie went for the wad of Kleenex she had on standby in her pocket when she heard the news. "Bless you, Mitchell Bailey," she whimpered looking up at the ceiling. Kinsley wanted to tell her she needed to turn her sentiment downward in order to get more direct acoustical properties, but it didn't seem like an appropriate time.

"And to my daughter, Kinsley Bailey, I bequeath my personal residence located at 4 Eagle Rock Lane, all properties and items included therein, my beloved dog, Petunia, and the contents of my safe deposit box located at Town Bank and Trust. There are no restrictions or contingencies upon the above mentioned."

Safe deposit box? Aunt Debbie never said anything about a safe deposit box. The sniffling woman next to her, who happened to be conveniently avoiding eye contact, had apparently been keeping secrets. *No contingencies or restrictions? That was promising.* He could have been a bastard and said she had to live in the house in order to keep it or that she had to keep that damn dog. She had free will over all of the above, including whatever was in that safe deposit box.

Mr. Brian finished the last few legal jargons of the document and pressed stop on the recorder. Chief Whitman stood up and shook the lawyer's hand while Aunt Debbie crumbled up her used tissues and stuck them into her purse, even though a trashcan was two feet away. Kinsley waited her turn for the formality of saying goodbye to Mr. Brian, but when he approached to shake her hand he handed her a key instead.

"Ms. Bailey, here is the key to the safe deposit box. To review its contents, you'll need to take a photo ID, your copy of the will, and the death certificate with you for proof. Please do let me know if you have any questions. I will be in touch once I get all the final paperwork on the deed to the house completed."

"Yes, Mr. Brian. Thank you for your help." Kinsley exited the office and stood outside the door to wait for her aunt. When Debbie spotted Kinsley waiting around the corner like a spider, she began speed walking out of the building as if it was on fire. Kinsley jogged behind her in an effort to catch up. "Hey, you didn't say anything about a safety deposit box. What's that about?"

"That's for you to open when you're good and ready." Debbie dug through her purse.

Why was she so anxious?

"You know what's in there, don't you?"

"It's not for me to say. You just make sure you take a peek before you high tail it out of town in that fancy Japanese car of yours."

"BMW's are from Germany," she explained.

"Well that's even worse. The Nazis came from there." Debbie shoved her key into the driver's side door of her Buick and threw her purse on the passenger seat before flopping down in the driver's seat.

Kinsley grabbed the car door so she couldn't close it. "I don't understand why you are in such a rush to get away from me right now! You practically had to hog-tie me to get me at the Holy Redeemer with you! Are you afraid of what I might find in that box over at the bank?"

"I don't know what you're talking about. I have a busy schedule to keep today, that's all. I got an appointment for a wash and style down at the Best little Hair House at one."

Her face was indifferent. She wasn't going to give anything away.

"Fine, Aunt Debbie. I hope to see you before I 'high tail it out of here' by the end of the week." Kinsley slammed the door and headed over to her own car.

Grabbing her phone, she saw it was already past eleven-thirty. Bastian would be at the house in a little over an hour.

That gave her enough time to stop by the grocery store to pick up a few more things. She was sick of eating tuna fish. She should probably pick up some dog shampoo too, so Petunia wouldn't smell like river water when Bastian came over. Might sweeten the pot for him to take the mutt or at least she would be clean when she got dropped off at the shelter.

Maybe I should buy a few treats too. Shelters don't have money for those sort of things.

***

Bastian turned his black Jeep Wrangler right onto Eagle Rock Lane at about 12:45. His meeting with Kinsley was in fifteen minutes, and one thing the Army taught him well was never to be late reporting for muster or for a meeting with a woman. *If you aren't early, then you're late.* If he'd been early arriving at his own house after his last stent of work in Afghanistan, he might have been able to stop his wife and daughter from leaving to go live with his best friend. Using an old copy of a billing slip for Mitchell's address, he spotted the log cabin home along the right side of the road. What he didn't expect to see was Kinsley chasing some four-legged floppy thing around a tree with a hose and a sponge.

Bastian parked along the side of Eagle Rock Lane in front of the house's mailbox. After turning off the ignition, he sat and watched as Kinsley did some sort of quick footwork and leapt for what appeared to be a basset hound. The top on his jeep was down so he was privileged enough to hear her cursing and telling the dog to get its "flabby ass over here." Kinsley's squatted stance signaled that a sprint for the dog was in the works, and after a heartbeat, she went for it. Since the pooch was quicker than her adversary, she darted in the other direction around the tree she was tied to while Kinsley gracefully belly-flopped onto the ground. Laughing to himself and realizing she didn't know she had an audience, Bastian decided to go ahead and head towards where she was sprawled on the ground.

Kinsley banged both her fists in the dirt and pushed herself up so she sat on her knees. "Alright you rotten sagging mutt! You win! I was trying to give you a bath so the man coming over here would be suckered into saving your ass from being delivered to the shelter! You better hope he likes dirty little dogs that smell like swamp water!" Bastian fought to control his laugh. The dog stood wagging her tail and gave one loud bark to let Kinsley know she was calling her bluff. Immediately, the dog's focus turned to him and three barks followed.

He grinned wide as Kinsley's head followed the direction of the dog's bark, and she smacked her hands against her thighs. "Great! So exactly how much did you see and/or hear?"

Bastian decided to have a little fun with the situation. "Oh, just you doing a face plant on the grass and calling me a sucker." After slipping his sunglasses to the top of his head and keeping a stern line to his lips, he slipped his hands in his pocket. He knew keeping his hands restrained was essential. Otherwise, he might reach out and touch something on her that would make him want to get his hands on more than the guns she had in the house.

"I wasn't calling you an actual sucker. What I meant was that maybe you were a sucker in the sense of having a big old soft spot for a beautiful Basset Hound dog that is in need of a new home." She held up her hands to feature Petunia much like a game show girl would showcase a new Toyota Camry.

"Sorry, dogs are against my lease." Kinsley let out a sigh and he figured he should probably let her know he really wasn't angry, but rather amused. His stern mouth cracked a grin and her shoulders slumped into a relaxed state. "Here, let me help you up."

Bastian walked over and held out his hand. This move was against his better judgment, but his mother raised him better than to let a woman sit on the ground without offering her some assistance in getting to her feet. She reached up allowing him to help her in getting out of her defeated position in the dirt.

"Thank you," she said, standing and wiping her hands on her shorts. Her hair was up in some sort of messy version of a ponytail. Through the spots of mud and dirt, he could see a grey tank top with the picture of a crab holding a sign that read, "Dirty Dick's Crab House." Her mid-thigh jean shorts revealed a set of knees that were also covered in crud. She was perfect.

"What time is it? I thought you were going to be here at one."

"I am a little early. I prefer to be early rather than late. Habit from the military, I guess." He pointed to her tank top. "Nice shirt."

She rolled her eyes. "Oh. I was going to change before you got here. I started giving that damn dog a bath twenty minutes ago. I thought I had the perfect plan of tying her to that tree and sating her with treats, but as soon as she saw the hose it was all over. And you're early. As you probably saw, I was getting ready to give up." She had a loose piece of hair that had fallen from her ponytail in front of her eyes. As her hands were covered in dirt, she huffed and puffed, attempting to move it out of her line of vision.

"Here, let me get that for you." Bastian reached out and tucked the loose strand behind her ear. He liked the sharp intake of breath his touch caused before her face screwed into a serious expression.

"Thank you." She walked over towards the tree and began the task of untying Petunia from the maple. Bastian decided to make himself useful and rolled the hose up on its stand. As the dog ran circles around Kinsley, making the process of undoing the knot more difficult, Kinsley's chin dimpled, and her brow scrunched. She certainly still wore her expressions on her face like a bright blinking light. He remembered that about her from long ago. She was terrible at lying and hiding frustration due to her expressive facial features. Not that she hid much from anyone anyways; she usually told it like it was.

Once the dog had successfully wrapped the yellow synthetic rope around Kinsley, pinning her against the tree, she at last got the knot free and started weaving her arms around the massive trunk to unwrap the tether. When the last loop released from the tree, the dog darted to the back porch with the rope trailing behind her.

Kinsley walked up to Bastian and pointed at the wound hose. "Thanks for doing that."

"Am I correct in thinking the dog was part of the inheritance too?" He cocked a brow while she leaned over to pick up the sponge and dog shampoo from the ground. The crevice of her cleavage became more visible with her bend. Bastian had to snap his gaze up from the tempting flesh in front of him. This was a business meeting. He didn't need to be thinking about her lady parts, visible or not.

"Ding, ding, ding. Yep, another jackpot I got from the inheritance, Petunia. I guess if you don't want her, then I am stuck with her until tomorrow. After that, it's off to the Staunton Humane Society!" she yelled towards the porch.

Bastian sucked his teeth as people do before delivering some bad news. "You're stuck with her until Thursday. The shelter in town is closed on Wednesdays." The mass of flesh, which was now laying exhausted in front of the sliding glass door entirely too proud of herself, appeared to be smiling while she panted.

"Of course it is. Well, you came all this way to see some guns. Come on in." As she stepped on to the porch, she picked up a giant blue bath towel that he supposed was meant for Petunia and wiped herself off. "Are you thirsty? Can I get you anything to drink?"

"Ice water would be great. I've been in Waynesboro since

eight on a few business meetings. I haven't had anything to drink since this morning."

Kinsley opened the refrigerator and grabbed bottled water. "You could have rescheduled for a later time or tomorrow. I would have been okay with that." She handed him the bottle.

"Nah, I could tell the other day you were pretty intent on getting out of here as soon as possible. I don't mind." He screwed off the cap and nearly drank the entire bottle in three gulps.

"Geez, you look like me after fifth period."

He pulled the bottle from his lips. "Fifth period?"

"I'm a teacher. I have to teach five fifty minute classes in a row before I get a break. As soon as the fifth period bell rings, I'm usually knocking the kids down to get to my water bottle and use the bathroom."

"I thought you worked on ships. At least that's what Mitchell had said." Her smile faded at the mention of her father, and he kicked himself mentally for bringing him up.

"He didn't keep too up to date on anything that happened with me. Do you want another?" she asked pointing to the bottle.

"No, this is good for right now. So where's this collection?"

"Garage, follow me." She led him around the corner of the kitchen to the small hall containing two doors. The doorknob refused to budge in her hand. "Sorry, it seems to stick." She shoved her shoulder into the door, almost toppling into the garage as it opened. Bastian grabbed her arm and cradled her against his chest to keep her from falling.

"Jesus, you okay?" He could wrap his entire hand around her bicep. Instead of releasing it once she was safely on two feet, he held her against his torso for a few moments. Her arms were thin, but muscular. She must do strength training, but not the body building kind. The kind meant to keep women long and lean.

Kinsley peered down at her arm and scrunched her nose when he didn't release it right away. The acknowledgement made him loosen his grip and put his hand back at his side.

"Thanks. I'm not on my A game today. Petunia went swimming in the river this morning, making me late for the appointment with the lawyer. Then, I had to run a few errands before I failed miserably at giving her a bath. Come to think of it, I don't think I've eaten anything today either, which would explain the dizziness." She stepped into the garage and flipped on the light.

Bastian stood there with eyes as wide as milk saucers. Taking in the massive collection of firearms mounted on the wall, he let out a whistle. "Damn, you weren't kidding." He stepped onto the cement flooring and walked over to assess the weapons. "A Bacon .30 caliber pistol, a German six shot revolver, a French 12mm pinfire?" After sounding like a kleptomaniac that just found the key to the city, he stood silently. Several long minutes passed with him not saying anything and rubbing his chin.

"Well?" she asked, standing behind him.

He let out a huff and turned around to face her. "As far as I can tell, you have about ten to twenty guns here I am almost certain Tommy will want to take off your hands. I can go to the shop and price list them all so we can get an idea about the value, and then possibly work out some sort of bulk sale deal. The other guns will most likely need to be sold piece meal, which will take some time unless we find one hell of a buyer. I can talk to Tommy about maybe doing a consignment sort of situation on those guns where we house them until they are sold and take a percentage, if you're interested in getting out of here quicker than three months."

"Three months?"

"That's about how long I think it would take to find individual buyers for most of these."

"Oh no, I can't do that. I have to be back to work in a little less than a month, and I'm only supposed to be here until the end of the week. If he would entertain a consignment option, that would be phenomenal. And of course, I'll do a bulk deal. These guns don't mean squat to me. If anything, they're a reminder of things Mitchell found more important than my mother or me."

Bastian stood there for a breath, regarding her warily. He wasn't too sure what she meant by her statement, but he figured since she had her ass handed to her by a sixty pound hound dog, now wasn't the time for her to elaborate. "Okay, let me take a couple of pictures. You got anything to write on? I need to make a list of what I see here and take a few shots of the weapons I'm not too sure about."

"Yes, absolutely. Hold on a minute and I'm sure I can find something somewhere in the house."

Chapter Seven

Kinsley scuttled into the kitchen, rummaging around on top of the fridge and counters for a notepad. On the coffee table in the living room, she found a pen next to the stack of yearbooks, but no luck on the paper. Before she began climbing the stairs, her eyes shifted in the direction of Mitchell's bedroom door.

What the hell? Why not? Figuring there was no time like the present, she changed direction and opened his door. His bedroom was outfitted simplistically. A double sized bed sat in the middle of the room, neatly made with two pillows and a white blanket beaded with a fabric design. A large light wooden dresser sat at one end of the room next to a window at the front of the house. On top of the dresser, she found a light blue notepad scripted with "Mitchell's Messages" on the cover. She grabbed the notepad and turned to leave but something caught her eye.

A photograph of her on college graduation day in a cap and gown sat on the nightstand next to his bed. She walked over and picked up the pewter frame adorned with a diploma scroll. She wasn't sure why or how he had this photo, but now was not the time to try to figure it out. Now was the time to sell off his shit piece by piece so eventually the memory of Mitchell Bailey would disappear as if he never existed. She set the frame back on the nightstand and walked out, closing the door behind her.

Upon returning to the garage, she found Bastian admiring some sort of pistol. His thick fingers caressed the barrel. The memory of those same fingers sliding across her cheek twenty years ago froze her in her tracks. Unprepared for the flashback or the sensation accompanying it, she gripped the pen and notepad until her knuckles turned white. Watching him gingerly rotating the gun to inspect its every angle, she found it so odd to see a metal object used for protection, war, or killing off turkey buzzards being handled as if it were as delicate as a butterfly's wing. Fortunately for her, he was too engrossed in the weapon to pick up on her body language or notice she was strangling the pen.

"This is amazing, Kinsley. I had no idea your father had this extensive of a collection. Whenever he talked about it at the shop, he always referred to it as a modest hobby. He had to track these guns down."

His voice reverberating off the cement walls jerked her from her trance and unglued her feet from their current position. She held out the notepad and pen to him, desperately hoping her palms hadn't left dampness on the paper from their earlier death grip. "Here you go. Yep, Mitchell clearly had at least one love in his life."

Bastian returned the gun to its position on the wall and took the items from her hand. She hailed a silent hallelujah when he didn't wipe the notebook on the side of his jeans to remove any sweat. Placing the pen between his teeth, he tapped the notebook against his palm. His expectant stare made her assume he was waiting for her to say something or leave him to his work.

Mentally wrestling over what sort of witty expression she could muster that would make him simultaneously desire her and hate himself forever before she sashayed back into the house like a boss, she badly hoped such an adage existed. Sadly, her stomach decided to chime in and growl instead. Being that she hadn't eaten all day and burned about seven hundred calories chasing Petunia around the backyard with the hose, the gurgle was the loud, drawn out obnoxious type that squealed like air being slowly let out of a balloon.

Any optimism that her stomach symphony remained inaudible to her present company was crushed when the corners of Bastian's lips turned upwards. "Hungry?" he asked with the pen still gripped between his teeth.

Although he had grown up in the same southern town as her, he had obviously forgotten proper gentlemen etiquette on ignoring situations in which women accidentally had bodily functions occur in their presence. Well, she hadn't forgotten her southern upbringing and knew it would be rude to eat in front of company…or to grab the Bic Retractable and stab him in his perfect pecs. "Are *you* hungry?"

He removed the pen from his mouth and stared directly into her goddamn soul. "Starving."

"Clearly, I am too. Do you like barbeque chicken?"

"Of course."

"Good…do you know how to grill it?"

He smiled. "I'd like to think so."

"Perfect, I'll get the charcoal started. I can grill, but I have the uncanny ability to burn the outside while the inside stays raw. Do you have anywhere you need to be right away?" God she hoped he didn't read too much into her invitation.

"Nothing's going on of too much significance," he said, shrugging his shoulders.

"Okay. I'll get the grill going and the food prepped while you do whatever it is you need to do in here. I could use some company that doesn't involve Aunt Debbie, a four-legged pain in the ass, or Tic Tac Pie."

"You met Ida Robinson, eh?" he laughed. "Her Tic Tac pie

is famous in these parts."

"Filling a pie crust with chocolate pudding and lining the top with orange and green Tic Tacs should be considered an abomination. I'll be in the kitchen, so come on in when you're done."

Kinsley headed to the kitchen to retrieve the chicken breast out of the fridge. Semi-confident she recovered from the staring, sweaty, stomach gas snafu, she breathed a sigh of relief as she grabbed a bottle of barbeque sauce from the cupboard and a small bag of charcoal from under the sink.

Once on the porch, she placed the briquettes in the base of the grill and gave them a good soaking of lighter fluid. She used a lighter she found in a jar that held grilling utensils, and the coals quickly ignited with a swift touch from the flame. Placing he lid on the grill, she went upstairs to clean up and change out of her muddy clothes while the charcoals did their thing. After scrubbing with warm soapy water, she slipped into a pair of grey yoga pants reserved for Pilates classes and dateless Saturday evenings. She also thought it best to change her Dirty Dick's tank top for something with a little less innuendo, and slipped a purple extra-long loose racer tank over her camisole.

After washing her face and redoing her sorry excuse for a ponytail, she decided she looked well enough put together without seeming like she put too much effort into it. Twenty years later his type probably still involved cupie dolls that wore makeup to go outside and get the mail. She wanted to show him she was comfortable and beautiful *au naturale* and had no need to get gussied up just because she was having lunch with a man...even if it was Bastian Harris.

Back on the porch, she lifted the lid to find the coals already a perfectly uniform grey. The door connecting the garage to the house opened and shut with a thud behind her. Like a traitor, her heart began to speed up and regrettably she wished she had put on some sort of lip gloss or at least a quick swipe of concealer. Bastian sauntered through the kitchen and onto the deck where she was focusing all her attention on repositioning the coals for the fourth time.

***

"I think I got everything I need for now. I wrote down the guns I know Tommy will want so I can get that offer for you tomorrow," he said, handing her the notepad.

"Great. Thank you again, by the way. I appreciate you making the trip out here."

"Not a problem. I'm guessing this could be pretty advantageous for the both of us. We have an identical Smith and Wesson Victory model on sale at the shop for eight hundred dollars. If all your guns are about that quality and rarity, I think you're going to be pretty happy." Bastian took advantage of her focus on the coals to survey her change in wardrobe. Unfortunately, she had picked a shirt that ended below her bottom so he couldn't see the obvious tightness of her workout pants and lacked a sexual slogan. *Too bad.* He was kind of hoping for lunch with a view.

"Can I get you another drink?" she asked, placing the lid back on the grill. "I think the grill's ready."

"Another water would be great." He followed her into the kitchen where she fished him another bottle from the fridge. As he drank, she prepped the raw meat with salt and pepper.

"I must admit, my agenda for getting you to stay is not entirely honorable."

Oh? Bastian cocked one eyebrow.

"I've eaten tuna fish for the past two days, and I was getting sick of it. Grilled chicken sounded on point when I was at the store, but I'm garbage at cooking it. I don't get much opportunity to grill at home."

Okay, maybe not the hidden agenda he had hoped.

"Why's that?" He took a long swig from the water bottle

and leaned his hip against the stove to watch her massage the seasonings into the meat. "Doesn't your husband grill for you?" May as well turn the conversation to answer a few of his curiosities. When he was around her for the first time at the shop, her calm and disinterested demeanor had him thinking she must be married or seriously involved with someone. But a few times in the backyard and just a few minutes ago, he could see her steely exterior slip a bit. He was pretty sure she was staring at him in the garage too.

She laughed. "No, I don't have a husband. Never had one. I guess you could call me a spinster." She smiled while flipping the chicken to season the other side.

"No, my Great Aunt Agnes is a spinster. You don't get to claim that title until you're unmarried and own at least seven cats. You don't even want that dog, so I don't think you're ready to get that label yet."

She moved to the sink and washed her hands. "It's not that I don't want her. But I don't think I could take care of a dog. My life is pretty busy, and I don't have anyone to help with something like that."

"What about a boyfriend?"

She grabbed a kitchen towel, drying her hands. "I don't have one of those either. More trouble than a dog." She didn't speak for several moments while folding the towel and placing it on the counter before picking up the plate of chicken. She snatched a set of tongs out of a mason jar on the counter and pointed the utensil at him. "You got a girlfriend?"

Bastian thought it sounded like more of an accusation than a question. He decided to use the question to his advantage to see if he could get her to come undone again. "No, I don't have *a* girlfriend." She nodded as if it were something to consider. "I have many."

She snorted with laughter, "Not much has changed then, huh?"

Ouch. Not exactly the reaction I was looking for. He took the tongs and plate of raw meat out of her hand. "What's that supposed to mean?"

"Just that the Bastian I remember from a long time ago also had the unfortunate dilemma of having too many women to court." She walked over to the sliding glass door and pulled it open. He followed her out onto the deck while she lifted the lid to the grill and placed it on the hand railing.

"Court? What are we in fifteenth century England now?" Using the tongs, he picked up pieces of chicken and placed them a few inches apart on the grill.

"Do you need the sauce?" she asked, pointing in the direction of the kitchen.

"No, not yet. You put it on the last few minutes of cooking; otherwise, it will burn into an un-eatable mess."

Kinsley stood beside him with her hands on her hips. He knew she wanted to say something because she was chewing on the side of her mouth. He somewhat enjoyed watching her impenetrable demeanor peel away like the shell of a peanut. Reading women as well as Bastian knew he could, he silently and slowly rotated the chicken, knowing she could only keep her question in for so long.

"So what my Aunt Debbie said was true then?"

"That depends on what your Aunt Debbie said." He crossed his arms over his chest, holding the tongs upright. This was probably going to hurt. Small town gossip usually did.

"That you were sought after by more women than insect repellant at a Fourth of July picnic."

He snorted. "I don't know where your aunt gets her stories from, but no, that isn't exactly true. I'm one of the few unmarried men over thirty and under fifty in this town. Divorcees out number us by twenty to one. The ratio makes it seem like I'm getting bombarded." Okay, so maybe he was exaggerating a little. The ratio was more like five to one, but he didn't want to seem like an arrogant prick.

He broke from the conversation to hang the tongs on the side handle of the grill and straightened up to take in the view from the porch. The gentle sound of the river flowing was soothing to the ears. The lush green vegetation that bordered its edges swayed softly along with the breeze. The farmland behind the house also appeared in good health and didn't smell of fertilizer, which was a plus since the day was so windy. "So you really wouldn't consider keeping this place?"

She leaned onto the hand railing to take in the view too. "Nope. This house doesn't mean anything to me. Plus my life is my home back in Hampton Roads, not here."

"I know, but you could at least keep it as a getaway house. Be near family and old friends every once in a while."

"The only old friend I've run into here, present company excluded, is Frank Goldman, and I'm in no mood to rekindle anything with that greasy sleaze ball."

"So Frank did his usual modus operandi, huh? You know he's not the only agent there. I mentioned him because you knew him. Sharon Wilson is the one that actually helped me find my rental. She's pretty easy to work with." Seeing her eyebrow move in a high arch of assumption, he added, "On real estate."

Bastian's cell phone rang, halting their conversation. He grabbed it off the holder on his hip. It was Tommy. *Probably calling to ask why I'm not back at the shop yet.* "Excuse me a minute," he lifted the phone up to his ear and headed for the other end of the porch. "Bastian Harris."

"Hey, Bass. When's your ass getting back here so I can go get some lunch with Darlene? She's riding my case about when I'm gonna be by the hair salon to pick her up."

"Sorry, Tommy. I'm still at Kinsley Bailey's house itemizing the gun collection. She has a lot I think you'd be pretty interested in."

"You're still there? Well, how much longer you think it's gonna be? Twenty or thirty minutes?"

"Well, we just got the chicken breasts on the barbeque." That led to some marked silence.

"Just put the chicken breasts on the barbeque?"

And here we go. Bastian prepared himself for whatever zinger was getting ready to come his way. "Yeah, she asked me to stay for lunch."

"Ohhhh," Tommy intoned. Bastian could hear the smile in his voice. "So she asked you to stay for lunch, huh? And you said yes too? Very interesting."

Bastian tilted his head down and lowered his voice. "It's only lunch."

"Sure it is man. A sexy woman who you know from a 'long time ago' asks you to put meat on her grill and it's just lunch."

"Quit being a pervert. And tell Darlene to pick you guys up something and bring it to the store. I'll be back in a little while." And when he got back, the first thing he was gonna do was put Tommy in a headlock.

"Alright man, I'll let you crap on my scheduled lunch date this once 'cause I'm an understanding kind of guy and know you haven't been laid in a looooong time. But Bass, a word of advice…"

"What's that?" Bastian rubbed his brow already regretting taking the bait.

"Make sure you wait until the last minute to put the sauce on the breasts. Nothing women hate worse than when your sauce gets all over their breasts too early." With that, Bastian hung up and headed over to Kinsley. She was sitting on the porch swing, drinking a beer. One leg was tucked under her butt while she used her big toe from the other leg to rock herself.

"Do you need to get back to the shop?"

"Not for a little while. The only thing I have to do today is teach a shooting class at six."

"My Aunt Debbie told me she took your class and has become quite a shot. Says she got rid of a couple of turkey buzzards due to your tutelage. Do you want a beer?" she asked, holding up her bottle. It was already two o'clock, and his class didn't start for another four hours. He could have one beer.

"Sure, I'll take one." Kinsley got up from her spot on the swing and retrieved a Corona from the fridge.

"Do you want a lime in it?" she called from the kitchen.

Bastian walked into the house to answer her. "Absolutely, if you've got it."

She produced a lime in a sealed plastic bag and a sharp knife from one of the drawers. Not wanting to hover over her, Bastian made his way to the massive built-in bookcase behind the living room couch. "Wow, your dad studied a lot about guns." He paced along the length of the couch, reading various titles of hundreds of firearms books aloud. Another set of books stacked on the coffee table refocused his attention. He snagged the one on top and realized they were yearbooks. "This is from middle school, isn't it?"

Kinsley had been walking towards him with both beers in her hand and paused at his question.

"Taking a walk down memory lane?" He flipped through the pages. "What year was this one?"

"Seventh grade," she said, regaining her momentum.

"My God, I haven't seen my yearbooks since I left and went into the Army. Hey, there you are," he said holding up the book and pointing to Kinsley's picture.

"Yep, there I am." She took a long pull from her beer, practically gulping it, and placed his on a coaster.

He flipped two more pages and found his own picture. "There I am. Jesus, we were such babies. Hey, do you remember spending all those summer days at the pool with...oh, what was your friend's name again?" Closing the yearbook and putting it back down on the coffee table; he stood upright to find her glaring at him squinty-eyed. He'd only seen a woman look at him like that before when he'd forgotten an anniversary or a birthday.

"Yeah, I remember," she took another gulp of her beer. "Her name is Erin."

Bastian picked up his own bottle. "Do you still talk to her?"

"Nope. We lost touch after high school when we went to different colleges." Although he was pretty sure it wasn't her birthday, her eyes stayed tiny and staring through him like lasers. "What college ended up snatching you?"

"James Madison University. It's probably time to flip the chicken." She turned around without another word and headed out to the deck. So much for changing the subject. He couldn't be sure what he'd done to piss her off, but she definitely had looked like she wanted to hit him over the head with that yearbook. Best he cook the chicken to perfection.

Kinsley sat on the porch swing while he continued to play chef. "What did you major in at JMU?"

"Chemistry and Engineering."

"Double major? Damn girl. Please don't take this offensively, but why are you teaching with papers like that?" Bastian put the lid on the grill and hoped the funk she was in had subsided enough for him to sit next to her on the swing. Just in case it hadn't, he decided it best to leave the tongs with the grill.

"None taken. I spent a few years in the Peace Corp and then worked for a major ship builder. I travelled a lot." She looked out over the yard and shrugged. "After a while it took its toll. I also think not having a family of my own made me want to work with kids. So I got my teaching license. Now I work with sixth grade."

"I would think teaching middle school would make you not want to have kids. I remember being an asshole at that age."

She chuckled. "Some days I want to run and get my tubes

tied, but most days it isn't so bad." They sat in silence for a bit, before she laid a doozy on him. "How old is your daughter?"

He sucked the inside of his cheek. "I see your Aunt Debbie talked to you about more than my dating habits." She cocked her head and smiled. "She can be pretty informative."

He sighed inwardly. Although he loved talking about his daughter, he despised the inevitable questions about the mother that usually followed. "Jodi is eight years old, getting ready to turn nine. She lives with my ex-wife, Linda, and her new husband, Mark, in Raleigh, North Carolina."

To his surprise, she detoured from the wife questions and kept the conversation on Jodi. "How often do you get to see her with them living so far away?"

"Alternating holidays and one week over the summer. She'll be here in less than a week for a visit to celebrate her birthday. She's a bit bummed to be missing the Founder's Day Parade this year. If you were staying longer, I'd introduce you." Whoa. Where'd that come from? He didn't introduce women to his daughter.

"When's her birthday?"

"August sixth."

"She's a Leo, like me. My birthday is August thirteenth, another reason I don't want to be stuck here then."

"I get it." Bastian rose to get the barbecue bottle and basting brush. Something about her leaving set a rock in his gut, but he couldn't voice it, didn't even want to acknowledge it. Instead, he painted the sauce on the chicken.

Chapter Eight

The familiarity of the situation struck Kinsley like a lightning bolt. She never watched him grill in middle school, but in science lab, she would sit at her table and observe him mixing solutions or dissecting whatever poor animal had been soaked in formaldehyde. Longing after your true love while he sliced into a pig gut took devotion.

"I'm gonna go make a salad to go alongside the chicken," she called out and bolted into the house. She needed to get away from the memories to clear her head and shove her ass back into reality. Kinsley once read an article about certain senses triggering memories, which had a profound emotional effect on the test subjects. Hypothetically, the thought of decaying pig flesh coupled with the smell of charring chicken should've kept her secure from dangerous thoughts, but the power of seeing her first love again after twenty years must have trumped all those disgusting little details that usually made people dry heave. Too bad for her.

Once safely inside, she put her beer on the counter and placed her hands on either side of the sink. "It's been over twenty-years, Kinsley. Get a grip," she murmured. She rewashed her hands, grabbed the lettuce, tomatoes, and cucumbers out of the fridge, and began washing and chopping the veggies. By the time she had finished with the tomatoes, Bastian was coming into the kitchen with a plate of beautifully grilled barbecue chicken. The site of the entrée made her mouth water. Definitely not the well-built, blue-eyed man coming through the door.

"Quick, close the door or Petunia will be all over us while we eat."

Bastian maneuvered across the kitchen and slid the door closed, blocking a very depressed Petunia. "Got it."

"Thank you for grilling. If you want to set the chicken over on the table, I'll plate up the salad. Italian dressing okay?"

"I ate MRE's for several years while out in the field. You could squirt mayonnaise on it, and I'd still think it was a delicacy." They set the silverware and plates on the small table that was barely big enough for two. His massive size made it feel even more inadequate.

"So the Army, huh?" she asked as she dug into her salad. "What did you do there?"

"I was in weapons maintenance."

"That explains all the gun knowledge. During combat? Which ones?"

"Pakistan, Somalia, Jordan, and stationed in a few other places where shit was going down, but not much was heard about it on the news."

"Is it an 'I'd tell you, but I'd have to kill you' situation?" She laughed, cutting her chicken.

Bastian pushed the chicken breast around his plate. "Yeah, something like that."

"How very James Bond," she joked. The rest of the lunch revolved around neutral topics. Kinsley wanted to stick to subjects that didn't involve failed marriages or other touchy areas as much as possible. Even with the most mundane subjects, he had the remarkable ability to say things both with his mouth and body that had her unraveled more times that afternoon than she could count. She didn't like it and she needed to take control of it. So, she redirected her efforts and focused on getting reacquainted with an old friend instead of a first love. As soon as she approached him from this angle, the tension she had felt since the first time she saw him at Five Points melted away. Their conversation became effortless and comfortable, like it had been all those years ago. When she wasn't yearning for him or scribbling, 'Mrs. Bastian Harris' all over her papers, they had a great friendship.

A memory popped into Kinsley's head toward the end of lunch, and she couldn't suppress the giggles.

Bastian paused with fork in mid-air. "What's so funny?"

She leaned in her chair with her arms crossed, smiling. "Do you remember the time we used your mother's laundry basket to go sliding down the stairs? And you got grounded for crashing into the drywall with your head?"

A loud rumbling laugh barreled from his chest. "Yep, I remember that. We could've been on that show where all those idiots shoot themselves out of cannons or walk on broken glass." He waved his fork at her like a pointer. "Here's another one, I also remember us sneaking out in the middle of the night when you were at Erin's to drink those warm wine coolers."

"Oh my God, I'd forgotten about that. Jesus, I got so sick!"

"I don't know how a person can forget throwing up eight times in the bushes off of three room temperature wine coolers."

Kinsley's laughter faded into a faint smile. "I don't know. I'm sure it's easy to forget a lot of things that happened that long ago." Not wanting to delve deeper into the topic of forgotten moments, she stood up and began clearing the table. Bastian went onto the deck to treat Petunia to a leftover chicken breast. As Kinsley placed the last dish on the drying rack, he came into the house with the empty plate in his hand and a new girlfriend wagging her tail at his feet.

"I think you've made a new friend forever on that one," she said, pointing to Petunia.

"Be that as it may, it is still against my lease."

"Can't blame a girl for trying." Kinsley shrugged and leaned against the sink. "Well, Bastian, it was great catching up. Thank you again for cooking lunch."

"Thanks for the invitation. And you cooked too."

"I didn't cook. I chopped."

"Either way, I appreciate the offer. I'll get back to the shop to price these things for you so we can start on Tommy's offer. I should be able to have them for you tomorrow. Do you want me to stop by sometime in the afternoon?"

"Sure, same time?"

"That works for me." He checked his phone. "I've got to go and get ready for class. Have you ever taken a shooting course before?"

"No, I never really had a desire to get into guns. Plus, I don't have a turkey buzzard problem."

"Well, if you want to give it a go before you head out of town, just let me know. On the house." He slipped his phone back on its holder and fished his keys from his wallet. "Until tomorrow."

Kinsley walked him to the door and echoed, "Until tomorrow." When she swung the door open, she about jumped three feet in the air as she found her Aunt Debbie standing in the threshold with an amused expression on her face.

Shit!

"Well now," Aunt Debbie said, putting her hands on her hips, "What are you still doing here? I thought Kinsley told me you were coming over around one." She twisted her wrist to read the time on her watch. "It's after four." Her eyes darted back and forth between them.

"Aunt Debbie, I thought you were getting your hair done." By the look of her tight new curls and the smell of ammonium thioglycolate wafting through the doorway, she had gotten a perm.

"I didn't like the way we left things this morning so I wanted to talk. I just finished up at the Best Little Hair House. But if you two are busy, I can come back another time."

Bastian interrupted, "No, Ms. Debbie, don't you worry about it. I was actually leaving to head to the shop for class. I saw you signed up again. More buzzards?"

"No, now it's two damn opossums. I gotta get those suckers 'fore they knock over my trashcans again. I need a refresher course."

"What's the deal with this town?" Kinsley asked, throwing her hands in the air. "You all are allowed to run round your yards shooting animals?"

"If it's a nuisance animal on her property, she can choose to trap it or kill it," Bastian said, flipping his keys around his finger. "Kinsley, thank you again for lunch, and I'll see you tomorrow around one. See you tonight, Ms. Debbie." Bastian squeezed between Kinsley and the older woman and walked without shame or apology to his jeep.

Debbie turned back around grinning much too enthusiastically. "I thought that was his jeep parked by the mailbox. Lunch, huh?" Without waiting for an invitation, she barreled through the front door. Kinsley sighed and closed the door behind her. Walking into the living room, she found Debbie going through her pocketbook while sitting in the same recliner she had taken up residence in before.

"He was here to see the guns and neither of us had eaten. That's all. Well, that was all until you showed up and made it seem like more." Kinsley flopped down on the couch next to Petunia and soothed her frustration by rubbing the dog behind her ears.

"And he's coming by tomorrow too, huh?"

"Yes, to make an offer on some of the guns."

"Round lunch time again too. I find all this to be real intriguing. Seems like someone else in this town wants to go fishing for some Bass." She was the only one laughing at her innuendo.

"That someone isn't me. Besides, it appears you're the one who wants to go fishing. Taking the shooting course again, Aunt Debbie?"

Debbie's jaw dropped. "Excuse me? Popping off flying birds and shooting an enormous rat are two different kinds of targets. I need to get my A game in check so I can nail those suckers on the first shot. Besides, I could be that boy's mother...or much older sister." She waved it off. "Now, about our words this morning outside the lawyer's office. I'm sorry that I ran away from you, and I'm sorry I didn't mention the safety deposit box before. But it's not my place to talk about that."

Petunia let out a giant snore before repositioning herself to allow Kinsley the privilege of petting her belly. Kinsley obliged. "What's in the box? What's the big secret?"

"That's for you to discover in your own time. Between you and Mitchell. I came round to apologize for my dishonesty by way of omission the other day. With your mama already gone and Mitchell being fired-up like a piece of pottery as we speak, I don't think it right for you and me to be on the outs. We don't have much family left."

Kinsley took her aunt's words to heart. All the family she had known from before didn't seem to want her around. Her aunt didn't have an agenda, as best as she could tell, and wanted to keep her close solely for the sake of family, a concept Kinsley didn't know too much about. "It's alright Debbie. We're good. I'll go check out the box later this week when I have time."

Kinsley was in no hurry to see what was in there. Debbie's tone led her to believe it wasn't cash or stock certificates, but something else. Something personal from Mitchell. She wasn't ready to make a special trip to the bank to discover what because it truly didn't matter to her that much.

"I know you're going to find a realtor tomorrow, but what are you doing tonight?"

"Oh, I don't know. I can try giving Petunia a bath again." The dog's head jerked up, and she hopped off the couch.

"Giving the dog a bath? Those are your plans? I think not. You're coming to the shooting class with me."

"What?"

"Yes, ma'am. With all them guns in there you are bound to end up having to keep one or two of them. Besides, this world isn't as safe as it used to be. Shouldn't you know how to protect yourself?"

Kinsley cocked a brow. "In the event of a malicious turkey buzzard roosting or opossums thieving from my garbage cans, I am sure I can call a park ranger to take care of it."

"Well, there have been a few break-ins round these parts lately. Sylvia Nickels got her house broken into, and they stole everything, even her dead stuffed dog, Trixie. Poor thing was getting ready to move into Eastover Active Living Community and had to buy all new electronics to replace the ones taken."

"She stuffed her dead dog?"

"I didn't understand it either, but my point is they'll take anything not nailed down. Luckily, the people being burgled haven't been home during the robberies. I'd hate to think what'd happen if they were. That's another reason why I sleep with my pistol by my bed."

"For burglars? Are you sure it's not to shoot any squirrels stealing your acorns or woodpeckers drilling a hole in the trunk of your maple?"

"No, sassy pants, for protection." Debbie wagged a finger at her. "You're coming to the class. End of discussion."

"Aunt Debbie, I really don't—"

"Don't you 'Aunt Debbie' me. We just said we was gonna

try to be more like family and family spends time together."

"Yeah by watching TV, seeing a movie, or getting ice cream, not by going to a gun shooting class!"

Debbie shook her head in pity. "Boy, you have been gone from Staunton a long time."

Chapter Nine

Aunt Debbie made Kinsley change a total of three times before she was wearing an outfit "suitable to shoot a paper perp full of lead." Apparently, blowing holes in a black silhouette target required a hunter green tank top, boyfriend jeans, and beige flip flops, "cause you still want to look feminine." Debbie also insisted on driving them to Five Points because her car was "crafted in the good ole' U.S. of A" and Kinsley's Nazi tuna can would most likely crumple like aluminum foil if it ran over a squirrel. Kinsley spent the entire twenty minute trek to the gun range explaining her 'Nazi' car had front, side, curtain, and knee air bags, collision warning system, night vision with pedestrian detection, parking distance sensors, and a wicked ass set of cup holders.

Debbie somehow maneuvered her Buick tank into one of the few remaining spots at Five Points. It was a quarter until six and the parking lot was almost full. Kinsley got out of the car and noticed a woman with long red hair exiting a ford pickup. The redhead carried a black box as she walked to the door. Not too far behind her was another woman, maybe Kinsley's age but a bit heavier, toting in another pistol box.

"Hey Aunt Debbie," she called back to her at the trunk of the Buick.

"Hold on a minute, sweetie. I gotta get Pete." She continued to rummage through the trunk.

"Pete?" *Sweet Jesus, who was she riding around with in her trunk?*

"Pete's what I call my pistol. It's a Beretta Tomcat, a real beaut." She lifted a small black box from the trunk and slammed the lid shut.

"Why am I only seeing women walking into the gun shop?"

"You're not blind. You tell me," she said giving her a wink. Debbie headed for the door with Kinsley on her heels.

"I don't have a gun to shoot. Are you going to let me borrow yours? Your, uh, Pete."

"Oh no, sweetie. They have rentals you can use for the courses. I plan on getting my optimum time with Pete. Them opossums don't know what's coming for 'em."

Kinsley and Debbie walked into the lobby of Five Points into a crowd of about ten women, all older than twenty and younger than fifty. This must have been that whole ratio thing Bastian was talking about earlier. Half of them looked more like they were getting ready to go to a nightclub rather than a gun class. Kinsley had never been too a shooting range before, but she couldn't imagine them including a crop top with visible tramp stamp as reasonable attire. The brunette to her left clearly felt otherwise. Kinsley grabbed a Five Points pen and twisted her disheveled hair, a trick she had learned in times of desperation at school.

Bastian and his cousin, Tommy, stood at the counter with all the women forming a straight line in front of them. Tommy checked each woman's driver's license and marked them off on the roll sheet. Afterwards, the women stepped to the right so Bastian could check their guns to make sure they weren't armed. Although his cousin was a bit of a looker too, you could tell the ladies were waiting for the moment when they could go up to the front of Bastian's line. He made small talk with each woman as he took apart their gun to check the chamber and safety lock before moving them one more step to the right where a young man in his early twenties was selling ammunition and passing out safety gear.

Kinsley and Debbie approached the front of Tommy's line. "Miss Debbie, I sure am glad to see you here again. And you brought a friend with you. Hey Bass, Miss Debbie brought a guest." Bastian was checking the chamber on the revolver belonging to crop top when he glanced up to see Kinsley. He was already smiling while he was lecturing Miss Mid-Drift on the importance of tying a rag around the rear cylinder opening so she wouldn't damage it while cleaning the barrel, but when he saw Kinsley, his grin grew a little wider.

"Hey, Miss Debbie. Hey, Kinsley. Taking me up on my offer?" He jerked his wrist, snapping the barrel of the pistol into place.

Offer? What offer? The only thing Kinsley could think about was how utterly hot it was seeing a man in a tight black t-shirt holding a gun. He was already fine to begin with, but while holding a weapon, sex just oozed off him. Not the most appropriate thought for a former Peace Corp member. No wonder it was all freaking women taking this class. "My Aunt asked me to come with her. Apparently, the turkey buzzards are getting aggressive, and she's worried about my well-being."

"I hope y'all don't mind, Bass. I know this is a class for people who already took the firearm safety course, but that doesn't come up again for another two weeks, and she'll be gone by then. So I was hoping it might be alright. We're working on our family time," Debbie said putting her hand on Kinsley's shoulder.

Tommy smiled, reaching for Kinsley's driver's license. "Not a problem. I'll do the firearm safety stuff with you while Bass works with people out on the range. Then, we can join up with them once you feel comfortable, sound good?"

"Yes, thank you," Kinsley said, nodding.

Tommy cocked his head over at Bastian with a devilish glint in his eye. "Sound good to you, Bass?"

Kinsley couldn't have been totally sure, but she thought Bastian was glaring at Tommy. "Sounds like a plan." Debbie moved to the right so Bastian could begin checking out her gun. "Does Pete need any ammo today, Miss Debbie?"

"Nope, Bass, I think I'm all ready to go," she said proudly.

"Alrighty sweetheart, you just step over there to where Mike is, and he'll get you all set up with your eyeglasses and ear protection." Debbie took Pete to the next counter, and Kinsley slid in front of Bastian empty-handed.

"I didn't bring a gun."

"Since all of the ones in your dad's house are antiques, I'd hope you wouldn't. Don't worry. We have guns we use as rentals for classes."

"How much is the rental fee and ammunition?" she asked, pulling out her wallet.

He put his hand up to stop her and leaned in close so the other customers couldn't hear. "Don't worry about that. I told you," he smiled that cheeky grin, "on the house." An electrical energy fizzled between them. She could get caught up in a moment like this. Her heart beat hard in her chest, each thump punctuating her thoughts. Yet she needed to stay focused on who she was dealing with: a former douche bag that had most likely grown into an adult douche bag and now had a gaggle of townswomen after him. She had gotten stuck in the "Bastian Tractor Beam" a long time ago, and she wasn't doing it again.

She smiled as she pushed off the counter and said simply, "Thanks." Turning her head to the left, she motioned at Tommy, who was watching them intently. "You ready?"

"Sure thing, sweetheart. Let me get a few things, and I'll meet you in the classroom." Tommy pointed to the left of the lobby where a white door sat situated between an entire wall of holsters. As Kinsley walked over to the door she noticed

Tommy glanced at Bass and lifted his eyebrows several times.

"Just remember, I have Darlene's number at the Best Little Hair House programmed on my phone. Don't embarrass me and don't embarrass yourself," she overheard Tommy say to his cousin. Bastian, in reply, grabbed a pen from his pocket, stuck it in the side of his mouth, and walked away toward the ammunition counter where his class awaited him.

***

Bastian wasn't too sure how Holly Writtle expected him to help her with aiming the gun when she kept grinding her backside into his groin. She stood in front of him with her legs two feet apart, her ass strategically pushed out about six inches, pointing her Glock at the target. With his arms reaching around hers and placed gently on top of her hands, he was trying to work with her on pulling the trigger during an exhale to get better control of the shot. Truth be told Mr. Writtle, Holly's father, had taught his daughter how to shoot when she was about ten years old. She could probably take out a soup can from a mile away if she wanted. However, she had a different agenda concerning her attendance at the Five Points Firearms class, and Bastian knew it. It was the same agenda she had with Carl Silver at the golf course and Trent Tatum at the A-Plus Driver's School.

Bastian watched her breasts slowly rise on the inhale, pause, and pull the trigger on the release of her breath. The bullet went straight through the center of the silhouette target—a perfect shot. Fast as a whip she unloaded her weapon, placed her Glock on the counter, and spun around to give Bastian a big hug. "Oh, thank you Bass! That was fantastic," she squealed. The embrace was awkward not only because her ear protection was right under his chin, but her crop top left no place for him to return the hug without putting his hands on her bare skin.

He really should peel Holly off him and keep walking

around to help the other women in the class. The sound of shots being fired in the range was loud, even with the ear protection on so he was sure one of them could use some pointers. He felt three taps on his shoulder and turned his head to find Tommy and Kinsley standing behind him with all their safety gear on. Kinsley had one half of her mouth cocked up and her arms crossed under her breasts. He knew what she was thinking. This scene suggested evidence of her Aunt's story. He placed his hands on Holly's shoulders to push her away.

"Um, I think Kinsley here is ready to try her hand at shooting," Tommy yelled over the shots. He lifted up a black gun case that held one of the many weapons they rented out for classes. "Ammo's in the box," he said, passing it over to Bastian.

"Okay, Kinsley, let's go down to the last aisle on the end." Bastian stretched his long tattooed arm and pointed to the left. A Hula girl with a waist disproportionate to her breast size lay on his inner forearm.

"Oh, no Bass. Are we done? I was hoping you could help me some more." Holly grabbed his wrist and pointed to the target doing her best to pout. "I want to work on head shots."

Both Tommy and Kinsley stood staring at Bastian, waiting for his response.

"Sorry, sweetheart. This is Kinsley's first time so I need to help her. You sure look like you know what you're doing though. Tommy can help if you need anything." Tommy took his cue and moved forward, turning Holly back around to her target.

"Lead the way," Kinsley yelled to him. Placing one hand on her back and the other on her hip, he maneuvered her towards the far portion of the walkway and led her all the way down towards the east end of the range. There were several empty stalls closer to the other shooters, but he bypassed all of them for the last one next to the wall.

"I figured it would be a little easier to hear if we were away from some of the noise, but you still need to keep your ear protection on." He tapped the earmuff lightly. "So, you've never shot a gun before, right?"

"Nope, first-timer."

"Okay, then we're going to work on your stance and position with the gun still unloaded. After that, we'll load her up, and I'll shoot a few times so you can see it in action. Then, your turn, sound good?"

Kinsley gave him a thumb up. Bastian set the gun case on the counter and put both his hands on her shoulders. Pulling her into his chest, he stood behind her and moved his mouth next to her right earpiece. "You always want to stand with your feet about shoulder width apart and one foot slightly further ahead than the other. This gives you more stability."

Starting at the base of her shoulders, he slid his hands down the backside of her naked arms until he reached her elbows. Goose bumps formed on her skin at the gentle caress, which made him laugh a little.

Without missing a beat, she turned her head, smacking him with her earmuffs on the jaw. "It's cold in here. That's all." She jerked her head and placed her attention firmly on the target. He lifted her arms up at the elbows, positioning them so they were slightly bent.

"Are you right or left handed?" She held up her right hand. "Okay, this is the hand you're going to hold the handgun with then. The arm of that hand is going to stay straight and pointed towards your target. Your left is going to be cupping the bottom part of the gun for more support and that arm stays a bit bent." He ran one hand down her right arm straightening it while his other positioned her left arm facing the same direction, but at a slight angle. "You spend a lot of time at the beach or something?"

He could see her eyebrows scrunch together. When he

sensed another head jerk coming his way, he backed up his face a few inches from her reach to avoid another smack to the jaw.

"Why?" she asked.

"Your skin is so brown." *And tight.*

"I tan easy, but yeah, I go to the beach a lot. Now can we do this please? The longer we wait, the more nervous I get about it." She focused on the target again. "I don't like guns. People get hurt messing around with them."

"People that don't know what they're doing get hurt messing around with guns. That's why I'm here. You're in good hands."

"Looked like Miss Mid-drift with the butterfly tattooed above her ass was in your good hands too."

Sensing her sassiness, he decided to give her a taste of her own medicine. "It isn't a butterfly; it's a swallow."

"Ha, I bet she does," she snickered. He knew she wasn't talking about the bird.

"I wouldn't know, but if you go downtown and shoulder tap any man within a fifty foot radius, chances are one of them could tell you. Now are you ready to keep going?"

"Yes, sorry. None of my business. Proceed Sensei." Bastian continued to help Kinsley with her footing and holding technique. After she had that down, he took the unloaded handgun from the box.

"This is a Sig Sauer 9mm. It's a good gun to start practicing with and for use in self-defense." He showed her again that the gun wasn't loaded and handed it to her. "It's not too heavy, but it'll get the job done if you need to shoot an intruder."

"What about turkey buzzards and opossums. I hear they're the real threat," she said, examining the gun.

"Very funny." Bastian took the gun from her and showed her how to load the magazine. "I know Tommy already told you this, but you never point a loaded gun at anyone you don't intend to shoot. Now if you want to take a few steps back, I'll go ahead and fire a round so you can get an idea of what to expect." Bastian took his stance in the aisle and positioned his body, arms, and hands exactly like he showed her. He winked and said, "Watch this."

***

Kinsley rubbed the goose bumps covering her arms. It *was* cold in there, and she refused to believe it anything else but chills and nerves. The ear protection cancelled out some of the noise, but the gunshots still rang clearly. She eyed Bastian as he took aim. Although she knew it was coming, the sound of the gun firing still made her jump. Of course, he nailed the target right in the center... all three times.

Showoff.

Unloading the gun again, he placed it on the counter facing the silhouette target. Kinsley couldn't help but shake a little as he motioned for her to take the shooting position. Poppers on New Year's Eve scared the hell out of her, and now she was going to shoot a gun cause Aunt Debbie wanted family time, even though she hadn't seen her since they first checked in. Kinsley positioned herself in the aisle with Bastian on her right.

"Okay, now load the magazine into the gun like I showed you, and rack the slide back with the weapon facing the target." She did as instructed and positioned to fire the gun. She visibly trembled holding the weapon in her hands. Mostly fear of the unknown. Yeah, Bastian fired it once before, but now she had to do it. Totally different.

"Okay, Kinsley. You've got this. Inhale, hold your breath for a second, and pull the trigger on the exhale. First time is always the scariest." He took a few steps away from her. She glared down the aisle, lining up the sights with the target. She knew chances were slim to nil of her actually hitting the damn thing, so why not just do it?

Inhale...Hold...Exhale...PULL!

The gun kicked a bit in her arms. The power nearly floored her. She had to adjust her footing to get her position in place, but she still held the gun up facing the target.

"You did it girl! Nothing to fear, but fear itself." He looked pretty pleased with himself, leaning up against the cement wall.

"I'm pretty sure FDR wasn't referring to taking out a paper target at a gun range when he gave that speech," she said quivering. She had made it, and now she knew what to expect. "I'm gonna keep going until the mag runs out."

Bastian nodded while she unloaded the remaining bullets on the paper target. When it appeared the magazine was empty, he removed the gun from her trembling hand and double-checked to make sure it was unloaded before placing it in its box. Kinsley hoped he didn't see her hand shaking when he took the gun from her. It would take away from the hard ass image she was trying to maintain, even though she felt like she could throw up a little in her mouth. Every nerve ending in her body was heightened times ten from the power of the gun. Bastian stepped around her while reaching overhead for a switch mounted on the wall. Kinsley's paper target came flying down the range on a rolling track.

She didn't hit the target. Not one damn time. "Well shit," she said examining the paper. Disappointment replaced her nauseated feeling. "The only holes in it are from when you took the first three shots."

"Don't worry, you'll get it. You just have to keep practicing," he hooked his thumbs into his jeans pocket, "and maybe a few more private lessons."

Kinsley never understood how Bastian was able to accomplish that same pose he had been doing since he was twelve. The physicality of it was simple enough, thumbs in pockets and leaned up against a sturdy object. It was a relaxed postures with a no hurry to go anywhere vibe. However, the energy radiating from his body emitted a sense of alertness and attentiveness like his partner was the only person alive to him at that exact moment. Foolish girls, like her younger self, would mistake it for romantic interest, but since she had been there and done that, she knew it was a weapon of mass destruction with a hybrid of Don Juan and Marque De Sade at the switch.

Determined to avoid that snare again, she made its ineffectiveness clear in her 'straight shooter' attitude. "How much do you charge for your services?" Okay... it came out as more of a schoolgirl squeak, but she tried.

"No fee, but I'm gonna ask a favor," he said before biting his lower lip.

Kinsley couldn't help that her eyes were drawn to the motion. It was like a vortex of hotness that made her think of dirty things she could do with his mouth. She snapped herself out of it and dragged her eyes away. She needed to stay focused. "What's the favor?"

"Ida Robinson has been on my ass for a month about going to her house for dinner. She cornered me this afternoon and said I was expected to arrive at her house promptly at six o'clock this Thursday."

"Is she serving Tic Tac Pie?" Kinsley gasped in horror. "If that's on the menu, you're on your own."

"No, thank god, she said something 'bout fudge. Anyways, I want you to come with me."

"Why? Can't you handle that little old lady by yourself?"

"Ida Robinson's brother is Lewis Writtle, who just so happens to be the father of a Miss Holly Writtle." When she didn't catch his meaning, he rolled his eyes. "Miss Mid-Drift. I'm certain it's a set up, and I don't want to end up sitting next to her for two hours. She can get pretty handsy under a tablecloth."

"Ah, so you want me to be on hands patrol? Like a bodyguard?"

"If you wouldn't mind. I don't want to ask any other

woman cause they might get the wrong impression. If I go alone, any part of me not visible from under the table is subjected to uninvited groping. You do this for me and you get all the private lessons you want before you leave here."

"God willing." She sighed and thought about telling him to figure out his own damn problems. She wasn't a shield for him to keep the wanton women at bay. *And what did he mean "they might get the wrong idea?"* Wasn't he worried about her ideas? But if she said no, he might think she had *ideas*. Ideas involving him and a stick of butter. Damn it if she was going to let him have the upper hand. "Okay, Bastian, you've got yourself a deal. What is the dress for the evening? Overalls or camouflage?"

He pushed off the partition with a gigantic smile and slid into her space. At most he was a foot away from her, so close that she could feel his breath on her lips. "Nice to see you didn't lose your spunk." He tapped her on the nose with his pointer finger, a move he had done frequently when they were friends so very long ago. It used to aggravate the hell out of her because it was such a tease. You could barely call it a touch, and she used to want to be touched by him so badly. "There's another two magazines in the box. Go ahead and get some more practice while I start getting people to finish up. Press the red button next to the target switch if you need anything." Without moving his face away from hers, he reached up, flipped the switch, and the target went whizzing down the aisle. He bit his lower lip again and headed down the shooting range towards the other students.

"Damn it all to hell," she said to herself. *How did this happen?* She was supposed to come into town, sell the house and all its stuff, and get the hell out of dodge. Now, she had to tag along to a dinner so he wouldn't get molested by Ida Robinson's loose niece. He must have gotten the wrong message when she asked him to grill that chicken.

Chapter Ten

S even in the morning came about too quickly and full of drool for Kinsley. She was woken up from a delicious dream of a half-naked, tattooed, faceless man waxing her car by Petunia's incessant salivation on her arm. After carrying her majesty downstairs to do her business, Kinsley decided to get ready for the day and tackle her realtor problem. Freshly showered, she slipped on a lavender colored spaghetti strap camisole and khaki Capri pants. She used a large round brush while blow-drying her hair to add a little extra body and swiped on some lip gloss. One good thing about summer—besides not having to work—sun-kissed skin left make-up unnecessary.

Kinsley hopped in her BMW and headed to town. Rather than try to hunt down a different realty office, she decided to go along with Bastian's idea of finding another agent at Blue Ridge Realty. Armed with a thermos of coffee in her kick ass cup holder, she parked in front of the office and waited much like a cop would do during a stake out. As luck would have it, Frank Goldman exited with an older gentleman wearing a business suit. They piled into a Ford Focus with the Blue Ridge Realty logo on the side and took off down the road.

Fueled by coffee, and the need to pee, Kinsley rushed from her car and headed into the office. A young secretary, no more than twenty years old, who had greeted her a few days earlier, recognized her. "Hello again, Ms. Bailey. Mr. Goldman stepped out of the office with an appointment. Was he expecting you?"

"Oh, no. I didn't have an appointment. I was interested in speaking with another agent if possible." The young girl gave Kinsley a knowing grin. It seemed Frank had a reputation.

"If you can hold on for a second, I can see if Sharon Wilson is available."

"Yes, that would be great, thank you. Um, do you mind if I use your restroom?"

"Not at all. Head straight behind me and you'll see the door marked 'ladies room' on the left."

Kinsley nodded her appreciation and rushed to use the restroom. Upon return to the waiting area in front, the young secretary informed her Ms. Wilson was available to meet and would be with her shortly. She sat down on one of the brown leather couches and began to flip through a magazine. They were all about home sales and interior design, which she found to be incredibly dull. Lucky for her, someone left an issue of *Hollywood Squealer* on the bottom of the stack so she happily skimmed through the pages and felt more in her element.

"Mrs. Bailey?" Kinsley looked up from reading an article about a certain New York debutante's supposed sex change appointments to find a tall, slender, blond-haired woman standing in front of her. She wore a black button down shirt with a grey pencil skirt and heels that Kinsley would bust her ass in if she tried to wear them. Everything about the woman reminded her of Princess Grace.

"It's Miss," Kinsley said, returning her smile and throwing the magazine onto the cheap coffee table. The tall blonde saw the magazine and rolled her eyes.

"Jenny, I thought I told you to get that trashy tabloid out of here."

Jenny popped up from her desk and ran over to the coffee

table to retrieve the offending entertainment.

"Sorry about that," she said, reaching out to shake Kinsley's hand. "I'm Sharon Wilson, one of the agents here at Blue Ridge."

"Nice to meet you, and thank you for meeting with me without prior notice."

"No problem at all. Why don't we step into my office?"

"Sure."

Sharon Wilson swayed and sashayed down the hall to her office like she was on clouds rather than three-inch heels. Kinsley wondered how a woman so classy and elegant could stand to work with that grease ball Frank.

Sharon's office reminded Kinsley of the one she used to have working at Northrop Grumman. The décor was modern but had elements of personalization and femininity scattered and hidden within its professionalism. A silver Tiffany lamp sat on a corner table that was draped in a silver and teal cloth. Accent pillows with hints of the same matching tones softened the chairs sharp corners. It all came together nicely and even kind of matched Sharon's outfit.

"Now, what can I help you with Miss Bailey?" Sharon said, motioning for Kinsley to have a seat.

"I was in here a few days ago. I spoke with Frank Goldman about listing a house I recently inherited."

"I see. And you aren't interested in listing the house with Mr. Goldman as your agent?" Her voice was as sweet as sugar when she said it, but Kinsley had a feeling this wasn't the first time someone came seeking an agent other than Frank.

"Not exactly, but the entire office was recommended to me in high regards. So I'm hopeful in finding another agent within this organization."

"Who may I ask sent you our way? We love referrals."

"Oh, um…Bastian Harris." Even though Kinsley didn't think it was possible, Sharon's smile spread a little further.

"How wonderful! I helped him find the rental house he's living in. I'll have to call him up and tell him thank you for the recommendation." She picked up a pen and wrote *Call Bass* on a light pink post-it note.

She calls him Bass? Kinsley didn't quite pick up the business relationship vibe from that name. "Yeah, anyways, I've inherited a house. It's at 8 Eagle Rock Landing. I'm interested in listing it as soon as possible. As is, fully furnished, or completely empty. Whichever will make the sale go faster. I'm a motivated seller, but I'm not inclined in making any repairs or changes that would cause me to stay in town longer than necessary. Would you be interested?"

"Of course. I'm familiar with the property. I'll need to come by to make some notes and arrange for an appraiser to come out. Sounds like you're willing to negotiate in the seller's favor if the offer comes in fast enough, am I correct?"

"Yes, I need to get back home. When could you come by to take a look?"

"I can come this evening around six-thirty, if that's okay with you. I might even already have a buyer in mind for the property."

Kinsley didn't dare get her hopes up. "Yes, that would be fantastic."

"Great. Here, let me get you my card. Give me a call if anything changes, but other than that I'll see you tonight at six-thirty." Sharon slipped the card between her manicured fingernails.

"Thank you again, Sharon. See you tonight." Kinsley put the card in her purse and headed out the door, praying Frank hadn't decided he needed to return to the office. She wanted to start cleaning the house ASAP. It wasn't in terrible shape, but it needed to be at its most presentable before Sharon showed up. If Sharon didn't want to represent the house, she would be up shit creek without a paddle.

***

True to form, Bastian arrived at Kinsley's house ten minutes before one o'clock. He tucked a folder under his arm containing his cousin's offer on fourteen guns he wanted from the collection and a contract for housing the rest of the weapons on consignment. As he headed up the sidewalk, he heard Madonna's "Express Yourself" blasting from inside. He knocked on the door with no response and then a second time with more force. Still nothing. He tried the handle, but it was locked.

He started to search around in the bushes and flowers for anything that looked out of place and might be hiding a key. A cement frog caught his attention. Kicking it over, he revealed it was in fact real and lifting it off the ground did not produce a key underneath. However, the rock next to it stuck out like a sore thumb. He picked up the stone and felt that it was made of plastic. Jiggling it a little, he heard something metal rattling around inside. After twisting the bottom, a key fell into his palm.

He placed the rock next to the frog and tried the key in the lock. It worked like a charm. Slipping the key into his back pocket, he slowly opened the door. "Kinsley," he called over the music. He closed the door behind him, but she was still nowhere to be found. He walked down the hallway into the living room, but movement in the right side of his peripheral vision caused him to jerk his head that way. There she was in tiny, tight black shorts and long yellow, rubber dish gloves mopping the floor. Her butt wiggled and moved to the beat of the music as she danced and scrubbed the linoleum.

Glancing over his shoulder, he spotted the stereo blasting the wretched music. Oblivious to his presence, he watched her sing into the top handle of the mop like a microphone. He figured his best bet to not totally scare the hell out of her was to turn off the music. He walked over and pressed the pause button. The absence of music made her stand at attention and swing around with the mop, screaming louder than a cat during mating season.

"How the hell did you get in here?" she yelled, out of breath.

"Sorry, I knocked a bunch, but when I heard the music through the doors, I figured you couldn't hear me. I found your key holder. And by the way you should get a new one. I could tell that rock was fake a mile away." He reached in his pocket and dangled the key in front of her.

Kinsley leaned the mop against the refrigerator and snatched the key with one of her rubber-gloved hands. "You nearly gave me a heart attack!" She slammed the key down next to the stereo and proceeded to pull off the gloves. Eyeing the folder tucked under his arm, she asked, "Is that the paperwork you're supposed to be dropping off?"

"Yes ma'am. Tommy would like to buy fourteen firearms outright and he's agreed to hold the rest of the weapons on consignment for you. I went ahead and printed out all the information and comparable pricings for the ones he wants to buy so you can see his offers are balanced with the going rates. There's also a contract in here regarding holding fees and advertising for the other guns as well as percentages of sale prices he expects to receive."

While handing her the folder, he was able to admire the low cut scoop neck of her red tank top. She had worked up a mild sweat from all her dancing so that a soft glow coated her cleavage. Bastian had to slip his gaze back up to her face before she caught him taking a peek.

"He's agreeing to house all the guns?" she asked surprised.

"Yep, all of them. He's happy to do it." Bastian wasn't going to tell her that he argued with Tommy until eleven-thirty last night about taking all the guns. At most, Tommy wanted to consign about twenty because he said they didn't have the room to store them all. After thirty minutes of explaining how profitable it would be for Five Points to have its hand on all the weapons, Bastian finally told him he didn't care if he had to keep some of the guns shoved up his cousin's ass, they were doing it no matter what.

"Wow, I wasn't expecting that. That's great, Bastian. Thank you and please tell Tommy I said thank you to him too." The booklet was filled with printouts from similar and duplicate weapons, asking prices, and what the guns sold for. She flipped through its pages. "Not a problem. Hopefully it will help you get out of here sooner rather than later...like you want." He swallowed and cocked a brow at the shiny floor. "So what's with all the cleaning?"

She closed the folder and put it on the counter by her gloves. "Oh, I have a realtor coming today at six-thirty to see about listing the house. I'm trying to get it spic and span for her."

"That's good. Who did you end up going with?"

"Sharon Wilson over at Blue Ridge. She says she helped you find your rental." Her hip cocked to the side. "Interesting how every female in Staunton seems to know you on some personal level."

Bastian took a step towards her, holding back a smile at her response. "What I find even more interesting than that is how you got on the subject of me with Sharon Wilson."

"Oh give me a break. She asked who referred me to the agency. I told her you did and she spilled the beans about your 'professional relationship.' She even doodled your name on one of her post-it notes so she could call on you personally and thank you."

Sensing she wasn't going to be buying his potential upcoming story about keeping business strictly professional, he decided to play along with her little game. "Well, I do look forward to receiving her gratitude then."

Kinsley gave him a smirk and turned to grab the mop.

"I can see you're busy here, so I'll let you get back to your Madonna impre—um, mopping. Check over that paperwork when you get a chance, do some research, and call me sometime tomorrow on whether or not we have a deal."

Kinsley's face turned a slight shade of red. "I'm only playing that CD cause every other radio station I could get was either country or some hybrid of bluegrass and Christian."

"You may want to take a break and get a cool drink. Your face is almost the same color as your shirt." He tapped her on the nose. "Make sure you lock up behind me." As he turned to leave, he hit the pause button so that Madonna was once again expressing herself. He showed himself to the front door, hearing Kinsley run over to lock it behind him.

He smiled as he walked down her front path at the enticing woman in a red tank top dancing to Madonna.

***

How did she always get into these embarrassing situations? He kept showing up all suave in his tight black t-shirt and smelling like Cool Water cologne, while she was either face first in the dirt or dancing with a damn mop. God was definitely a man.

Kinsley mopped, swept, dusted, and vacuumed everything she possibly could without taking a break. Despite busting her ass for hours to clean and keeping an eye on the clock, Sharon Wilson still showed up before Kinsley had the opportunity to change out of her dingy clothes. How the woman managed to have flawless make-up and not a single hair out of place after a full workday was beyond Kinsley. After teaching school for six hours, her eyeliner was smeared, and she usually had a stain somewhere on her shirt. Feeling once again at a disadvantage, Kinsley sucked it up and began showing Sharon around the property.

Like a good tour guide, Kinsley pointed out all the amenities that could increase the probability of a quick sale while trying her best to hide anything that could result in a reverse effect. When she showed Sharon around her father's bedroom, she did her best not to pay attention to her picture on his nightstand.

After doing a walkthrough of the second floor, Sharon asked to see the garage as she explained that was often a great selling point for a male. Kinsley escorted her there and flipped on the light.

"Wow! Are these your guns?" Sharon asked, pointing to the wall of weapons.

"Technically, yes. They're mine from the inheritance."

"Are you a gun person?"

"Not in the least. Five Points Firearms is helping me sell them. I hardly know diddly about guns; well, except for what I learned last night at the shooting class."

"Oh, so that's how you know Bastian Harris. You've taken his weapons class." Sharon cocked her head to the side when she said it, as if Kinsley was just another Bastian Harris gun groupie.

"No, Bastian and I grew up together." Kinsley set her straight. "We're old friends from a long time ago. We reconnected when I discovered all these guns I needed to get rid of and my father used his company to help with some of the repairs. He offered to show me how to shoot, so I stayed for one of the classes."

"He's very good at what he does," the agent said smiling before continuing to inspect the garage.

"So I hear."

Sharon walked the perimeter before turning to face Kinsley again. "Well the good news is, I can sell this place. I have a family relocating here from Pennsylvania that hired me to help them find a house. They don't mind it not being turnkey and don't want to live too close to town. I think this is something I can pitch to them and get them eager about. You're lucky because they're in a hurry too. Can I come back tomorrow to get some pictures when the lighting is better?"

"Sure. How about ten-thirty?"

"That'll work for me. I'll also need to bring some paperwork so we can lock it down that I'm officially representing you and this property. A few things to sign." Sharon reached out and shook Kinsley's hand. "Just make sure to try and tidy up a bit before I come so the pictures are the best we can get. I'm going to try and have everything listed by the afternoon and sent to the family."

Kinsley squeezed her hand a bit more aggressively than she intended. She had been scrubbing all freaking afternoon. What did she mean "try and tidy up a bit?"

"Will do," she said as Sharon jerked her hand from the vice grip. She felt like grabbing the rubber dish glove and slapping the woman with it to let her know she accepted her challenge. Competitiveness rippled off her like heat waves over asphalt in the middle of July. However, she was in a predicament that had no allowance for being choosey. Whether or not she liked this Sharon person, she was her only hope at getting out of Staunton.

Chapter Eleven

A quarter to six on Thursday showed up faster than a zit the day of prom and equally as unwelcome. Between staying up until three in the morning tidying up again for Sharon-I-Have-a-Stick-Up-My-Ass-Wilson to come take some photographs, meeting with the lawyer to get the final deed paperwork signed, and dropping off the gun forms to Tommy, Kinsley barely had any time to get ready for her job as hand monitor at Ida Robinson's house. She had almost forgotten about her arrangement with Bastian until she ran into him at Five Points, and he reminded her exactly why he would be picking her up shortly before six.

She had intended on going by the bank to see what was in that safety deposit box, but she would have had to forgo a shower and shaving her legs in order to make it home in time to get ready. Since a black and blue floral dress was her only attire left clean and suitable for a dinner party, going without shaving her legs wasn't an option. She hadn't even had the opportunity to return the three missed phone calls from Aunt Debbie. The woman would have to wait until tomorrow.

Kinsley spritzed on one final spray of Miss Dior before she considered her outfit complete or as good as it was going to get before Bastian showed up. Thank God the French pedicure she had treated herself to prior to arriving in Staunton held up. Her polished nails peeked from her silver thong flip-flops, which matched the pretty stitching on her summer dress. Kinsley was loading up Petunia on a new bowl of Purina when she heard a knock at the door.

She glanced at the digital clock on the stove. "Ten to five," she muttered as she reluctantly padded to the front door holding the cup of dog food. "Early as usual." Up until this point, she had only seen Bastian in his Five Points attire of tight black t-shirt and jeans. When she opened the door, the sight of him almost took her breath away. He wore a white button-up shirt that hung below a brown belt with a silver buckle. Instead of jeans, he had on form-fitting khaki pants and brown boat shoes. About to make a smart ass remark on how he didn't need to put on airs to impress Ida Robinson, she noticed he kept the sleeves on his shirt rolled up to his elbows. Although the hula girl remained hidden, several of his tattoos stuck out beneath the roll at his elbow. Leave it to Bastian to pull off tattooed badass meets college preppy.

Nevertheless, she needed to make a cynical remark in order to counter the fact that he had seen her jaw drop to the floor at the sight of him. "Didn't you know you aren't legally allowed to wear Abercrombie after the age of twenty-seven?"

The side of his mouth cocked up. "Tough words coming from a grown woman wearing a dress from the Little Miss section at Old Navy."

She glanced at her dress, offended. "Hey, this is from Emilio Pucci."

He laughed, apparently finding her retaliation amusing. "You look really pretty, Kinsley."

The flattery made her stomach do a little flip. Despite the comment, she needed to keep her head in the game. Even though he swayed Aunt Debbie into thinking he was elusive and a non-dater, the women's behavior at the gun class and Sharon

Wilson's doodle of his name was enough to affirm this man knew how to smooth talk the ladies. A talent he was born with and had clearly worked to the point of perfection over the years. "Thanks, you look great too. Come on in for a minute. I need to grab my purse and make sure Petunia is set."

Bastian walked in and closed the door behind him, following her into the kitchen. "I thought you were supposed to take her to the shelter today."

Kinsley leaned over and dumped the cup of food in front of a very appreciative Petunia. "Yeah I was, but I got caught up with the realtor and then the lawyer. I'll drop her off tomorrow. Hey, do you think they'll let me bring all this dog food I got her? She seems to like it and I don't want to waste it by throwing it out. And her dog bed and toys? Can she take those with her or is it like prison where they aren't allowed any outside contraband?"

"I'm sure they would. But I'll bet fifty bucks that she doesn't go to the shelter tomorrow." Bastian laughed. "Or the day after that."

"You're on pal. I have no room for a dog in my life. I'm too busy drinking booze and fighting off bachelors. So you better stop by the ATM cause I don't take checks, credit cards, or IOU's." Kinsley rolled up the top of the dog food bag and moved to the sink to wash her hands. "So besides for Ida and her handsy niece, Holly, who else is going to be at this dinner?"

"Not sure. I was told to show up. Ida doesn't know you're coming, but I'm sure she won't mind."

"You didn't tell her you were bringing somebody?" Bringing an unannounced guess in the south was about as rude as showing up to the event with no pants on.

"Nope. Better to ask forgiveness than permission. Besides, I figured if this is a deliberate set up, it will teach Ida to mind her own damn business."

Kinsley shrugged her shoulders and grabbed her purse. "Are

you driving or am I?"

"I'll drive. I put the top on the jeep cause I know how you ladies are about your hair."

"How gentlemanly. Lead the way," she motioned forward, "and for the record, if there's Tic Tac pie, these shoes offer a lot of support and I won't hesitate to hoof it home."

"Dually noted. After you." Bastian let Kinsley walk ahead of him and waited for her on the porch as she locked the front door. The ride to Ida's house didn't take too long. They spent the majority of the time arguing about the cliché lyrics Kinsley felt were present in a majority of country songs.

"I'm sorry. I just don't think that sexy farm girls ride on tractors like Tawny Kitaen did on the hood of that Camaro or that going to a hootenanny in a barn makes you forget that your girlfriend left you. That seems to be what most of those songs are about."

"I disagree. They're also about hanging with your boys at a bonfire and beer," Bastian rebutted while turning the station back to Country 101.4. As Kinsley was about to provide a dissertation on the lyrical diversity of groups like Train and Imagine Dragons, Bastian pulled his jeep into the driveway of a one story rambler that had two fake pig statues situated along the walkway. "Although I would love to hear your take on modern day music of the angsty persuasion, we have arrived at our destination."

Kinsley started to unbuckle her seat belt when Bastian grabbed her hand. "I know I didn't say so before, but thank you for coming with me. And I apologize in advance for any culinary mishaps Ida may have on the menu."

She paused at his touch and the sincerity in his expression, but the moment was short lived. "Wait a minute. I thought you said she was serving fudge. What other kind of weird shit is this woman known for concocting?"

At that moment, the front door swung wide open and Ida

Robinson came onto the front porch. She had a lobster oven mitt on her left hand and an apron that read, 'Kiss My Rump Roast,' hung around her neck. She waived the mitt frantically at the car. "Bass. I'm so glad you made it. You're a little early...and I see you and Kinsley decided to ride together."

Bastian and Kinsley climbed out of the jeep and walked fearlessly into the inevitable torture.

"Yes, ma'am. I'd forgotten I had arranged a dinner with Kinsley before I accepted your invitation. I didn't want to be rude and cancel. I hope it's alright." Bastian reached down and attempted to grab her hand, but she already had her purse in an iron grip. He clasped around her wrist instead and practically dragged her towards the house.

Ida scrunched up her nose. "What the heck do you mean? I expected her to come. Debbie told me she invited her."

Aunt Debbie popped her permed head out the front door. "Kinsley, you got my messages! Good, I was worried you hadn't listened to them when I didn't hear from you. I'm glad you could come to dinner." Debbie trod onto the top porch step next to Ida.

Out of the side of her mouth Kinsley whispered, "It appears, Sherlock, it wasn't the set up you thought it was."

"Is that Bass Harris I hear?" came from inside the house. Seconds later, Holly Writtle, aka Miss Mid-Drift, and a man in a Budweiser t-shirt joined Ida and Debbie on the porch. Holly looked pleased to see Bastian, but less than appreciative he was holding another woman's wrist. Kinsley struggled not to roll her eyes. *How could she have such a sour puss on her face with her date right next to her? Does this woman have no couth?*

Bastian whispered through clenched teeth, "Don't get ahead of yourself now, sweetheart. That's Chuck, Holly's brother. And no matter how hick you think this town might be, I'm guessing he's not her date for the evening but yours."

Damn Aunt Debbie for trying to play matchmaker and

damn Ida Robinson for whatever culinary crap she was going to force feed Kinsley. She fought not to look back at the jeep and headed inside for the inevitable.

The dinner started normal enough. Kinsley was less than pleased she was instructed to sit next to Chuck while Holly practically sat on Bastian's lap. But she guessed it could have been worse. For instance, she could have been set up with a man who was missing his entire row of top teeth. Lucky for her, Chuck was only missing three on the right upper side. He treated Kinsley and the rest of the table to some dinner entertainment by showing exactly how his false teeth slipped in and out. Thank God there was wine, even if it was Snow Peak Peach Boones. Fortunately, Ida Robinson stuck to making pot roast and new potatoes for dinner, so not everything at the table—excluding Chuck's choppers—made her want to vomit.

Dinner conversation with Chuck was about as stimulating as listening to a lecture on the growth rate of fungus. Turned out he was the manager of the very lucrative You Toss It, We Trash It junk removal company. He'd recently divorced his wife when she decided to go "tramping all over town" and ran out on him with the Assistant Manager of the Piggly Wiggly. Every so often, Kinsley would glance across the table at Bastian. He didn't wear the expression of a person who'd been recently violated and Holly had both her hands on top of the table so there was no immediate need for an intervention.

"Your aunt tells me you're a teacher and do some sort of science research involving bird dookie," Chuck said, interrupting her thoughts. That last part caught the attention of everyone at the table.

Holly snickered. "Bird crap? What sort of research involves lookin' at bird crap?"

Kinsley's eyes darted around the table and landed on Bastian. His hands were folded over his mouth, hiding a smile. His shoulders shook a bit too. He was either choking or laughing. She hoped it was the first.

Call me out, Miss Mid-drift and prepare to be amazed.

"Well, it's actually an environmental study. The amount of pollution present near local public beaches has a direct ratio with the amount of trash we find within a seagull's waste and digestive track. We're able to determine which toxins are present in larger amounts at the ocean and in turn are consumed more by birds, either causing illness or death. We report these findings to the EPA," she paused and smiled at Holly, "that stands for the Environmental Protection Agency, which then relates the information to companies using those materials to package products, and thus, influences the materials they use to pack and ship their products. Then those companies can report their efforts on being 'more green' and receive a tax write off for using more environmentally friendly, but more costly materials."

Everyone at the table stared at her like she'd admitted setting worms on fire was her hobby. Of course it was complete an utter bullshit, but she hoped she had spun the web so intricately that none of them would call her bluff.

"You get all that from lookin' at bird shit under a microscope?" Holly's sarcastic tone implied she was not fully convinced.

"And their stomachs and intestines," Kinsley answered while pouring a third glass of wine. Like hell if this belly button country bumpkin was going to one up her in the intelligence arena.

"Man, you must be really smart then, huh?" Chuck patted the mound in his gut where the pot roast was likely giving him grief.

"She always has been," Bastian responded.

"Oh, you two knew each other before now?" Holly asked, pointing between Bastian and Kinsley.

Bastian nodded. "Yep, we've known each other since the

sixth grade."

"Did you two ever...you know...date?" Holly picked her napkin off her lap and placed it next to her plate. Her hand shot under the table fast, and Bastian straightened like he sat on a tack. He appeared as stiff as a mannequin while Holly looked a bit too at ease about potentially giving a man an erection in front of her family members. Kinsley recognized the silent plea for help and chugged the hell out of her water glass.

"Nope, never dated. Just friends. Good friends in middle school and then fell out of touch in high school. Ida, may I please run to the kitchen to refill my water glass?"

"Sure thing, honey. Would you like me to do it for you?" Ida asked, starting to stand up. Kinsley held up her hand and motioned for her to sit down.

"No ma'am. You have done enough. The kitchen is this way, correct?" She pointed to the hallway behind Bastian.

"Yes, sweetie. Brita pitcher's in the fridge."

Kinsley rose, pushing in her chair and headed around the table. Down the hall, she found Ida's quaint country kitchen interesting. It was decorated in red and white picnic tablecloth patterns with figurines and pictures of roosters as far as the eye could see. She popped open the fridge and filled her glass with cold water from the pitcher. Figuring Bastian's crotch was in serious jeopardy, she wasted no time hurrying out to the dining room again.

As she came behind the couple, she noticed Holly's arm slowly rubbing back and forth, her hand on Bastian's upper thigh. As there couldn't be anything more embarrassing than telling a table of strangers she examined bird poop for summertime employment, she had no hesitations about what she was getting ready to do. Kinsley scrambled towards the table and dug her right foot across the wood flooring to add realism to the illusion that she tripped. Conveniently enough, her glass of freshly poured ice water happened to be in her right hand, directly next to Bastian. The fake tumble sent Kinsley stumbling in between Miss Mid-drift and Bastian, causing her water to spill onto Holly's hand and into Bastian's lap.

At the shock of the cold, Bastian leapt out of his seat with a giant wet stain on the crotch of his khakis, while Holly's hand shot into her own lap. "Holy Shit, that's cold!" he yelled, grabbing his napkin from the table.

"Oh, Bastian! I am so sorry! My flip flop must have gotten caught in something."

The ever-so considerate Holly attempted to grab her napkin and assist Bastian with dabbing at his groin. He recoiled.

"No. Thank you, Holly. I've got this." Bastian jerked his head at Kinsley with his nostrils flared. She guessed this wasn't quite what he had in mind when he asked her to come to his rescue. Chuck sat at the table laughing with his arms crossed over his chest. Luckily, his teeth stayed firmly in place.

"Miss Robinson, I'm sorry, but I think we're going to have to call it an evening. I'm totally soaked."

"Oh really? That's a shame. You'll miss dessert." Ida's bottom lip quivered.

"Yes ma'am and I'm all torn up inside about it. But I better hurry up and go home to change."

"Yeah, something that cold probably made your boys nestle up inside your stomach," laughed Chuck. "Kinsley, you can stay, and I'll give you a ride home after dessert."

Kinsley wanted to tell him she would rather eat glass, but knowing Ida's affinity for making people eat weird ass stuff, she figured she should keep that to herself. "Thank you for the offer Chuck, but no. Bastian has to come by my house tonight to pick up a few of the guns his cousin is buying, so I'll have him run me home."

Ida hung her head a little lower. "But what am I gonna do with a dozen squares of Velveeta Fudge?"

Kinsley froze. "Did you say Velveeta Fudge? As in the

processed cheese blocks?"

"Mmm-hmm. Sounds funny, I know, but it's the perfect combination of sweet and salty. I'll wrap some up in a Tupperware for y'all." Ida hopped up from her seat and waddled towards the kitchen.

"I'll help you Ida," Debbie called after her. "Don't worry, I'll make sure she packs the smaller squares," she whispered out of the corner of her mouth while she passed Bastian and Kinsley.

"Bass, I hear you're pulling the float on Saturday for the Staunton High ROTC club. You need a ride along buddy?" Clearly, Holly was determined to make some headway with Bastian this evening.

"Yeah, Bastian. Why don't you give her a ride?" Kinsley teased. He shot her a sideways glance to tell her to shut up.

"That's real sweet of you to offer to keep me company, but I have to carry a bunch of the kids' gear and such in the car with me. Won't be any room."

Kinsley wanted to remind him that his lap was always an option, and Holly seemed to have gotten quite comfortable with it under the dinner table, but she held her tongue. Ida and Debbie returned from the kitchen with a small plastic box containing large square blocks impersonating normal fudge. Kinsley knew the true evil that lay within.

"Miss Ida, dinner was wonderful. Thank you for inviting us." Bastian reached his arms around Ida and gave her a giant bear hug, after which he bestowed Debbie her fair share too. When he turned towards the table, Holly stood up and held out her arms ready to receive her embrace. Instead, he shook her hand. After Kinsley hugged her aunt, and before Chuck could try to grab her boob, she hauled ass through the front door to Bastian's getaway chariot. Bastian came jogging behind her. "You're so gonna get it for that."

"What? You told me to be on hand patrol. So I was. I had

to think fast and that was the quickest way to get her hand off your junk." She smiled sweetly. "By shriveling it up with ice water."

"For your information, she wasn't jerking me off under the table. Her hand was on my thigh, up high, at the crevice where it meets my pelvis."

"Well, excuse me for being a few millimeters off. I thought I was doing you a favor." Kinsley grabbed her cell phone from her purse to check for messages after they got in the jeep. The only missed calls were from Debbie inviting her to dinner. She put her phone in the center console cup holder and her purse with the fudge on the back seat. "Now, where can we throw that fudge so no one will find it and it won't poison any wild animals or plants."

Bastian threw the shifter into reverse and backed out of the driveway. "I'm not helping you destroy the evidence. Not after you poured an entire cup of ice water on my groin."

"You're seriously mad? I helped you out. I stopped you from being molested in a room full of people, and we both avoided having to eat cheese fudge. I think you owe me a thank you, you ingrate."

"It amazes me that when you have to come up with a bullshit story about the scientific relevance of bird poop, it spews forth from your mouth like Shakespeare. But when I ask you to be on surveillance for a woman getting too frisky with my boys, all you can think of is pouring water on my pants."

"You knew that story was bullshit?"

"Please," he said, giving her a pointed look.

"Well, I'm sorry you're so upset. You can retract your original offer of free shooting lessons since you're less than pleased with my end of the bargain." Truth be told, she wasn't too bummed about that part.

"No, no. A deal's a deal. You got her hand off me and out of that dinner faster than I could have done on my own. Come by the shop tomorrow after six and I'll work with you."

They both sat quietly as they drove down the dark wooded road. But the silence was interrupted by the sound of muffled giggles before morphing into full on laughter. "Shut up, Kinsley. It wasn't that funny."

"You should've seen your face when that water hit your pants. It reminded me of that time we were in gym class in eighth grade and that kid, Raymond Drewer, grabbed onto your gym shorts to try and break his fall during volleyball and accidentally pantsed you."

"For Christ's sakes, you remember that?"

"My mind is like a steel trap. And who could forget those bright red briefs you were wearing?" She snorted she was laughing so hard.

"My shorts only got down to my thighs before I yanked 'em back up! You make it seem like they went down around my ankles."

"Ah, it was a fantastic day." She sighed, her laughter subsiding.

"Thanks a lot. What makes you say that?"

"Because it was one of the few days I remember where Bastian Harris was human."

"What's that supposed to mean?" He almost sounded offended.

"What I mean is you," she paused trying to find the words, "You and your perfect hair, baby blue eyes, and smooth talking that could have charmed a nun out of her Fruit of the Looms. You never tripped, never looked less than immaculate, and not once did I ever see a zit. You didn't seem real. Seeing you in action was like watching an episode of Beverly Hills 90210."

His brows drew together. "If I was such an asshole, why were we friends for so long?"

"I never said you were an asshole. You were just exhausting to be around sometimes. I couldn't get through a damn day without humiliating myself somehow. You, on the other hand, were like a boy band heartthrob and living a charmed life. Yikes. It was nice to be reminded that you were mortal like the rest of us, despite your flawless skin and trail of groupies."

"Boy band heartthrob, huh?" His tone changed from offended to mildly amused.

"Oh, Jesus. I am not taking this walk down memory lane with you. A man who practically got a hand job under the table from a woman sitting eight feet away from her aunt and four feet away from her brother does not need his ego boosted. You know what you looked like then. You know you're easy on the eyes now. Every girl, including me, was madly in love with you back then, so let's try not to let your head get any bigger by discussing it."

His brows rose to his hairline and his eyes went as wide as saucers as he turned from the windshield to stare at Kinsley. "You were what?"

Kinsley blew air between her lips. "Oh don't act like you didn't know."

"I didn't. You never said anything." With the only interior light coming from the dashboard, it was not easy to see, but Kinsley could still make out his stoic face. That sort of pissed her off.

"Are you for real? I didn't say anything? I thought sticking my tongue down your throat in Erin's basement would have communicated that clearly enough, but I guess I should have made a giant poster board in glitter glue and puffy paint for clarity." She slammed her hands on her thighs. "And as if being in your perfect presence didn't make me feel awkward enough, you totally blew me off afterwards. Why would I have said anything? I was already sufficiently humiliated without adding that little cherry to the top of the sundae."

Bastian turned the jeep onto Eagle Rock Lane. The short distance from the entrance of the road to Kinsley's house was driven in silence. Kinsley sat chewing on the side of her cheek, contemplating the extremity of her verbal diarrhea. She must have looked like a fucking lunatic, yelling at a man for things that happened over twenty years ago. He clearly didn't remember any of it because it didn't mean to him what it meant to her. She blamed him for it when they were thirteen, but she couldn't fault him for his honesty now.

She took a deep breath in and exhaled as Bastian parked in her driveway. "Look Bastian, I'm sorry for what I said. I shouldn't have yelled at you for what you did, or didn't do, when we were younger. Instead of keeping my mouth shut about how I felt, I should have said something. Assuming you would put two and two together just because I kissed you, which you obviously don't even remember, was my problem. I guess I remember it more vividly, or at all, because of how I felt about you, or at least what I thought those feelings meant." Her insides twisted and she blew some hair out of her eyes as she worked to get out the next part. "I don't want to argue or come off as some deranged, jilted old friend because we still need to work together so I can get out of here as soon as possible. I hope you don't hold what I said against me. It's not your fault you don't remember my attempt to tell you how I felt because you weren't emotionally there with me. But we're adults now and it's all good, okay?"

Bastian sat motionless in his jeep, staring straight ahead. His stone silence confirmed the issue was not resolved.

"Good night, Bass." She grabbed her purse from the backseat and slammed the door. Under the porch light while searching for her keys, she realized she had left her phone in Bastian's car. Luckily, he was still in the driveway, watching to make sure she got in the house. Jogging over to the passenger side, she swung open the door. "Sorry, I forgot my phone."

Pushing up on her tiptoes, she leaned in towards the middle console where the cup holder trapped her phone. "I didn't say I don't remember," he broke the silence between them like a hammer on rock.

Kinsley stared up at him. "What?"

He was still staring straight forward with his hands on the steering wheel. "I never said I didn't remember. You assumed it."

"Oh, I'm sorry. I just thought that—"

Suddenly he bent down towards Kinsley, who was still leaning over the seat in the middle of the car, and cupped her chin with his hand. "We'd finished swimming. You were standing in front of the refrigerator, drinking a Coke and shivering. I put my towel around you and you kissed me."

A tingling sensation took over her chest and halted her breathing. No action or anything he had said in the past few days even remotely suggested that he remembered what happened between them, but...he did. Floored by this revelation and with all the memories buzzing around in her head, there was only one thing clear as day that came to her mind to say. "It was a Sprite, actually."

Before she could react, his mouth was on hers. She was focusing on the awkwardness of her position during the kiss, but forgot the discomfort when his tongue began to glide rhythmically into her mouth. Her knees felt weak and her feet were moving like Mikey's in *The Goonies* when the cheerleader dragged him into the dark cave and kissed him.

His hands slipped around to the back of her neck as his mouth made love to hers. She wanted to return his touch, but she was supporting herself on the seat since her ass and legs were sticking out the side of the car. Their lips broke apart only for a moment, long enough for them to breathe and think. Clear their heads before they did anything they might regret. Instead, they dove for each other again. The lip lock continued for maybe another twenty seconds, but it felt like an eternity, partially because she was time warped to the summer before eighth grade. Although he had become a more skilled kisser, his mouth was still familiar.

Finally, they pulled apart. Panting he whispered inches away from her mouth, "Good night, Kinsley. I'll see you tomorrow around nine to start removing the guns."

She leaned out of the car and held up her cell phone to reiterate why she'd come back to the jeep in the first place. A feeble attempt at restating her original intention. She stumbled like an inebriated person to her front door. Once she was able to wiggle the key in the lock with her unsteady hands, she stepped in the house and turned to look at the Jeep. Only his silhouette could be seen, but she knew from the burning in her chest and the pulsating sound of her heartbeat in her ears that he was staring right back at her.

Chapter Twelve

On the drive home, Bastian had time to break down what had happened play-by-play. He hadn't planned on kissing Kinsley, especially with half of her body hanging out of the car. Not the most romantic way to kiss a woman for the first time. Well, technically the second time. He had completely forgotten about their make out snafu the summer before eighth grade until Holly Writtle asked if they had ever dated. As soon as Kinsley buzzed in with, "We were good friends in middle school and fell out of touch in high school," the memory of them making out against that washing machine came flooding in like a tidal wave.

The trembling of her lower lip from the cold, the blue polka-dotted bikini she always wore every time he came over to swim, and his battle with whether or not he should press his luck and try for second base. Hearing her confess how much she used to like him, he was glad he'd kept his hands on her shoulders instead of following his urges and placing them elsewhere. That probably would've made her feelings of rejection far worse and the ability to return to friendship status nonexistent.

In the past twenty years, Kinsley had become a magnificently beautiful woman. Under normal circumstances, it would have no weight on Bastian's decision whether or not to pursue her. In all honesty, it probably would have kept his playful flirting from becoming anything more since his pin-up ex-wife proved to be a vindictive she-devil. Hearing her complain about his preteen perfection, and the way she clumsily jogged back to his car, reminded him that inside that gorgeous body was the girl who used to flip him off when he tried to help her up from the floor at the roller skating rink.

When she leaned in to reach for her phone and he caught a whiff of that delicious floral scent she was wearing, it was all over. He had to kiss her and he wasn't sorry that he did it this time around. The sound of his cell phone ringing disrupted his thoughts. Not wanting to take his eyes off the road, he answered it without checking the screen. "Bastian Harris."

"Hi daddy." It was the sweetest voice Bastian had ever heard in his life. No, correction. The sweetest voice the Lord had ever put on the planet, his daughter.

"Hey Jodi, baby. How's my girl?" He always loved it when his daughter called. He talked to her at least twice a week during the school year. Teaching shooting classes in the evenings made it difficult to speak with her before she went to sleep. That's why he loved summer. Her bedtime was later and he got to talk to her in the daytime when she would have been in school during the year.

"I'm good," she said with a smile in her voice, "Whatcha doing?"

"Driving home from dinner at Ida Robinson's house. Do you remember her?"

"Yep. She's that nice old lady who watches me when you have to work and always makes us those weirdo desserts."

"You got it babe. No weird desserts tonight though." He wasn't going to tell her about the processed cheese fudge. He didn't want to frighten her. "I'm excited about you coming to stay with me for the week."

"Me too. I tried to get Mama to let me come a day early so I could ride in the parade with you, but she said no because Mark has to work and she needs him to help with the drive." Of course Linda needed Mark to help with the drive. The woman never did anything by herself. Growing up as a doppelganger for Michelle Pheiffer made her learn very quickly that she could get about anything she wanted by flashing a smile. Such a charmed life ended up handicapping her, which Bastian should have seen from a mile away after he discovered she didn't even know how to put gas in her car. But like every other sucker before him, and the giant ex-friend sucker after him, he let her ineptness slide because of her beauty and decided she was the type of woman he wanted on his arm. Her inability to be self-reliant especially affected their home life while he went on tours. His best friend, Mark, stepped in at some point to fill the void.

"Oh, that's okay sweetheart. There's lots we're going to be able to do when you come visit. I've scheduled a couple days off work so we can spend some extra time together before you go to school. Any special requests for your visit?"

"Yep. I want to shoot a gun."

"What, like a Beebe gun?"

"Nope. A real one. I want you to take me to your work and teach me how."

"Not gonna happen Jodi," Linda interrupted from the background.

"Oh, come on Mama. If anybody can teach me, Daddy can."

"Your mom's right, sugar bug. You're too young. I can show you how to shoot a Beebe gun, but not a real gun. You need to be older." Bastian hated agreeing with her mother, but she was right on this one.

"Okay, fine. But if you aren't gonna teach me to shoot a real gun, then I want to go to Princess Playtime, and Disney World, and Washington DC to see the White House…and

McDonald's."

"Why not Paris and the Australian Outback too?" Jesus, how much time did she think she was staying with him and where exactly did she think he lived?

"If we have time, we can go to those places too. Mama wants to talk to you, okay?"

"Alright sweet pea, love you."

"Love you too, Daddy." Bastian could hear the phone being passed between hands before Linda spoke.

"Hello, Bastian."

"Hey, Linda. What can I do for you?"

"Just wanted to confirm our drop off time on Sunday. We'll be at your house around twelve o'clock. Then you'll bring Jodi home the following Sunday, right?"

He resisted growling into the phone. "Yep, that's the usual run of things. Just tell Mark to stay in the car and we'll be good to go."

She huffed. "Really, Bastian? We haven't moved past this yet?"

"I moved past your choices a long time ago. It's Mark I'm still raw about. You don't take another man's wife. You don't break up your best friend's marriage. He needs to stay clear of me."

"You were gone so much; there wasn't much of a marriage there to break up."

"My job and its travel requirements kept you in the lifestyle which you demanded to remain in."

"I'm tired of this argument," she sighed. "Mark is Jodi's father about eighty-five percent of the time now. Hell that seems to be about how much it was even when we were married. How do you think it makes Jodi feel that you won't be around him?"

"I'd like to think that when Jodi is old enough, she would understand my position. I treat her mother with respect and dignity. I don't trash talk either of you or discuss our relationship when Jodi is around." He ran his hand through his hair. "You were once my wife and are the mother of my child; there are certain courtesies you deserve. I owe her STEP father, the best man at my wedding who decided to take advantage of me being gone so much, nothing."

Linda let out another huge sigh on the other end of the line. "Fine, Mark and I will be there with Jodi on Sunday. See you then, Bastian."

"See you then." Bastian hung up the phone and threw it on the passenger seat. He was getting ready to turn on the radio to listen to some music about hot girls straddling tractors to take his mind off the argument when his phone rang again.

"Bastian Harris," he barked in the phone.

"Hey, Bass. It's Tommy. What are you doing?"

"Driving home from Ida Robinson's house."

"She trying to set you up with Holly again or was she force feeding you crap on a cracker?"

"Yes to both. What do you want?" He gripped the steering wheel tighter.

"Cameron Quinn from Waynesboro Gun and Sports Supply called. They've signed the addendums to the contracts, but want some provisions added to a couple of the clauses. I need you to drive up there tomorrow and finish up the paperwork so we can get this deal moving."

"Okay. Did they fill you in on the specifics of the stuff they want changed?"

"Yep, I've written down all the changes I've agreed to, but I need you to go initial off on everything. Can you be there by nine?"

"Yeah sure." He did a quick rundown of tomorrow in his head. "Wait, oh shit. I'm supposed to be at Mitchell Bailey's house at nine to start getting all those firearms for the shop."

"Mitchell Bailey? He gonna be there in spirit or something?

Don't you mean Kinsley Bailey?"

An image of her leaning over his passenger seat popped in his head. He pushed it aside fast. "Yeah, you know what I meant. I already told her I'd be there. Can you go to Waynesboro?"

"Sorry, brother. I have to take mom to her dialysis appointment at nine-thirty." Bastian had almost forgotten Tommy had a standing appointment to take his mother to her treatment at Riverside Dialysis every other Friday. He and his sister, Rita, alternated weeks chauffeuring and keeping her company for the couple of hours. A few times Bastian had to step in and take her when Tommy was sick or had something else going on. He did not envy their situation, but he did admire their patience and love for his aunt.

"Damn, I forgot about that. I'll give Mike a call and see if he wants to pick up some overtime and get the guns from Kinsley."

"Sounds good to me, man. We'll have to open late tomorrow. I'm still at the shop wrapping up a few things. Stop by and get the notes I have from my conversation with Cameron. I'll help you get out all the packing materials for Mike so he knows what he needs to take with him to the Bailey house to move those guns without fucking them up."

"Okay, I'll turn around. See you in a few." Bastian hung up the phone and made a U-turn on Newell Road. Returning to work at eight o'clock wasn't his idea of fun, but then neither was driving to Waynesboro instead of Kinsley's house. He was hoping he might get to see her in her pajamas. Although he figured her for a boxer and t-shirt kind of girl instead of lace nighties, it still would have been nice. He'd give her a call once he was done at the shop to let her know Mike was coming instead of him. Calling her minutes after he had kissed her senseless to tell her he wasn't coming over after all might be mistaken for a dick move.

***

On Friday morning, Kinsley didn't mind heaving Petunia down the stairs so much. Before she knew it, the lyrics of Prince's "Kiss" were coming out of her mouth while she brewed the coffee. She never sang. Ever. Well, except for that time at the funeral home…and that time she was dancing with the mop when Bastian scared the shit out of her. Damn, Staunton was making her a pretty musical person.

Although Kinsley had gotten in bed around ten last night, she didn't fall asleep until two in the morning. Thoughts about her kiss with Bastian in the jeep and uncontrollable fits of smiling kept her awake until the wee hours of the morning. As she sipped her Starbuck's Breakfast Blend, she realized she needed to get in check about this whole kissing situation. The fact that she hadn't kissed a man for over a year probably had something to do with her mild obsession about last night. And he remembered their kiss in the laundry room. That was the best part of all.

Although her body was pinging at the memory of his lips on hers and the way he fisted his fingers through her hair with need, she was an adult. She knew the difference between acts of love and acts of lust. There was no question in her mind on which one this was. What wasn't there to desire? He was tall, blond, built like a brick house, and beautiful. Her craving was only sweetened by the fact that this man used to appear in her thoughts every waking moment of her preteen years. If she slept with him now, hypothetically speaking, it would be like she was championing a conquest twenty years in the making. Such a feat would be worthy of a medal. Maybe she could have one made. That was, *if* she slept with him. Hypothetically. No, a medal was a silly idea, but printing up a certificate on her home computer was doable.

Kinsley made sure to go for the gold with effortless "I just woke up and I am always this beautiful when I do" undertones.

She wore a form fitting white V-neck shirt and a loose plum colored skirt. After a quick battle with the hairbrush and a swipe of lip gloss, she was ready to greet Bastian at 8:50. But at 8:55, when he hadn't shown up yet, she started to get a little worried since he was notorious for showing up early. Petunia barking at the back door pulled her away from spying out the front peephole. After she let in the world's most useless pooch—maybe she should print her off a certificate too—there was a knock at the door.

With a bounce in her step, Kinsley hurried to answer it. "You're late—" she started to say, swinging open the door. Her girlish smile faded when a man, who wasn't Bastian, stood on her front porch with his hands in his pockets. She recognized him from the night she went to the shooting class. "Hi, um, can I help you?"

"Yes, ma'am. I'm Mike Pedersen. I work at Five Points. Bastian couldn't make it over here this morning to collect the firearms so he sent me instead."

"Oh, okay." She swallowed down a lump that had suddenly stuck in her throat and collected her whirling thoughts. Automatically, she said, "Let me open the garage door for you so it's easier to move the guns to your van."

Mike nodded and headed down the sidewalk, where the black van with the the Five Points logo professionally painted in white lettering idled. She closed the front door and headed to the garage. At first, Kinsley tried to dismiss the eerily similar feeling produced by this situation; however, with each passing step, her agitation grew. She had no struggle opening the door leading from the house into the garage with her shoulder this time because, quite frankly, she was pissed. *Is he seriously trying to blow me off? Again?*

Kinsley flipped on the light switch and pushed the button for the garage door to open. Mike backed the van up to the house and organized lengths of bubble wrap and packaging tape. Curiosity got the better of her so she decided to go ahead and ask, "Did Bastian say why he couldn't come today? I saw him last night and he said he'd be here at nine. Everything okay?"

"Yes, ma'am. He had some business to tend to with someone named Cameron." Mike continued to organize his supplies while Kinsley stared into space and contemplated. She remembered he said his daughter's name was Jodi, and his ex-wife's started with an L... Laura... Linda... something like that, but he never mentioned any Cameron. Did he break his engagement with her to go see another woman? No, not possible. Men didn't do that at his age...did they? Kiss one female so senselessly that she couldn't have recited her ABCs afterwards and then twelve hours later see another woman? That would be even quicker than when he started going steady with Melissa Childress.

"Excuse me a moment," she said, turning on her heels. Like hell if she was going to keep quiet about it this time. She had made that mistake before. Either Mike had his story mixed up or Bastian had found a miraculous way to evolve into an even bigger bastard than he was in middle school. She picked up her cell phone to see that she had received a text message from Bastian.

Kinsley, I didn't want to call b/c I was working late last night & was afraid you'd still be asleep this morning. I can't come over. Sending Mike. Got to go to Waynesboro to see Cameron, manager of store we're doing the online merger with. Be around this afternoon to see how things went.

Kinsley released the breath of air she was holding while she read his message. So Cameron was the manager of that store he had mentioned at lunch. A little smile crept up her face at the realization she was getting all upset over nothing. He wasn't running for the hills or ignoring the situation. He had something pop up and would be by later. Just as soon as her eyes illuminated with a shred of relief, she caught herself in a most dire predicament. She had gotten upset! She was on the cusp of panicking over Bastian Harris, which meant he had regained a certain level of power over her after one measly kiss—albeit a hell of a kiss. That may have been the way things between them operated over twenty years ago, but to hell with that flying now.

She dropped her phone down on the counter and ran her hands through her hair. So furious with herself that she couldn't hold a steady hand, she decided getting out of the house was the only way she was going to calm the train wreck in her mind. She jerked her head to the right and saw Petunia chewing on a rubber bone.

"Come on Petunia, we're going to Gypsy Park!" On first glimpse, a bystander would assume that Petunia's total body weight consisted entirely of skin, fat, and floppy ears. However, a brain did add some heftiness, for as soon as she heard the word *park,* Petunia leapt up as if someone had lit a firecracker underneath her.

Kinsley flung open the door leading to the garage like a woman on a mission. "Mike!" she barked. He was only about ten feet away, but she was fueled with animosity and didn't care about her tone or volume.

He jumped at the unexpected sound. "Yes, ma'am?"

"I'm taking Petunia to the park! I'm locking the door leading into the house. You need to take a whiz or anything?" Kinsley usually didn't speak this abrasively to people, at least not to people she just met, but the anger ignited and rolled off her tongue.

Mike stood there, appearing like he didn't know quite what to do. "No ma'am. I'm fine. This should only take me about two hours at most."

"Good! Can you close the garage door on your way out?"

"Sure." Poor Mike. With his bubble wrap in one hand and some sort of rifle in the other, he seemed to be debating on whether or not it was okay for him even to breathe in this crazy banshee's presence. "You okay, miss?"

"Yes! I just need some fresh air!" Kinsley slammed the door and locked it.

Petunia remained vigilant at the front door while Kinsley changed into a pair of green running shorts and a black racer tank top. Coming down the stairs, she noticed a leash hanging on the coat hooks. As Petunia wriggled with excitement and Kinsley clipped it onto her collar, her phone dinged from its location on the counter.

She stood erect and stared at her phone from across the room. She could go over and check it. She *should* go over and check it in case it was Monica, Delilah, or Diane. Instead, she held up both hands giving it the double middle finger, grabbed her keys and Petunia's leash, and was dragged by the dog out to her car. Was this whole situation worthy of a double middle finger salute? No, but it made her feel better nonetheless. Once Kinsley placed Petunia in the backseat, she punched Gypsy Park into her GPS and gave Mike a curt nod before peeling wheels out of the driveway.

Chapter Thirteen

At some point on the ride to the park, Kinsley lost control of the situation and Petunia ended up maneuvering her way into the front seat. Since Kinsley fully intended to drop her off at the shelter that afternoon, she figured every dog should have one last fun ride. Petunia took full advantage of Kinsley rolling down the passenger window and hung her head out the entire way. Nothing but ears and spittle flapped in the breeze.

Kinsley coasted into the parking lot of Gypsy Park beside the duck pond. This place was one thing she'd missed about her hometown. Expansive in scope, it hosted massive playgrounds, a community pool, and a gazebo where local bands would play on Friday nights in the summertime. Jogging trails wrapped around and wove through it too. Anticipating Petunia making a mad dash out of the car, Kinsley grabbed her leash in one hand and the keys in the other. Getting out of the car mimicked the choreography of a pirate with a peg leg doing a sea time jig. After she had gotten Petunia appropriately unwound from her left thigh, they headed down the paved trail into the wooded area of the park.

Petunia must have been saving her energy the past six-plus days for their visit. It amazed Kinsley that a hound dog who spent at least twenty hours a day sleeping, the other three eating, and the remaining sixty minutes scratching, could dash down the trail with the energy and enthusiasm of a marathon runner. Luckily, the burst of liveliness was short lived and being dragged down the walkway only lasted about a quarter of a mile before Petunia pooped out. Around the half-mile marker, Kinsley was pretty much towing the bag of fleas through the park.

Getting ready to heave Petunia over her shoulder before animal services was on her ass for cruelty, good fortune decided to smile on her. Devine park providence placed a dog watering station by a park bench that was only about twenty feet ahead of her. "Come on Petunia, I'll grill you a steak when we get back to the house. It may be raw in the middle and Cajun style on the outside, but you're a dog so I'm sure you won't mind."

Apparently, "park," was not the only word in Petunia's vocabulary. She was fluent in "meat" vernacular too. The word "steak" had her powering through the last twenty feet to the water spigot.

Kinsley cranked the silver handle until lukewarm water ran into a lower basin attached to the fountain. After two refills, Petunia hopped up on the bench and settled in for a breather. Kinsley sat next to her and patted her on the head as the dog closed her eyes and began to snore. It was the perfect spot for resting: the sun shimmering through the trees, birds tweeting, and cute little senior citizens doing tai chi in a clearing over to the right.

Kinsley decided to use the moment of peace to try and assemble some clarity on her feelings from this morning. She didn't like that believing Bastian had blown her off for another woman had such an impact on her. That kind of emotional reaction indicated she was developing some sort of attachment and she was *not* willing to let that happen. Fall for it once shame on him, fall for it twice shame on her. She needed a strategy to handle this entire situation. There were only two options she had at this fork in the road: continue with Bastian in an entirely professional capacity, or trust she was older and wiser than before and could handle casual sex with the first boy that ever broke her heart. *Talk about a slippery slope.* If she selected option two, she needed to dig her heals in so that a metaphoric rockslide didn't take her down.

Spreading her arms along the back of the park bench, she tilted her face towards the sky. Her eyelids drifted closed as the warm sun's rays washed over her. With her hand on Petunia's torso, she slowed her breathing so the rise and fall of their chests ended up in sync. The thumping of Petunia's heartbeat on her palm and the sound of blue jays signing in the trees swooned her into relaxation. That was until she heard a familiar voice behind her. "Hey, Kinsley."

She blinked, allowing her eyes to adjust to the intrusion of light. As the black blobs dissipated, she found a very taut Sharon Wilson standing in front of her. She wore a hot pink sports bra that was moonlighting as a running shirt and a pair of black Nike spandex shorts below her flattened stomach. Her blond hair was piled high on top of her head with only a hint of dampness from sweat at the hairline. Kinsley hated women that didn't sweat during workouts; it wasn't natural.

"Hi, Sharon. I didn't know you were a runner."

"I've been doing it seriously now for the past five years or so. It's sort of my addiction, I guess you could say."

"I see." Kinsley didn't know you could take running seriously. It wasn't a career or charitable obligation. It was simply putting one foot in front of the other a lot faster than normal. Sharon stood in front of Kinsley with straight legs, bending over to touch her toes. Although Kinsley had developed quite a bit of flexibility from her years in Pilates, she still couldn't touch her nose to her knees like this showoff. She tried her hardest not to stare while Sharon went through her lunges and stretches. Her eyes needed to remain on Sharon's face since the Nike running shorts were wedging into unflattering crevices. Kinsley cleared her throat and diverted her gaze. "Do you have Fridays off?"

"Oh, no. I rarely take a day off. Slows down the momentum. I usually go in at one on Fridays, but I'm going to have to go in a bit earlier today since they're closing down Main Street at twelve."

"They're closing down Main Street?" Kinsley's forehead crinkled. This was news to her. "Why?"

"To get ready for the parade. They block everything off early. Most of the businesses on the street close up early too since not much foot traffic comes in with the whole place coned off."

Kinsley peered at her watch. It was already ten-fifteen. She would need to get back to the car soon if she was going to make it to the Town Bank and Trust before everything shut down for the parade. "How's the listing for the house going?"

"Funny enough, I was going to give you a call later today. The family moving here from Pennsylvania got the pictures and is very interested. The father said he'd like to come on Sunday to take a tour. You think I can show it on Sunday afternoon, say around two o'clock?"

"Yes, most definitely!" It was one of the first good pieces of news she had gotten in the last few days. Maybe she could get out of here by Monday. Tuesday at the latest.

"Great. Oh, and I spoke to Bass last night to let him know about your referral. If we can sell this house he gets half off his next month's rent for sending us the business." Sharon stood on one leg while touching the heel of her other foot to her spandex butt cheeks.

"You spoke with him last night?" That was odd. He had told her via text message that he couldn't call her because he was busy at work.

"Yep, for about twenty minutes or so. The Blue Ridge

Realty float is behind Wilson Memorial High's ROTC float, which Bass has graciously volunteered to pull with his jeep. He's a very sweet guy." Kinsley couldn't be entirely sure due to the running, but it looked like Sharon Wilson was blushing.

"That's nice." Kinsley bit out the platitude right before Petunia stretched her legs and let loose a loud fart that scared away the flock of birds behind them. She woke herself up for a brief second before returning her head to Kinsley's lap.

Sharon snickered a little and grabbed her ear buds, preparing to continue her run. "Okay then, these next two miles aren't going to run themselves. I'll call you later to confirm the showing time on Sunday. Will I see you at the parade tomorrow?"

"Not sure if I'm going yet." Kinsley slipped from underneath Petunia's head and stood with leash in hand.

"I hope to see you there. Talk to you soon." Sharon gave a little wave and continued down the trail as if no effort was involved.

Kinsley tugged on Petunia's leash and, luckily, the mutt obliged by hopping off the bench. The two walked side by side down the walkway to the car. Petunia's fat padded feet pounced off the asphalt with less energy than before, but still obvious enthusiasm. Hopefully, she could keep it up until they got to the car. Kinsley needed to hurry if she was going to make it to check out that safe deposit box.

By the time she arrived home, Mike had already finished loading up the guns and left to deliver them to Five Points. Kinsley got Petunia settled inside and grabbed the safe deposit key off a hook by the stereo. She picked up her cell phone to see what had caused her earlier double finger maneuver.

It was from Bastian.

Everything ok

Staring at the screen and chewing on her bottom lip, she dismissed the thought of a flirty text as soon as Sharon Wilson popped in her mind. In the matter of a few hours, Kinsley had ridden a bipolar rollercoaster about this man. Excited to see him one minute, angry with him the next, and now he didn't seem like the pinnacle of honesty. Not having enough time to call to let her know he wouldn't be around, but having enough time to chit chat with Sharon Wilson for twenty minutes was a load of garbage.

Her decision was easy. Option one of the professional relationship had a bright, blinking neon sign flashing "Over Here Stupid." There was too much of a history for her to remain unbiased. She could say she was going to use and abuse him before riding her beamer off into the sunset all she wanted, but the truth was she didn't think she could do it. She never had clinger issues with any other men before, but this man had found a way into her heart when it was just developing. His nails sunk deeper than others, which meant his hold would be greater.

She let out a sigh and picked up her phone.

Everything went great. Mike got all the guns. No need to stop by later. She threw her phone in her purse and was halfway out the door when it dinged again.

Okay. What about your check?

She would like to believe she could tell him to stop by, give her the check, and take a hike, but she knew it was wishful thinking. He'd show up and his piercing eyes would get to her like they had all those years before. Only this time, they wouldn't be thirteen. Immaturity wouldn't keep her from going too far.

Tell Tommy to mail it to my Aunt Debbie. She'll make sure I get it. Thanks for everything, Bastian.

Not wanting to be disturbed anymore, she turned her phone off and headed to the Town Bank and Trust. She'd had a savings account there until she was eighteen, so she knew where to find it. Careful not to park on Main Street for fear of being blocked in, she ended up on Second Street and walked the three blocks to the bank.

The lobby hadn't changed much in the past twenty years. The grey and green marble floors were still the same. Eight teller windows constructed of wooden paneling and gold framed glass stood on the far end of the wall. A few desks for loan managers and opening checking accounts sat in rows off to the left and right. Kinsley saw a balding, middle-aged man in a suit filling out paperwork behind one of the desks. His desk plate read, "Bank Manager: Edward Mahoney," so she figured he would be the best person to ask about the safety deposit box.

"Excuse me?"

The man stopped scribbling on his papers and smiled. His nose reminded her of a stork's beak. "Yes, ma'am. How can I help you?"

"I need to get into my father's safety deposit box. It was willed to me. I have his death certificate here along with a copy of the will that was given to me by his lawyer." She handed over the paperwork and fished her driver's license from her wallet.

"Absolutely Miss. I'm Mr. Mahoney, the Bank Manager. I'll need to make a copy of all these documents and your photo ID."

Kinsley handed over her driver's license and sat in a leather-studded chair across from his desk. Townies staggered in and out, making withdraws or deposits and, of course, every teller knew them by name. That didn't happen back in Hampton Roads. Kinsley watched the patrons and their interactions during the twenty minutes it took for all the documents to get copied, verified, and certified before she was led to the room of safety deposit boxes by Mr. Mahoney. "Here we are, box 234. Do you have your key with you, Mrs. Bailey?"

"It's Miss, actually. And yes, it's right here," she said, lifting the key.

"Okay, do you see these two locks? Your key unlocks one

of them; the bank has the other key. You need both of them in order to remove the box, so anytime you want to come in here to open it, a bank representative will need to be with you. Then you'll be escorted to one of our rooms where you may view the contents in privacy. So if you will please go ahead and place your key in the silver lock and I will place the bank key in the bronze. Then, we can get you all set up." He waved at both locks. "After you have a chance to look through it, we can meet again to discuss if you would like to carry on renting the box. Mr. Bailey was paid up through December."

Kinsley and Mr. Mahoney unlocked the box and removed it from its position on the wall. It was the smallest size the bank offered, like a child's shoebox. He walked her down the hall to "Box Room A" and opened the door for her. It was a small room with a table and two chairs, like the furniture in the lobby. Mr. Mahoney placed the box on the table. "I'll be right outside when you're done reviewing what's in here, and we can have that discussion about how you'd like to proceed. And there's no need to rush, but just letting you know we're closing down at twelve today to get ready for the Founder's Day Parade tomorrow."

"No worries. I'm sure it won't take that long."

Mr. Mahoney excused himself and left the room. With the door closed behind her, Kinsley took her key, unlocked the box, and flipped the top up on its hinge. Inside was a yellow 3x5 envelope with one word written on the outside in sharpie, "Kinsley." Whatever was in this box was enough to make Aunt Debbie haul ass from the lawyer's office the other day. It was time to find out what all the fuss was about. She pulled the envelope free and used her key to slice open the top. Upon opening it, she saw it was lined notebook paper. A letter...from her father...to her.

She unfolded the paper until it laid flat. The handwriting showed age, maybe arthritis, so this must have been written in his later years. After taking a big gulp, she started reading.

Dear Kinsley,

I'm sorry you had to come all the way to Staunton to deal with everything. The last time I saw you, you called me a whore of a bastard and said you would use your designer shoes to dance on my grave. If you're reading this, I hope your feet aren't too swollen.

Right now you're probably wondering why I decided to leave you all my stuff even though we haven't exactly had a typical father/daughter relationship. You've probably asked yourself on many occasions why I stayed away. To be honest, I tried calling your house at least once a week after your mother died and one time made it all the way to your front door. Unfortunately, I never finished dialing, and I couldn't knock on your door. Taking down dangerous suspects without a second thought was easy, but when it came to telling you the truth I always chickened out.

Just in case I never got around to facing my responsibilities before the Good Lord called me home, I decided to write a letter and leave it in this box here for you. Because you deserve to know the truth even if I can't tell it to you face to face. Kinsley, you are not my biological daughter. You are the daughter of Jim Bailey, my brother.

The letter dropped onto the table. Somehow all of the air had been sucked out of the room and Kinsley struggled to breathe. Mitchell wasn't her father? Her Uncle Jim was her father? What the hell happened? Why hadn't her mother ever said anything to her? This had to be a lie. One final punch to the gut from the whore of a bastard. After taking a deep breath, she picked up the letter and continued reading.

I didn't find out about this until you were almost eight years old. We both know that even though your mother was a great woman, she had demons she battled regularly.

Her behavior was not easy on our relationship. I'm sure I could've done more for our marriage or tried to persuade her to get help, but I did the best I knew how at the time—disappearing into my work.

Although your mother and I fought a lot, we still found comfort with one another from time to time. During one of her more rational moments, she agreed having more children wasn't a good idea since there were times she could barely take care of herself. I decided a vasectomy was the best option so we could fix the family we were barely holding together. It required testing. Two days later, I got a phone call from the doctor. It turned out that your mother and I didn't need birth control...I was sterile. Knowing you were still at school, I left work to talk your mother. I asked Jenean what was going on. I didn't want to believe it. You looked so much like me that I didn't think it was possible. But then I saw the panic on her face, and I knew no medical miracle had occurred. You were not mine.

Bile began to burn Kinsley's throat. She wanted desperately to believe this confession was a ruse. In the story of her life, her father was the villain, not the victim. The nausea produced tiny beads of sweat above her lip. Using the letter, she fanned herself briefly before resolving to read on.

When your mother and I first got married, I had an old Dodge Dart permanently parked next to my gun collection in the garage. My brother Jim and I used to spend hours fixing it up. When Jim was laid off from his job at the paper mill, he decided to utilize his free time working on the car instead of finding a job. While I was out earning a living, Jim decided to do more than work on the engine. Afraid to ask a doctor to help her and in fear of destroying our marriage, they decided neither you nor I were to ever find out.

The room started spinning and I couldn't think clearly. All I could do was start packing. With my car full of clothes and the trunk full of guns, I went over to Jim's house and beat the hell out of him in front of his first wife, Patty. I'm not sure if she ever knew why it happened, only that is was so bad I didn't ever come around again before she died ten years later. I never spoke to him again until his second wife, Debbie, called me to say he was dying of cancer. It wasn't until then that I forgave my brother for what he did, because that's what you do when someone dies.

I don't know if I waited too long, but when I finally felt strong enough to see you again, your mother refused to let me anywhere near you. She said I should suffer for walking out. She threatened to order a paternity test and ruin my career by revealing the scandal. I wasn't willing to put you through the whispers and gossip I knew this town could dish out. So I kept my distance, signed the checks, and sent you away when you came to the police station to try and talk to me. Unfortunately with time, my sadness turned to anger. Because of her, my daughter hated me. Taking the house was not the classiest move I could have made, but years of watching her play the jilted wife while she held my future and yours under her thumb was unforgiveable. As twisted as it seems, it was a way to get even with her. What did I have to lose from taking claim to the house? You already hated me.

I shouldn't have made the choices I did. I should have fought for you, even if you weren't my daughter. I was too worried about my career, afraid of what people would think. I don't expect over twenty years of hurt to disappear by one long letter. I don't expect you to believe me either, which is why I hope you speak to your Aunt Debbie. I only hope that one day, knowing what you now know, you'll find it in your heart to forgive me. I love you and am so proud of the person you have grown up to be. If making the choice to stay away had anything to do with you turning out the way you did, then as much as it would kill me, I would do it all over again.

With love,

Mitchell Bailey

Kinsley placed the letter back in the safe deposit box as gingerly as if it were a bomb. The room shrunk. The air dissipated. She couldn't catch her breath. She stood up and opened the door leading into the hallway.

"Mrs. Bailey, are you all finished up?" Mr. Mahoney sat behind one of the smaller desks positioned outside of the rooms, ready with a file of paperwork in hand. "Mrs. Bailey?"

She gripped the doorframe tight. "It's Miss!" She screeched, turning around and grabbing her purse from the table before storming down the hall.

"Miss Bailey, I need to put the box back with you, and we need to discuss the rental agreement before you go!" He chased after her at a jog.

"Not now!" she said, throwing her hand in the air to stop him. She needed to get the hell out of the bank. Everything seemed to be running in slow motion, except for her. People wouldn't move out of her way fast enough in the lobby. She weaved through the throng, making a mad dash to get money before it closed early. She had to get to her car. She had to get to her aunt's house.

Her father had to be lying. Kinsley's mother was always a bit off her rocker, but an affair? Threatening to destroy him and take her away if he didn't maintain the persona of abysmal ex-husband? That all didn't seem plausible. Sure her mother had her issues—okay, so there was that one time her mother ripped her phone off the wall when she got caught cheating on her math test in fourth grade. And yes, maybe she made Kinsley quit Girl Scouts when she was eleven because she thought the other mothers were putting rat poison in the coffee at meetings. She went a little bonkers from time to time, but she usually snapped out of it in a week or so. There was no way she was capable of keeping up such a façade for so long.

Kinsley jogged to her BMW. Once in her car, she grabbed her phone and pushed the power button. Bastian had called and left a voicemail, but that wasn't her concern right now. She scrolled through her contacts until she found Aunt Debbie's number.

"Hello?"

"Hey Aunt Debbie. Guess where I'm leaving from."

"Oh, please tell me it's Bass Harris's house! If that little trollop, Holly Writtle, gets him 'fore you do then I have to pay Ida ten bucks." Nice to know her Aunt was placing bets on her love life.

"Nope, I'm now leaving the bank." She waited for a response. For the first time since Kinsley had been back in Staunton, Aunt Debbie was speechless. "Yep...just left. Did some light reading. Are you home? We need to talk."

"Yeah, darlin'. I'm home. Come on over. I'll fix you a strong drink and we'll sit out on the porch and talk."

Kinsley surveyed the digital clock in her car. "A drink? It's only noon."

She laughed. "Honey, if Mother Teresa had left Town Bank and Trust reading that letter, she'd be having a stiff drink too. It's 121 Buffalo Gap Lane. I'll see you in a few minutes."

Chapter Fourteen

Kinsley drove up Debbie's driveway and parked directly behind her aunt's Buick. A huge maple tree sat off to the left, the perfect perch for turkey buzzards. Aunt Debbie rested in a rocking chair on a porch that wrapped around her one story rambler. It was quaint with beige siding and bright blue shutters. White painted flower boxes lined the base where its poles met the porch and overflowed with orange and yellow zinnias. The flowers were fragrant and added a homey touch to the already inviting atmosphere.

Debbie rocked in her chair, sipping a glass of lemonade. In anticipation of Kinsley's arrival, she had set a tall glass filled to the brim with ice and yellow liquid placed on the table next to her and sweating from the summer heat.

"Hey, Aunt Debbie." Kinsley plopped into the rocker next to her Aunt and slid her keys on the table by her drink.

"Hey sweetie." Without saying another word, Kinsley leaned in her chair and began to rock. They sat like that for a few moments: silent, rocking, and taking in the view. Buffalo Gap Lane was part of a neighborhood called Eastview nestled in the hills on the outskirts of town. Although the higher elevations had eventually been bought by a developer and now housed the more prominent citizens of Staunton, the older homes owned by the modest income constituents still rested at the base of the hills. Eastview even went so far as to build an alternate entrance so the rich homeowners didn't have to get depressed entering their neighborhood and driving past $150k homes.

Parched from her earlier walk and the heat of the day, Kinsley picked up her glass and took a big swig, which led into a coughing fit. "What is this?"

"It's called a Stump Lifter. What? Don't you like it?"

She was sure her face turned red from all the coughing, and spit shot out of her mouth. "I thought it was lemonade. What's in it?"

"Well, lemonade's in it along with some beer and vodka. We drink it down at the VFW on Bingo nights."

When her coughing subsided for good, she stared at the glass in awe. "And you drive home afterwards?"

"Course not, I have my godson come pick me up. Part of his rental agreement for staying with me. Geez girl, can't you hold your alcohol?"

"Of course I can, but it looked like regular lemonade. I wouldn't have taken a big gulp if I'd known it was two parts booze." Truth be told, Kinsley couldn't hold her liquor. She was frequently the reliable source of entertainment for Delilah, Monica, and Diane whenever they ventured to a bar. Last June, when they all went to Plaza Del Torro to celebrate the last day of school, she got up on stage and sang a Shania Twain song, smacked a bus boy on the ass, and was asked to leave the establishment.

Despite the fact that this particular drink should have a flammable sign on it, Kinsley sipped. She was still thirsty after all. Placing the glass on the table, she turned towards her aunt. "I'm guessing you know what that letter said."

"Yes, ma'am. Mitchell wrote roughly eight different drafts of that letter and had me read every one of them." She nodded.

"So...is it true?"

"I married your Uncle Jim about seven years ago. He'd never tell me why he and Mitchell didn't speak. He only said they had a falling out and it was best to let dead dogs lie, so I obliged. Debbie put her glass next to Kinsley's. "When Jim started being unable to eat and feeling ill, we went to the doctor and found out he had stomach cancer. He went through surgery to remove the tumor, but the cells had already spread into other parts of the lining in his stomach. Even with chemo, the prognosis wasn't good. So after a lot of consideration, we decided he should remain as comfortable as he could for as long as possible."

Kinsley sat straighter in the chair and said softly, "I'm sorry."

"Thank you." Aunt Debbie took another swig from her cup. "One day, the pain was getting to him. You know stomach cancer's excruciating, what with the eating issues, and you get twig skinny. After a double dose of pain meds and finally feeling some relief, I guess he realized the end was coming quicker than we'd hoped. He didn't want to die with a secret. So he told me about what happened with your mother, Jenean. Even through all the agony of the cancer and the discomfort that he suffered from, that was the only time I'd ever seen that man cry."

Aunt Debbie wiped at her eyes with the back of her hand and gave a small sniff.

"Anyway, he'd confessed he and your mother had a few weak moments on a couple of different occasions while your daddy was at work, but they decided after the fourth or fifth time to call it off. He thought it was a demon secret he was going to have to keep locked up tight, and hopefully, never have to deal with it again. But a month or so later, your mother announced she was pregnant. You came along and as far as all parties were concerned, you were Mitchell's child. Apparently everything was fine, until one day about eight years after you were born, your father showed up where Jim lived with his first wife, Patty, and beat the living snot out of him. They didn't speak after that. Not until I called Mitchell to let him know Jim was dying."

"And then he came to the house," Kinsley filled in for her aunt.

"Yep. Mitchell showed up at our house that afternoon and they settled their differences. Jim was certain it was a last ditch effort to let him pass without guilt, but Mitchell showed back up at the house every day for the next three weeks to help me with the yard, fix what needed fixing, and get Jim's affairs in order. That was when your father and I became friends and stayed such even after Jim passed a month later. My word, that was five years ago."

"Why didn't he ever come tell me after Mama died?" Her stomach dropped with the heavy dose of liquid fire she'd sipped. "If she really had him that scared and she wasn't a threat anymore, why not extend the olive branch and an explanation face-to-face?"

"Darlin', when your mama passed you came hauling ass into town madder than a fire ant whose ant farm got shook up. You had a scowl on your face and your arms crossed all the time. You were unapproachable. And Jesus help us when you found out your father was moving back into the house. You know why your daddy did that? Why his name was never taken off the deed?"

Kinsley felt like a lost child who couldn't tell the locating officer her phone number because she hadn't memorized it. She just shook her head.

"Cause he was paying the mortgage on it the whole time. Up until about two years ago, when it was paid off. If he didn't take it back, you'd have find out he'd been making payments over the last twenty some years and start asking questions. He wasn't ready for that yet, especially after you called him a son of a whore."

"It was a whore of a bastard," she smirked. "At least that's what he said in the letter. I was so angry at him that I kind of blacked out when I made that scene in the front yard." Kinsley put her head down and stared at her lap. Needing something to do, she started picking at her cuticles. "What about my mother? Do you know if she did those things...blackmailed him and told him to stay away? Do you know that for certain?"

"Honey, about four months after I laid my Jim to rest, I got antsy and decided I was gonna talk to your mama about it. I had gotten to know Mitchell and the toll this whole screwed up situation had on him. I mean, he lost his wife, the little girl he thought was his child, a brother, and then, he was taken to the cleaners by his ex. I was gonna reason with her that you had moved out of town and it was time to let Mitch repair his last broken relationship." One more swig of the twisted lemonade had Aunt Debbie rocking even more on her chair. "She told me to go to hell and mind my own business. When I backed out of her driveway, she tried throwing a flower pot at my car."

Kinsley lifted her head, raw and more than a little shell-shocked. "I remember her crying, locking herself in her room, and sometimes have paranoia, but I didn't know she was capable of anything like this. She was diagnosed as being bipolar about three years before she died and was being treated for it. Why didn't she ever come clean?" She was asking the question more to herself than her aunt.

"Well now, she'd been tellin' this lie for over twenty years. You grew up believing the man who you thought was your father deserted you. How do you straighten out a lie like that? What would you have done if she'd come to you and told you she had an affair, another man was your daddy, and she blackmailed her ex-husband to keep the checks rolling in?"

Her mind reeled, thoughts flying in and out like a swarm of angry wasps. "I don't know what I would have done, but at least I would have had the chance to make a decision. I wasn't even given the option. I find it all out after they're both dead. I was robbed of telling my mother how angry I am at her and telling my father…" she sucked in a breath, "well, I don't know what I would have told Mitch, but I don't even get a chance to figure out what to say cause he's dead now too. All of my choices, from when I was eight all the way to now, were taken away by selfish people who couldn't own up to what they did wrong." Kinsley grabbed the glass of lemon-flavored kerosene from the table and took a big gulp. At least she could claim the burn from the alcohol was responsible for the water stinging her eyes.

"I understand you're angry. Hell, I'd be madder than sin too. But there's nothing you can do to change any of this now, except work on healing yourself, holding onto the family relationships you have, and moving on. I know I'm glad to have you around," Aunt Debbie smiled wide. "And you're pretty good company to keep when you're not pissed off or singing in a funeral parlor."

Kinsley couldn't help but laugh at that last part. "Can we please never talk about that again? I can't carry a tin in a tune pot with the lid on."

"You mean carry a tune in a tin pot with the lid on?" Debbie asked, and cast a suspicious eye. "Have you eaten anything today?

"Nope, didn't have time. Mike came from Five Points to pick up the guns, I took Petunia to the park, ran into Sharon 'watch me stretch' Wilson, and went to the bank. I haven't eaten a thing yet." She picked up her glass and finished it off.

"I think I need to get you something to eat then. Come on inside and I'll make you a sandwich and a cup of coffee. I forget you skinny ladies are easy drunks."

"A coff of cuppy sounds great." Kinsley stood, trying to use the handrail on the rocking chair to steady her. Not the smartest of moves. Thank goodness Aunt Debbie had the alcohol tolerance of a frat boy. She helped Kinsley straighten up and led her into the house.

***

It was already five o'clock, hours past the time Bastian thought he'd be driving back into town. The contract meeting ran a hell of a lot longer when Cameron Quinn's silent financial supporter stepped in saying he wanted his own attorney to check over everything before it was all signed and sealed. Even after the lawyer left around noon, Cameron requested to take Bastian to lunch so they could discuss in further detail the possible layouts for the website and the bidding software and credit card companies to use. Considering this was the partner in a deal projected to pull in an additional six figures yearly over Five Points current profits, he felt he couldn't refuse.

Bastian glanced over at his glove compartment. Inside laid Kinsley's check for the fourteen guns Tommy purchased from her. He went ahead and grabbed it when he was at the shop last night until about twelve-thirty in the morning. He'd planned on bringing it to her when he was done in Waynesboro, but then she sent that text message telling him to have Tommy put in the mail. It also sounded like she was saying goodbye, which didn't make any sense to him.

Eagle Rock Lane was only about a mile ahead; maybe he would just drop by and tell her he was in the area. And he could find out exactly what was going on with her. He'd thought last night had ended pretty fantastic on his end, considering he'd had a hard on to hell and it wasn't from a woman gyrating on his lap. She was also supposed to come by the gun range that night for one of her freebie private lessons, but the subtext of her message made him lean towards the possibility of her not showing up.

That solved it. He would stop by, hand over her check, say he was passing by on his way to the gun shop and didn't know whether or not she was coming to her lesson. Those all sounded like legitimate reasons to show up at a woman's house who basically told him not to bother. Jesus, he was pathetic. He didn't know what it was about this woman that made him rationalize playing the fool in order to see her. Plenty of women in town would be thrilled to have him roll up in their driveways, and he wouldn't need to be packing a check for over ten grand to feel welcomed either.

Bastian flipped on the blinker and turned left onto Eagle Rock Lane. A few minutes later, he parked the jeep on the side of the road next to her mailbox, opened his glove box, grabbed the white envelope that held her check, and got out of car. On walking around the front of the jeep, he realized his plan was in the crapper when step one—knock on the door—was rendered moot. Kinsley was on her knees, bent over in front of the house, gardening. A pile of weeds sat to her right, while small potted plants of yellow and gold rested on her left. She had apparently been at it for a while as a sheen of sweat coated her skin and dirt smudges covered her arms.

"Hey, Kinsley. Gardening?" He flinched the instant it was out of his mouth. *What a stupid question. Of course she was gardening, she wasn't building a rocket.*

She leaned back to sit on her feet and sniffled. Rising from the grass, but still not facing him, she began to pull off her gloves. After swiping the dirt at her knees, she turned around. A smudge of soil streaked across her left cheek and a piece of mulch stuck in her braid that lay over her shoulder. Her face was slightly red from being out in the heat so long and her eyes were blood shot and glassy.

"Hey, you alright?" He reached for her, but curled his fingers in when she took a step back.

"Oh, I'm fine. Allergies I guess. What can I do for you, Bastian?"

Okay, something was definitely off. "I know you said to have Tommy stick the check in the mail, but I'd already grabbed it last night, thinking I'd see you at some point today before your gun lesson." He held out the envelope to her. "Did you forget we were supposed to meet tonight at the shop?"

Not making eye contact, she took the check from his hand. "No, I didn't forget."

Bastian stood there with a furrowed brow before speaking again. "Oh-kay so were you going to show up, or did I read the subliminal message of your earlier text correctly?"

Kinsley still wouldn't look at him. "I hadn't forgotten about it but I think I just lost track of time. I was going to call you and cancel." She stared at her hands, turning the envelope corner to corner repeatedly.

So he had understood her hidden intent. She was telling him to have a nice life.

"Okay, Kinsley. Sorry to have bothered you. You be careful going home." He was getting ready to leave when she stepped forward and grabbed his arm.

"Wait." Her fingers dug into his bicep like she was holding on for dear life. As soon as he titled her face up, she released her grip. Words seemed stuck in her throat as she looked away again, refusing to make eye contact.

"I'm a little bit confused here, Kinsley. You came to dinner with me last night, granted it was to Ida's house, but it was still dinner. We said goodnight...the way we said goodnight...I mean I thought it was pretty fucking fantastic." He ran a hand through his hair trying to find the right words. "And then today you tell me to put your check in the mail and thanks for the help. You want to give me some sort of clue about what's going on here cause I'm starting to feel like an asshole."

Biting her lower lip, she at last met his eye. "I found out today that my dad is not my dad."

He took a step closer, unsure he heard her right. "What do you mean?"

One tear ran down her cheek, leaving a streak on her face

where it washed away some of the soil. "I went to the bank today because part of my inheritance was a safety deposit box. I went to see what was in it and found a letter from Mitchell. The letter said he left my mother and I when I was eight because he found out he wasn't my father." She swiped away the tear, making the dirt smudge more. "His brother Jim was. Then, my mother told him she would ruin his career and move me away if he ever told anyone and didn't keep sending her money."

His eyes widened. "Holy shit, are you sure that's true?"

She nodded. "Yes, I went to see my Aunt Debbie today and she confirmed everything. She said Jim told her that I was his child a few weeks before he died."

The lost expression on her face urged Bastian to hold her until she felt better. She wasn't sobbing, only one tear had slipped out, but she was obviously overwhelmed by all of it and needed some comfort. Instead, he slipped his hands in his pockets and took another step closer. He tilted his head down and said into her ear, "Jesus, Kinsley. I'm really sorry…I don't even know what kind of consoling you give someone when they find out something like that."

Kinsley rested her forehead on Bastian's chest without saying a word. Her arms were still at her sides when Bastian removed his hands from his pockets and wrapped his arms around her. They stood there in the front yard not saying anything for several moments. With his chin resting on top of her head, Bastian glanced up and saw that she only had planted two groups of flowers and still had several more to do. He rubbed her back for a bit and then pulled away. "Let me help you finish the flower beds. I'm surprised to see you planting since you want to leave in the next few days."

Kinsley glanced at him with eyes no longer on the verge of tears. "Aunt Debbie said it would help with curb appeal for selling the house. I have a potential buyer coming on Sunday."

"At the rate you're moving it will take you 'til then to get it done, and you have a parade to go see tomorrow. Yours truly is in it. So let's get this finished up."

She smiled slightly. "Okay, but I get to use the gardening gloves."

Chapter Fifteen

Kinsley wiped the steam from the mirror in the upstairs bathroom. She had taken a quick enough shower last night to rinse off the dirt and film of sweat, but she needed to scrub a second time and shave to feel clean. She stared at her reflection in the patch of mirror that wasn't foggy. Putting both hands on either side of the sink, she leaned in and examined the small red rash on her chin. Bastian needed to shave; his prickly facial scruff had done some damage.

Last night after they finished working in the flowerbeds, Bastian came inside to get a drink while Kinsley jumped in the shower to rinse off. Even though her hair was wet, she had on no makeup, and wore comfy pajama pants and a big t-shirt, she asked him to stay for something to eat. Luckily, Aunt Debbie had sent her home with a Tupperware bin full of cold cuts and cheeses so she made him two sandwiches and one for herself. They sat on the couch with Petunia wedged between them, talking about anything and everything as long as it had nothing to do with safety deposit boxes, letters, or paternal questionability.

When it hit nine o'clock, she leaned her head against one of the couch pillows and listened to Bastian talk about his daughter, Jodi. He was so excited that she was coming to stay for a whole week. Since school was getting ready to start, it was the last time for a while that he'd get to see her that long. When he started chatting about the business plan of Five Points and their online partnership with Waynesboro Gun and Sports Supply, the lack of sleep from the previous night and the emotional roller coaster of the day caught up with her. Her eyelids became heavy and she drifted off to sleep before feeling a blanket being wrapped around her.

She jolted at the touch and stared up at Bastian standing over her. "I'm gonna head out Kinsley. Thanks for the sandwich, and hopefully, I'll see you tomorrow at the parade." He bent over the coffee table to grab his keys. Unsure if it was from her exhaustive state, or perhaps she could place the blame on thinking it was a dream, Kinsley got off the couch and followed him to the door.

Bastian turned around. "What are you doing? Go back to sleep. I can let myself out."

Without a second thought, Kinsley grabbed the collar of his shirt and pulled his mouth down to hers. She wasn't too nice about it either. Frustrated about her shit life, she needed some sort of release. Plus, he'd helped her plant flowers for two hours, which kind of made him a not-so-bad guy in her opinion. She knew this decision went against everything she'd worked out about keeping things professional, but a sleep-deprived woman of thirty-three, who just found out her uncle was her father, could hardly be held responsible for her actions.

Kinsley placed both her palms on his chest and shoved him against the front door. Bastian dropped his keys on the floor and cradled her face in his hands while her mouth relentlessly took control over his. His stubble ground into her chin, but the sting of it made her feel good, alive, and helped her forget she was abandoning her scruples.

Bastian grabbed underneath her bottom and hoisted her up, pushing away from the door. The space allowed Kinsley to wrap her legs around him while he turned and pinned her in the corner between the doorframe and the wall. Tearing his mouth from hers, he began to trail hungry kisses along her neck as she breathed heavily into his ear. With his lobe so close to her mouth, she drew it in between her teeth, not-so-gently sucking and biting the flesh in intervals. Against the thin material of her plaid pajama pants, she could feel his erection growing harder. He ground against her, alleviating some but sadly not all of her frustration.

As their lips met again, Kinsley slid her hand between them and grabbed at the bulge in the front of his pants. He moaned into her mouth, either from the pleasure of the touch or the exquisite pain she caused by teasing him. Want and frustration overtook her at the sudden absence of his lips.

"Kinsley." He panted her name like he had just finished a 5k.

"Hmm?" Her eyes half hooded from lust, her hand went on an expedition up from his groin to his neck, trying to coax him back into the kiss. He resisted.

"Kinsley, I think we should stop." Her lids snapped open. *What? Why should they stop?* She had moved on from professional to all kinds of personal, but she needed him to be a willing participant in throwing caution to the wind.

"Why?" She pecked small kisses around the corner of his mouth.

"Because Kinsley, you found out some pretty shitty news today, and I don't know if that has something to do with why you're kissing me. I mean, less than twelve hours ago you were telling me you didn't want to see me again." She kissed his lips again, to which he reciprocated for a few seconds, but then groaned and broke the lip lock. "Damn it, Kinsley, you aren't making this any easier. I'm trying to be an honorable man here. I don't want you doing anything because you're upset."

She rested her head against the corner of the wall. Wanting

to protest, she silently worried her argument would be confused for begging. No amount of desire would bring her to that level with this man…or any man for that matter.

"Believe me Kinsley, it's taking everything I have not to take you in one of these bedrooms and fuck you 'til you're walking funny tomorrow, but I can't do it. Not unless I'm sure you're doing it cause it's what you want and not for any other reason."

She rolled her eyes and breathed a heavy sigh. "Til I'm walking funny, huh? You're awfully confident."

He gave her a gentle peck on the lips. "To the point where you have to rent one of those little scooters to go grocery shopping."

She laughed and unwrapped her legs from his waist. He placed her on the ground and fished around the floor for his keys. Little had she known an audience had watched their affair. Petunia sat at the base of the steps the entire time, watching them. His keys rested next to her back paw. He leaned over to pick them up and patted Petunia on the head.

Placing his hand on the doorknob, he paused and looked back over at her. "See you tomorrow? At the parade?"

She stood frozen, watching him. "Maybe. I have a lot to get done before the house is shown on Sunday."

"All work and no play make Kinsley a dull girl." He tapped her on the nose before opening the door and walking out.

Kinsley rested against the doorframe. "What a day! Earth-shattering family secrets and going to bed cranky and unsatisfied. Great."

Trudging up the stairs, she headed straight to bed without passing go. She should have been awake for hours, but once her head hit the pillow, she was out like a light and didn't open her eyes again until nine the following morning.

Upon waking refreshed and clearheaded, she was glad Bastian decided to walk out. If she had been allowed to act off impulse, she would have thrown him down on the floor and humped him right there. Poor Petunia could have been squashed. She finished wiping down the rest of the mirror before drying off and slathering on lotion.

Kinsley slipped on a pair of beige panties with matching bra, cut off jean shorts, and a white baseball t-shirt with blue three-quarter sleeves. Being out in the sun so much yesterday had given her face enough bronze color that she didn't need any foundation or powder. She swiped on some mascara and clear lip gloss. After blow drying her hair, she put it up in a loose bun and ponytail combo with a few strands hanging around the sides of her face.

When she came downstairs, the clock displayed that it was already ten-thirty. If she cleaned, only stopping for food and bathroom breaks, she could have the house completely spotless in no time. A gnawing in her gut had her turning her head, staring at the door to Mitchell's bedroom. She hadn't touched that room the previous times she went on her cleaning rampage, but she needed to at least dust and vacuum it before the buyer showed up tomorrow. She went into the hall closet to grab the Pledge, a dust rag, and the vacuum. Pushing open the door to the bedroom, she found it as she had left it—sterile and untouched except for a little settled dust.

She propped the vacuum next to his closet and doused the dresser and nightstand with the lemon-scented cleaner. After wiping the top of the mirror, the sides, and the drawers of the dresser, she began dusting the nightstand...the one with her graduation picture. *How the hell did he get that?* She took the picture frame and laid it on the bed while she got busy wiping it. She noticed the golden handle on the small drawer of the bedside table was lopsided. Wondering if a screw on the back of the drawer was loose, she yanked it open. Inside she found a wooden box with the Five Points Logo burned into the top. Curious, she grabbed the box and set it on the bed. Pulling off the top, she found a revolver—a black one—that's the most she could tell about it. It made sense a former cop and gun enthusiast would sleep with a gun next to his bed. She popped open the chamber, saw it loaded, and immediately closed it back up before putting it in the wooden box.

Although the hammer wasn't cocked and she knew it couldn't be fired, thanks to Tommy and that gun safety course, she didn't want to hold a loaded gun. She finished dusting off the nightstand, said the hell with the lopsided handle, put the gun box back in the drawer, and closed it up. She was plugging in the vacuum when she heard a knock on the door. Petunia, oblivious to the sound of someone knocking, lay passed out like a bear rug in the hall.

"Some guard dog you are," Kinsley hissed. She stepped over the sleeping dog and peeked through the peephole. God help her! It was Debbie and Ida.

Plastering a fake smile on, Kinsley opened the door to greet her unwelcome visitors. "Aunt Debbie, Ida, what a nice surprise. What are you two doing here?"

Debbie steamrolled her way into the house. "We're here to pick you up for the parade of course. It starts at noon, so we've gotta get a move on if we want to get a good spot. Come on darlin', we already got lawn chairs in the trunk of the Buick. Lucky for us it's only gonna be a high of eighty degrees today! Perfect parade weather." Debbie wore a bright red shirt adorned with Mickey and Minnie Mouse. Her blue-jean sun visor hid perfectly the tight permed curls on her head. Ida's ensemble was a bit more modest, but not by much. She too donned a bright red shirt, but it was plain. Plaid shorts checkered in red and white reached lower than her kneecaps. Kinsley was pretty sure she used the same fabric as her kitchen curtains to make the pants.

"Aunt Debbie, I'd love to go, but I have to finish cleaning before the house gets shown to a buyer tomorrow. I'm sure you understand."

"Who's representing the house?" Ida chimed in.

"Sharon Wilson at Blue Ridge."

"Is the buyer a man?" asked Ida.

"Yes, a married man, but it's him that's coming to see the house."

"It could be covered in chicken crap and she'd still sell it to him. She's been the most successful realtor in these parts for the past four years at least. Men buyers are putty in her hands. You'll have an offer by Monday night." Debbie began shaping her hair in the hallway mirror. "Now go get your shoes on. I want to get a good spot in the shade."

At this point, it was clear that no amount of arguing was going to make these two leave without her. Kinsley guessed she could go for a few hours to get her mind on other things. Maybe cleaning wasn't that important since men apparently turned to chicken shit in Sharon Wilson's hands, at least that's what she thought Ida said.

"Fine, give me a minute." She stepped over Petunia and went to collect her brown suede sandals from the upstairs bedroom. After slipping them on her feet, she came down to find the two women discussing the two dirty plates on her coffee table.

"You have company last night, honey?" Debbie asked with her mouth partially cocked.

"Not company. Only Bastian Harris."

Ida Robinson huffed and puffed as she went into her purse and handed over a ten-dollar bill to Debbie.

Kinsley pointed at her. "You give that right back to her. Nothing happened last night. Holly still has a shot."

"Oh please," Ida snickered. "Soon as I saw how Bass was eyeing you from across the table all evening, I knew Holly had better chances of poopin' out a leprechaun than dating Bass Harris."

"That's not true. Leprechaun's are very tiny and can be

digested without you even knowing it."

Debbie looked at Kinsley like she had just pooped out a little green man herself. "Well, I guess if anyone would know about things being pooped out, it would be you."

Damn it. That stupid seagull story was gonna haunt her. Kinsley slipped her cell in the pocket of her shorts and stuffed a wad of cash in the other. After locking the front door behind them, she secured her keys around her belt loop.

The drive to the designated parking for the parade wasn't too bad, if you liked listening to two old ladies arguing about toilet paper brands while riding in the back of a Buick that drove over the hillsides like a boat in choppy water. The three of them each carried their lawn chair until they found a spot alongside the parade route that was in the shade for Aunt Debbie and close to public bathrooms for Ida. By the time they got situated, they had roughly twenty minutes to kill before the opening ceremony, so Kinsley decided to walk around and see what the festivities had to offer.

Vendors lined up along the streets with all their fried fair. She was tempted to be the first in line for the beer truck she saw setting up, but figured she should wait until at least noon to get something to drink. Lord knows alcohol was going to need to be involved if she had to spend the next two hours with Ida and Debbie. Kinsley bought a hot dog and a soda and made it to her seat in time for the opening festivities. Wilson Memorial High's band and flag team marched proudly down Main Street to start the parade. Weaving in and out of the smiling girls twirling their batons, members of the Staunton Order of Antelopes drove around in tiny cars wearing red bowling shirts and hats with antlers glued to them.

Different floats sponsored by organizations and businesses throughout Staunton travelled in neutral gear down Main Street. Kinsley's personal favorite was the float done by Moreland Berry Farms. They had men in overalls and straw hats standing behind giant blueberries. Unfortunately, for the riders of the float, they weren't given good direction on where to stand, so the giant berries happened to be waist high—a float of farmers holding blue elephantitis-sized testicles. Shortly after the berry display, Bastian's jeep appeared, pulling the high school's ROTC float. Decked in a tribute to America, the students were dressed to the nines in their ROTC uniforms and chanting a cadence. Bastian sat dutifully behind the wheel of the jeep waving to people, but always keeping one eye on the road, that is until he saw Kinsley sitting on the sidewalk. He smiled and waved specifically to her. Unfortunately, she responded by waving back and blushing, which did not go unnoticed by Ida or Debbie.

"Uh-huh, Holly has a shot my butt."

Kinsley, ready to make her argument against Ida's comment, was interrupted when an older man wearing an Order of the Antelopes hat came dragging a cooler over to where she was sitting. "Well hell, Debbie girl! How you been?"

"John Cletus! Where the heck have you been?" Debbie got up from her chair and gave the man a big hug.

"I was out in West Virginia visiting my son, Greg. I got something special for you, Mrs. Debbie." John reached into his red Coleman cooler on wheels and produced a huge slice of watermelon. Its pink surface glistened in the sun. Kinsley's mouth became dry at the sight.

"John, you naughty dog! You know we love your watermelon!" Debbie passed a slice over to Ida. "Kinsley, would you like one of John's watermelon slices?"

"Sure, if he doesn't mind." She smiled, taking a slice of fruit from John's hands. Debbie took a slice for herself too. "They look lovely."

"Debbie, I'll have to come calling at your place sometime just as soon as more fruit is ready. You ladies enjoy the parade." John tipped his horned hat at the three women and continued weaving in and out of parade gawkers with his cooler.

"That was nice of him," said Kinsley. She took a big bite out of the watermelon and noticed something was off. It tasted good, but watermelon wasn't supposed to burn, was it? "Aunt Debbie, why does this watermelon taste funny?"

"Oh, John seeps strawberry wine into his watermelons for a few days before he slices them open. A nice little summer drink in a nice little summer fruit, don't you think?" Debbie and Ida nibbled on theirs slowly.

"Wine-soaked watermelon, huh?" She continued to take big bites of her watermelon as she watched the rest of the parade. "Sure, why not?" Since she ate a hot dog, she could handle a little wine. The culmination of the parade was a float adorned with red, white, and blue tinsel and the Staunton official seal. All of the city council members and Miss Staunton herself rode on the final float, waving to the crowd.

As the traffic cleared off Main, patrons and vendors were able to begin walking the streets, buying food from different carts and memorabilia from moveable kiosks. Kinsley felt surprisingly relaxed, a little silly, even giggly. She glanced at her Aunt Debbie and Ida Robinson who had still only eaten about a quarter of their watermelon slices. Hers, on the other hand, was all the way down to the green part of the rind.

"I think I'm gonna walk around. Can I bring you two angels anything?" Kinsley asked, leaning over the arm of her chair.

Angels? Where'd that come from?

Debbie smiled. "No, sweetheart. You go on ahead. We like to stay here and people watch. We'll be waiting for you."

Kinsley explored the various booths down Main Street sidewalk. She wasn't exactly sure what she wanted to do, but she hadn't been to a street party in years.

"Miss… Miss… would you like a tattoo?" A woman with partially dreadlocked brown hair and a tie-dye dress tried to flag her down.

"A tattoo? At a parade?" she asked walking over to the

stand. The artist could seriously use a loofa and smelled strongly of patchouli, but Kinsley didn't care. She felt too relaxed to care.

"They're henna tattoos. Temporary, but last a few days. You interested? Only ten dollars and I can do something pretty on your calf maybe?"

"Sure, why not?" That seemed to be her mantra for the day. Kinsley sat and propped her foot up on a stool to give easy access.

The artist's name turned out to be Clover. Kinsley doubted it was her real name, but what the hell? While she drew a series of psychedelic designs from the outside ankle of her right leg up to her knee, she told Kinsley stories about living off the grid and supporting herself by travelling to artisan fairs and parades. Kinsley found the entire conversation engaging and praised Clover for her ability to live a life of not being tied down. That was something she could never do; she felt vulnerable when she didn't have WIFI.

As Clover was doing a final fan over the enormous design she had drawn on her lower leg, Kinsley felt a tap on her shoulder. It was Sharon Wilson. Her blonde wavy hair fell below her shoulders the same way they do in those Vidal Sassoon commercials. She wore a flowing summer dress with light pink lace atop of a nude colored slip. Even her toenail polish matched her dress. Kinsley didn't like her, but if she could sell chicken shit to a man then she was gonna have to deal with it. Kinsley was pretty sure she had royally screwed Ida's original euphemism.

"Hey, Kinsley. Good to see you here. Coming from a ball game?" she asked motioning to her baseball t-shirt. Although it was a legitimate question, the tone was mocking.

"Nope, I was cleaning the house when Aunt Debbie and Ida decided to drag me out." Kinsley felt a little too good to let a Barbie Doll stick figure in pepto-pink ruin her mood.

"We still on for tomorrow at two? I know Mr. Harper is excited to see it and Bass is excited for you to sell it."

Kinsley's smile dropped. "Excuse me?"

"Remember, Bass gets half off his next month's rent if we get a contract on your house. It's a referral policy we have at Blue Ridge. When I spoke to him the other night, he seemed stoked about it. Plus, I know he wants you to be able to get home."

Kinsley was at a clear disadvantage. She had her leg propped up adorning some sort of acid trip artwork and sat next to Clover the hippie. Clover looked back and forth between the two as if she was watching the Hindenburg explode. Sharon telling her about her phone conversation with Bass the other night when he said he didn't have time to talk to Kinsley was the driving force of keeping things professional. Yet, when he showed up at her house, she was so tired and upset that she let his handiness in the garden and skilled lips make her forget about it.

Kinsley plastered on a smile. "You're right. I hope for both our sakes this man makes an offer."

Sharon peered at Kinsley's leg art and lifted her eyebrows, amused. "Nice tattoo. I'll see you tomorrow at two, Kinsley. Enjoy the rest of the party." She nodded at both Kinsley and Clover before heading off into the crowd on her heeled sandals.

"Man, I could feel the negativity off that lady. Like a territorial thing." Clover swatted at the air as if there was a bee flying around her, trying to shoo away the bad ju-ju. "I don't need that type of energy around here. I'll have to burn some lavender and smudge my cart so I don't take it with me. Are you all having conflicts over the same man?"

"Not really…well…it's hard to explain and a long story. He isn't my man." Kinsley lifted her leg off the stool and handed Clover a twenty.

"Was he ever your man before? A soul-mate perhaps sent to

you by the universe?" Clover tried giving Kinsley ten dollars in change, but she waved her off, telling her to keep it.

"No, he never was my man and it's about time I found out why!"

Chapter Sixteen

Kinsley turned on her heels and stormed through the crowd. Although the parade exit turned left onto McCall Avenue, she headed straight down Main past the cones blocking off traffic from the parade route. If she was lucky, Bastian went back to the shop to drop off his jeep before heading over to enjoy the parade. He seemed like the kind of guy that would want to get star clings and tinsel off his car as quickly as possible.

She was done with people keeping information from her. Mitchell did it, her mother did it, and Bastian did it...and he was the only one left with a pulse, so he was going to give her some answers. Lucky for Kinsley's feet, Five Points was only about a quarter mile down Main Street past the parade barrier. She spotted his jeep parked in front of the shop. Bastian was kneeling over the front right bumper, peeling off the decorations from the ROTC. She stomped up the gravel of the parking lot.

"Bastian Harris!" she shouted out behind him with her hands on her hips. He turned around with a handful of miniature flags. "I have a bone to pick with you." She pointed her finger at him and stared squinty-eyed for added intensity, her teacher glare.

"Hi, Kinsley. It's nice to see you too."

"Don't you try and sweet talk me. Your words have no effect on this particular woman. You may be Superman, but I am kryptonite."

"What the hell are you talking about?" His line of vision drew south to her leg. "Did you get a tattoo?"

"Don't you judge me! You're inked up more than the Human Canvas I saw at 'Ripley's Believe it or Not' last year! He had a lot of piercings too, and his tongue was slit up the middle like a snake. He could even hold a pen with it. I got his autograph."

"He gave you an autograph with his tongue?"

She regarded him as if he were nuts. "No, with his hand."

He smiled at her. "Have you been drinking or something?"

"Ha!" She yelled a little louder than she had intended. "I haven't been drinking. I've only had a hot dog, a soda, and a slice of watermelon soaked in strawberry wine from a very nice man in an antler hat."

Bastian started laughing. "Kinsley, was his name John Cletus?"

Was it? She squinted to remember. "Yes, I believe it was."

"Kinsley, it wasn't strawberry wine. It's strawberry moonshine. His son makes it illegally in West Virginia. Its 160 proof. You could put a horse in a coma with enough of that stuff."

"And yet, I'm still standing. And stop distracting me; I have a bone to pick with you."

"As you've already said. Come on inside, I'll get you some water." Kinsley followed Bastian up to the store while he unlocked the three different locks on the door and disarmed the security system. He fixed the locks behind her and walked over to the counter to put down the decorations. Grabbing a paper cup from the water cooler, he filled it and passed it to her. "So, what's your bone?"

Kinsley took a big swig of water and put the cup down by the decorations. *Here it goes, now or never.* The droplets from the cup trickled down her hand. "Why didn't you want to be my boyfriend?" She had been waiting over twenty years to ask him that question and now it was out there. No taking it back. She hoped to God what she heard wasn't too brutal.

"What?" He leaned against the glass counter, crossing one leg over the other.

"In middle school. I kissed you, which you admitted you remembered. Then, you took me into that closet or whatever it was and we made out some more there. After that, nothing! You didn't say a damn word about it ever. I didn't even get a 'Kinsley, I'm sorry but I don't think of you that way.' I want to know what happened!"

He swiped a hand through his hair and blew out a breath. "Kinsley, I was thirteen. I don't have reasons for a lot of things I did between the ages of eleven and twenty. Who knows why I acted that way back then?"

"So that's it? That's the answer to a question I have had for the past twenty years? 'I was thirteen and did some stupid shit.' That's what I get?"

"I'm sorry it's not more complicated, but yes. I also gave a hickey to Suzanne Moffit while I was still dating her little sister. There's no philosophical reason for it other than I was fifteen and a guy." He shrugged. "We do stupid shit."

Kinsley stood there with her mouth agape in horror before she smacked him on the arm. "You really are an asshole!"

"Not quite. I was a straight, teenage boy who had girls throwing themselves at me all the time so I *was* an asshole. But what boy in that situation wouldn't have been?"

"A boy whose best friend just-so-happened to be a girl who threw herself at him. A boy in that situation should've behaved differently."

"Kinsley, you're right. You were one of my best friends. I

didn't want things to get weird between us but…" He glanced at her as if assessing her mood and said, "I couldn't help that I thought you were beautiful and went for it when you showed some interest. I thought I was doing the most respectable thing a thirteen-year-old could do, I pretended it didn't happen and then never let it happen again. If I didn't care about you so much, I would've been happy to have repeat performances before dropping you. But you were different. I wanted you to stay around."

She stood there with her arms crossed, glaring at him, and chewing on the side of her mouth.

"Kinsley, you have to take it or leave it. I'm sorry I don't have the type of answer you've been waiting for, but it is what it is."

Years of randomly questioning what had gone wrong with the first boy she had fallen in love with, a mystery that eluded her more than who shot Kennedy, was solved. He was a teenager with more blood in his pecker than his head and he was happy to dry hump any willing girl. That's why he kissed her and dragged her in that room. Then again, he also stopped and didn't let it happen again because she wasn't like the rest of the girls. He didn't want to lose her friendship. That was more important to him than her obvious willingness to fool around.

"Are you screwing around with me now, Bass? You told me the other night you couldn't call me to cancel our meeting because you were working late. But Sharon Wilson has mentioned on two separate occasions, and a bit smugly I might add, that she spoke with you for a long time that night. She told me she called to tell you 'thanks for the referral' and you went on and on about how hopeful you are that I sell the house quickly so you get your rental discount."

Bass rolled his eyes before pulling his cell from his back pocket. "For Christ's sakes! Women can be some caddy ass creatures. I talked to her for five minutes max and said that if you want to get out of here quickly, she was the woman that could sell that house for you." Bastian scrolled through his phone, and then turned to hold it up to her. It showed that he had received a call from Sharon Thursday night and the duration was roughly four minutes and sixteen seconds "Satisfied?"

She said nothing, merely stood there trying to figure on her next bone picking topic. She couldn't think of one.

"Kinsley, I know you're here out of necessity and will most likely be gone by the middle of next week. But like in middle school, I like looking at you and enjoy every word that comes out of your mouth." He smirked. "Even when it's telling me off. No matter what your Aunt or anyone else in Staunton thinks about me, I am *not* bedding every woman in town. I did have a few one night indiscretions right after I came home and found my wife and child gone, but messing around with random women is the last complication I need. To be clear, I don't feel like getting into a relationship now either. What makes this situation so perfect for us is that I think you're in the same boat as me."

So there it was, a polite way to say they could be friends with benefits until she left town. No awkward encounters afterward and the physical distance of their homes kept the possibility of a relationship void. Kinsley walked over to him and placed her hands on either side of him on the counter. "Let's spell it out here, we're both going for my latter option then?"

He put his hands on her hips and squeezed. "What's the latter option?"

Kinsley could do this if the cards were all out on the table. She wouldn't be blindsided, which would give her the ability to handle it. Plus, she wasn't thirteen anymore either. "That whole 'fuck me 'til I'm walking funny', but with the addendum of this being a temporary arrangement."

He leaned down and bit her bottom lip gently. "I thought all girls wanted to be respected."

She returned the nibble. "All except for me and Holly Writtle. Now, take me somewhere and make me need a scooter."

Bastian crashed his mouth to hers. He threaded his hands up into her loose ponytail, yanking it back so that her mouth opened wider. If Kinsley had thought she was pent up from not having known the touch of another person for over a year, that was nothing compared to his response. He grabbed and pawed at her, squeezing almost to the point of being uncomfortable. If she hadn't been so aroused, it would have hurt. As it was though…perfect.

Tilting her head to the side, he trailed kisses up and down her throat and collarbone while he moved his hand underneath her shirt. He squeezed at her breast, causing her nipple to tighten under her bra. Reaching around, he expertly unclasped the clasp in one swift motion. Suddenly, her shirt was up at her neck and he was licking and sucking her nipples with so much need she almost came undone right there in the lobby of Five Points.

Not wanting to be the only one on the verge of release, she massaged the front of his khaki shorts. At her touch, he bit down gently on her right nipple. Realizing it wasn't fair that he was torturing her on the skin while she had merely caressed him through material, she removed her hand from the outside of his shorts and forcefully shoved her hand down his pants. She took her thumb and ran it along the bulbous head, feeling the drip of moisture already present. He inhaled deeply through his nostrils before returning his mouth to hers.

Kinsley had randomly thought of this moment several times throughout her life. The one imagined day where she got the man that got away. She flipped through the file cabinet of her memories and decided some of the hottest scenarios involved her torturing him with her mouth. Wanting to savor every second and leave regrets behind, she pulled away from his kiss and dropped down to her knees. Pushing up his t-shirt to reveal washboard abs, she unbuttoned his shorts with one hand while the other explored the ridges of his stomach. She worked at the zipper until it came undone, reached into the opening of his boxer briefs, and freed him.

She took him into her mouth, having difficulty wrapping her lips around the girth of him. He was more than she had ever fantasized about, almost too much to take. She had to will her gag reflex not to betray her. She glanced upwards and found him bracing his body against the counter, his knuckles white from squeezing the glass. He was watching her, breathing through his teeth like he was mere seconds away from losing control. After several moments of tormenting him, he jerked his hips away and lifted her up underneath her arms.

With her legs wrapped around him and not breaking their kiss, he carried her to one of the doors behind the counter. It took him three different tries to enter the code for the door leading to the workshop. Luckily, right after he made a comment about ripping the steel door off its hinges, the green light on the security pad illuminated. He brought her to the first clear workbench in the room and laid her down gently, as if he was worried he would break her. However, his tactic with pulling off her shorts and underwear were of a more aggressive approach, like tearing open a present on Christmas morning.

With her naked from the waist down, he grabbed the back of her thighs and pushed them up until her knees met her chest. Lucky for her, she was used to this position from Pilates. Without asking and without any sort of gentlemanly etiquette, he devoured her. No thigh kiss working his way up, no nipple suck, and then working his way down. There wasn't any misapprehension about what it was that he wanted to dine on.

Kinsley tried her best not to be self-conscious, but he had

been so silent except for the heavy breathing when she went down on him. As soon as his tongue flicked her clitoris for the first time, the moaning and whimpering started without her control. It surprised her as she had never been a particularly vocal lover. Yet, she couldn't help herself. The sensation was too strong not to release some of the energy building up inside of her. She needed to be careful or she was going to be the first one to come undone in this whole ordeal. In all her fantasies, she was the driver. But then he slipped his finger inside of her and began moving it in circular motions while simultaneously licking her nub. Without thought, she lost all control and came to pieces in his mouth. She had to grab her knees to keep her legs from fluttering like a butterfly's wings.

After she came down from the outer orbit, he trailed kisses up her thigh and abdomen before reaching her lips. Pulling her into a sitting position, he made short work of the rest of her clothing. "Are you sure you want to keep going? You're not too drunk?"

"You're asking me now? Your tongue was inside me ten seconds ago!"

"My tongue is one thing. *Sex in the City* said you all don't consider that sex. I just want to be sure."

Saying nothing, she slid to the edge of the workbench. She took the bottom of his grey t-shirt, yanked it over his head, and threw it to the floor. Several tattoos she had not been able to admire before due to his pesky clothing and society proclaiming men should wear shirts in public, even if they were as delicious as him, decorated his chest. "I love a man who watches *Sex and the City*. You have a condom?"

Luckily for her, his shorts were still half way on his ass and he reached into his back pocket, producing a foil packet.

"What were you expecting to do here today?" she asked between kisses as he ripped open the square and rolled on the latex.

"Nothing here. I was hoping to get you back home and do it there." With the condom all the way on, she wrapped her hand around it and placed it at the ready.

"Would you prefer to stop and wait until then?" she asked sweetly.

"Fuck that. I'm taking you home and fucking you there too."

"I want to really need that scooter." She eased her bottom closer to the edge so that it partially hung off and guided him in. Her breath hitched at the stretching her body needed to do to accommodate his size. She sucked in air between clenched teeth.

Once he was fully inside her, he retracted and pushed slowly in again. He made several small movements like that until they were both at ease with the brand new sensation and could hold themselves together without shattering too soon. Although not in a power position, Kinsley wanted to regain control. She lay back on the workbench and grabbed its sides with her hands to brace herself. "Fuck me, Bastian. Hard."

As if her words were the sound of the shotgun at a race, he unleashed the tether on his control and drove into her. Her grip on the sides of the table was not enough to keep her from scooting to the wall, so he grabbed underneath her shoulders to keep her from moving. The rhythmic motion back and forth caused her walls to constrict as he relentlessly plunged into her over and over again. She was trying to hold on and savor every moment, but Bastian must have sensed she was close and trying to avoid the fall.

Although she had already come once, Bastian clearly wasn't the type to lose himself before he had sated a woman. He removed one hand from beneath her shoulder and began massaging her clit with his thumb while he continued to plunge inside her. The caress of his thumb while simultaneously rubbing her G-spot with his cock was enough to make her forget her need for dominance. She couldn't focus on anything but the pleasure between her legs. She climbed higher and higher, ever reaching for that peak, until she shattered all around him.

"Oh damn!" Bastian called out as he accompanied her with his own release. Although his speed slowed during his climax, his thrusts became more forceful. It was as if he was trying to reach some untouched place within her.

When they both came down at last, he flopped on top of her with his feet still on the floor. "Jesus Christ, Kinsley. I haven't worked that hard for anything since boot camp."

She wiped her hair from her face. "Worked? It was work?"

"No, it was work not to lose it the first time you touched me. And when you gave me a blow job...Jesus, I thought I was a goner." He lifted his head and looked around the shop. "Remind me to thank Tommy for insisting we get so many workbenches."

She laughed quietly. He softly kissed her nipples while she ran her fingers through his hair. "What about those private shooting lessons you owe me?"

He stopped sucking and glanced up at her, resting his chin between her breasts. "You don't think I settled my debt tonight?"

"Although you were faster than a speeding bullet," she bit her lower lip, "it's not the shooting deal we agreed on."

Bastian covered his eyes. "There's that mouth again."

Chapter Seventeen

"That is about the sexiest sight I have ever seen." Bastian leaned against the wall in the gun range, admiring Kinsley. She stood in shooting stance, arms stretched out and holding a 9 mm like in the previous gun class. Only this time, she wasn't wearing a shirt. Kinsley had unloaded three magazines in nothing but her jean shorts, bra, and a henna tattoo. She said she had fully intended on getting dressed for their private shooting lesson, but when she called her Aunt Debbie to tell her she wouldn't be needing a ride home from the parade, he couldn't resist hiding her shirt. She told him the only way she was going to shoot topless was if he set par. So they were both naked from the waste up and taking turns blowing the paper perp to smithereens. At least that's what Bastian was doing...what Kinsley was doing would probably translate into one hell of a shoulder ache or the intruder losing the tip of his ear.

"Don't try to distract me. I need to better my game so I can help Aunt Debbie with the possum epidemic." She held out the gun, aiming for the target. He slid his hands along her waist and down into her shorts. The flutter of her lower abdominal muscles at his touch made him smile. "Damn it, Bastian. How am I supposed to shoot when your hand is down my pants?"

Bastian pressed his face to the side of hers and sucked gently on her earlobe. "Just trying to make sure you can handle shooting under duress." He skillfully slipped one finger in between her lower lips until he could feel her moisture. His breath hitched knowing she was already wet.

"I highly doubt a robber is gonna be touching me there while he tries to steal my stereo." His finger hooked inside her and began a slow internal assault. His chest tensed and tightened against her bare back as he pushed his erection into her bottom. Giving up on the private shooting lessons, he watched Kinsley as she tried to concentrate long enough to unload the gun. He had this woman less than thirty minutes ago and already he was hungry for more. Unsure if it was the nostalgia of who he was with or that it had been so long since he had a woman in his bed, he felt like a teenager who had gotten laid for the first time. The insatiable appetite of needing a repeat performance as much as possible made him feel defenseless.

At first, he thought once he had her and had gotten the

curiosity out of his system, his craving would dwindle and he could gain better self-control. The exact opposite turned out to be true. Now that he knew what she looked like naked and felt like inside, his desire for her was morphing into an urgent need. He had to have her again and again until the day she drove out of town. All of her from the sexy woman who wasn't afraid to get on her knees in the middle of his gun shop along to the less self-assured version having trouble unloading the gun while he fondled between her legs. Once she succeeded, Bastian took her on the couch in the gun safety classroom, where he continued hitting the target.

***

Sunday morning came all too quickly. Kinsley hadn't slept in Mitchell's room before, which unfortunately for her faced in the direction of the sunrise. Sleeping in her dead father's bed was not something she was particularly excited to do, but after having sex on top of a workshop bench and flung across the arm of a couch in the classroom, sex on her dinky twin bed upstairs didn't sound appealing. Bastian offered to take her to his house, but Petunia needed to be let out.

While trying to block the sun's rays, she caught a peek at a most interesting display. Bastian slept soundly next to her on his stomach with his head shoved underneath a pillow. Only his illustrated arms stuck out from underneath. Kinsley rolled on her side and took the opportunity to examine the artwork he had obtained throughout the years. On the inside of his right forearm rested the outline of a child's face with his daughter's name and birth date encircling it. Right above his elbow, a black feather whose barbs had begun to break off morphed into the silhouette of flying birds. Below the elbow read, 'No Excuses, No Regrets,' in black calligraphy.

Kinsley propped her head on her fist and savored the moment by listening to the steady inhale and release of his breath. *How the hell did all this happen?* This was supposed to be a quick trip to dissolve her dead father's assets. Instead, she found her beliefs on her entire family structure were all kinds of messed up and she'd slept with an old friend from twenty years ago...repeatedly. No matter the strange turn of events, she couldn't help but relish it. This beautiful man, the first love of her life, rested in her bed, exhausted from the triple they hit last night. Something about all of it was so gratifying.

"Kinsley, stop staring at me and go back to sleep." His head was still buried under the pillow.

How the hell did he know? She tapped his arm. "Uh... sorry. Just admiring your tattoos."

He popped his head from under the pillow and had the most delicious display of bed head she had ever seen on a man. The stubble he had shaved the day before was already making an appearance too. "I'll show you mine if you show me yours again," he teased, giving her a lazy smile.

"As much as I would like to show it to you again, I have to get up and moving. Sharon will be here with the buyer at two, so I need to get the place cleaned." Kinsley threw the covers off and attempted to get up, but Bastian surprised her by hooking her around the waist and pulling her back onto the bed.

"Don't think for one minute I can watch you get out of bed naked and not try to take advantage. I haven't matured that much." Although she intended to protest his advances, her body betrayed her and she dipped her head so he could kiss her neck more easily.

As he slipped his hand up to massage her breast, Petunia started whining at the bedroom door. "Bastian, I have to let Petunia out." He grumbled quietly, but she definitely heard the complaints before he released her nipple from his grip. He kissed her one more time on the neck before rolling back over to let her get up. Kinsley stood in front of the bed slipping on her t-shirt and shorts.

"Knowing you're walking around commando isn't going to help my predicament any," he said, watching her dress.

She smiled at him before turning to see the horrific sight of her rat's nest hair in the dresser mirror. Smoothing it down as best she could, she still looked like she'd stuck her tongue in a light socket.

"It's so unfair that you men wake up looking like that and we wake up looking like this." She flipped a hand at where Bastian laid naked with only a white sheet covering the lower half of his body. One leg stuck out from underneath, drawing her eyes south. Either the early morning hours or his reaction to her partially naked form created a massive erection. His rippled abs leading up to his sculpted chest looked like something from the cover of GQ. "Okay, maybe not all guys wake up looking like that."

As soon as the knob turned, Petunia burst into the bedroom and dove on top of the mattress to lick Bastian's face. "See, this is how you should greet me when you see me. Not all yelly and finger-pointy."

"Sorry, that type of greeting screams 'relationship' and that's not what this is. This is casual sex. So I'm thinking a slap on the ass would be a more appropriate salutation. Come on Petunia," Kinsley called smacking her thigh.

Petunia bounded off the bed and followed eagerly behind her to the back door. She darted outside and off the porch to her favorite peeing spot by the tree. Kinsley started a pot of coffee while Bastian was getting dressed. After the coffee finished brewing and Petunia felt fully relieved, Bastian emerged from the bedroom. "Do you want some coffee before you leave?" she asked gesturing to the pot.

"Thanks, but I have to get going. Jodi is supposed to be here at noon."

"Have anything special planned for today?"

"Not really, only getting her unpacked and settled. I took a few days off at the shop to spend some time with her. On the days I have to work, Ida Robinson watches her for me." He walked over and wrapped his arms around her, burying his face in her neck. She threaded her arms around his waist. "Last night was amazing, Kinsley. It's going to be difficult not replaying it in my head today."

"Me too." The compliment gave her goose bumps. "I hope you have a wonderful visit with your daughter. I'll let you know how things go with the realtor." She cocked a brow. "Wouldn't want you to worry about your rental discount."

He chuckled. "I don't give a damn about the discount, but let me know how it goes. I don't want to get blindsided and find out you've sold the house and left town."

"Blindsided means without warning. You know I'm leaving at some point this week, remember? Contingencies of the casual sex plan." The rules of this hook-up needed to be reiterated on a regular basis.

He gave her a small close-lipped peck on the mouth in answer. "Just don't forget to call and let me know how it goes." He pulled his keys from his pocket and headed to the door. "Bye, Kinsley. I had a great time."

She didn't say anything, but gave a slight nod in agreement as he walked out the door. Grabbing a mug from the cabinet, she poured a cup of coffee, and started to wonder why he was worried about her leaving without letting him know. For all intents and purposes, she was a booty call. A one night stand that ended with three rounds of sex and eight orgasms...only three of them his. During her senior year of college, she actually had a random hook up ask her to leave less than twenty minutes after doing the deed because he wanted to get rid of her. Bastian wanted a phone call to find out when she was going home. As she snagged the milk out from the refrigerator, she decided she needed to snap out of it and quit dissecting his words. It was simply a request for a courtesy phone call. Maybe that's how people in their thirties did casual flings…with tidbits of respect.

Suddenly, with her spoonful of sugar in midair, she froze. She realized it wasn't what he said that was the problem, it was her. She was doing it again. Although it was twenty years later, and after sex as opposed to post-make out session, it was 1993 all over again. She was hoping something was there with Bastian that was nonexistent. "Get a grip, Kinsley," she groaned. Her cell phone buzzed letting her know she had a text from Bastian.

Circumstances aside, I'm glad we ran into each other again.

Placing her phone on the counter, she pushed it slowly away as if it would explode at the slightest jolt. Several moments passed of her staring at the phone with her cup of breakfast blend in her hand and second guessing her decision to sleep with Bastian. Even though they had put all the cards out on the table, she feared it might have been a misdeal.

Chapter Eighteen

Mark's Toyota 4 Runner pulled up in Bastian's driveway at exactly twelve o'clock. He grumbled at the window. "Nice to know the prick is still punctual."

Bastian opened his front door in time to see a knobby-kneed, blonde-haired, skinny-mini leap out of the backseat and come running up towards his porch. He hadn't seen Jodi in person since she came to visit during her spring break from school. She must have grown another two inches, but not gained an ounce.

"Daddy!" she yelled flying over the steps with wide-stretched arms.

Bastian caught her as she leapt into a big hug. "Hey, baby girl! I am so glad you're here. I've missed you so much. Give me some sugar."

Jodi planted a big wet kiss on his cheek before turning her head to hug him tightly again. He watched Linda getting out of the car as the trunk of the 4 Runner automatically lifted. Mark sat dutifully in the front seat, avoiding eye contact by occupying himself with his phone.

Pussy. He held back a sneer...barely.

"So Daddy, I was thinking about reasons you should teach

me how to shoot a real gun and I have three awesome ones."

"Lay 'em on me, baby." He grinned.

She smiled back at him so big that the freckles on her cheeks were close to folding in on themselves. Her blue eyes twinkled at the anticipation of having her plan succeed. Bastian couldn't get over how much more she looked like her mother with each passing year. Luckily for Jodi, one thing she didn't inherit from her mother was entitlement. Jodi had a lust for life and wanted to do everything on her own. Very different from the woman who was fighting with the rolling suitcase across the gravel driveway.

"Okay, the first one is that we're out here in the woods so there might be bears. How am I supposed to take down a four-ton bear with a bee-bee gun?"

"Honey, you wouldn't be by yourself in the woods. I'd be with you. And there haven't been any bear sightings, especially eight-thousand pound ones, in a while." Bastian placed her on the porch beside him.

She squished her eyes up at him for ruining her first reason. "Okay, fine. Reason number two is that Mark read on the internet there've been a bunch of robberies in Staunton lately. If I shoot a robber with a bee-bee gun, he'll just laugh at me and still steal your TV." Her hands planted firmly on her hips.

"Again peanut, I would be home with you. I'll be here to catch the robbers."

She rolled her eyes. "Okay then, reason number three is Martin Jenkins in my class told me his father lets him shoot a real gun and his daddy is a dentist! Aren't you worried 'bout how my classmates will talk if my daddy's job is working with guns and he won't even teach me to shoot?"

"Two weeks ago you told me Martin Jenkins was a booger-faced liar." Linda huffed as she hefted the suitcase onto the first step. Standing there in her tan chino pants and lavender blouse, she looked like a model from a dish detergent advertisement.

Putting her sunglasses on top of her head revealed she was just as beautiful as the day she left him. Bastian had secretly hoped as she got older, the beauty she had relied so heavily on for happiness would start to deteriorate. Unfortunately, no such luck.

"How are you doing, Linda?" Bastian asked, reaching for the suitcase.

"Tired from the drive, but happy for Jodi. She's been waiting a long time to spend the week with you. Sorry she couldn't come earlier, but she had gymnastics camp, ballet camp, and she got back from nature camp only two days ago. It's been non-stop ever since school let out."

"I understand she's got a busy schedule. Thanks for dropping her off and I'll bring her home next Sunday around noon." Jodi leaned into her father and wrapped her arms around him.

"Sounds good. Jodi, I want you to call me at least every two days to tell me how you're doing. I'm going to miss you." Jodi released her grip on Bastian and reached out to give her mother a hug. They squeezed each other for several minutes before Jodi let go and ran to the 4 Runner to say her goodbyes to Mark.

Linda stared at Bastian with a proper pout on her lips. "I wish we could get past this. Jodi knows you hate her stepfather so much that she has to go to the car to tell him goodbye. Have you said anything negative to her?"

"Just that he's an adult version of Martin Jenkins."

Linda rolled her eyes and headed back to the car. She gave Jodi one more kiss before letting her run up onto the porch to be with Bastian.

Jodi waived frantically. "Bye Mama, bye Mark! Don't worry and don't forget to feed Mr. Bubbles while I'm gone!"

Bastian inclined his head at his daughter. "Who's Mr. Bubbles?"

"My new pet fish. They got him for me yesterday. I really

wanted a dog, but Mama and Mark said I have to show I have responsibility with easier pets first. Plus, if this pet dies it can be flushed down the toilet. Mama said you can't do that with a schnauzer."

Bastian leaned over to pick up Jodi's suitcase and they headed inside the house. "Your mother is a smart lady. Now let's get you unpacked and have some lunch. Then, we can figure out what we're going to do for the rest of the day. Sound good?"

"Yep, but I already know what I want to do. I want to go to the movies. There's a new movie about a princess getting trapped in a wizard's kingdom and her only way out is by the kiss of her true love. Afterwards, we can go to the gun range and you can show me how to shoot a real gun so I can show that Martin Jenkins. Okay?"

Oh for Christ's sakes.

***

Kinsley sat in one of the rocking chairs on her Aunt Debbie's porch, sipping sweet tea and watching the last sliver of the sun slip behind the horizon. Petunia lay passed out next to her chair and resembled a brown mud puddle.

"What did your realtor have to say?" Debbie asked as she poured bourbon into her tea.

"The man who came to look at it thought it had potential. He wants to come back tomorrow around four o'clock for another walk through. Sharon says he's torn between my house and another one closer to town. She is trying to sway him towards my property."

Debbie offered up a silver flask, but Kinsley put up her hand to say no thank you. Kinsley and Petunia came to visit with Aunt Debbie earlier in the afternoon so they would be scarce when the potential buyer did a walkthrough. What was supposed to be a quick afternoon visit evolved into staying for dinner and sitting on the porch sipping tea sweet enough to give a person a cavity.

The vibrating song of cicadas filled the air off in the distance by the tree line. Aunt Debbie had no love for them. "Those damn bugs. I'll be glad when summer is over and they all die."

"You don't have a fondness for nature or wildlife, do you Aunt Debbie?"

"I don't like pests, plain and simple." Debbie took another big swig of her tea. "You gonna spill the beans or do I have to ask you?"

Oh Shit. Kinsley had been successful so far in keeping the topic of "exactly how did you get home from the parade" from being discussed. It seemed as though her time might be up. "What are you talking about?"

"I think you know." Aunt Debbie didn't falter. She wanted the gossip.

"Look, I just took Bastian up on his offer for private shooting lessons after the parade. We hung out for a while at the gun range and then he took me home. End of story."

Debbie scrunched her nose. "Honey, what in the hell are you babbling on about? I meant the situation with you and your daddy. I wasn't asking about Bass. But since we're now on the topic, why did you spit that out so quickly on one breath like you were at confession?"

"I'm Baptist, not Catholic, so I don't know what you're talking about. What religion are you, by the way?" Kinsley was trying her best to sway the conversation in a different direction, but apparently, her aunt was too smart for it.

"I'm Episcopal and I know when a woman spews out some mundane information about a man, and turns three shades of pink when doing it, that something was going on in that gun range other than target practice."

Kinsley didn't want to admit to her aunt of all people what

went down twice in the gun shop and once in her father's bedroom. But the memory of him helping her hit bulls eye five times made the corners of her mouth curl up.

Debbie smacked the arm of the rocking chair. "Hot damn! I knew it! You let Bass swim up your stream, didn't you?"

Kinsley's mouth dropped open. "Eww. That's crude, Aunt Debbie!"

"Crude-Schmude. Tell me, how was it? Is he every bit as sexy out of his clothes as he is in them?" She licked her lips in anticipation.

Kinsley gasped. "I'm really not comfortable having this type of conversation with you."

"Sweetheart, I'm sixty-four years old and haven't seen a naked man since before Jim got sick. Well, 'sept that time I accidentally walked in on my godson getting out the shower, but that doesn't count. I need to live vicariously through the young and big-mouthed. So tell me…how was it?"

Sensing this subject was not going to be dropped any time soon, Kinsley sucked her teeth and surrendered. "It was phenomenal."

"I knew it!" she said before leaning back in her chair and rocking in over drive. "I told Ida after we all had dinner that night you two would be getting together!"

"We aren't together. We're just…having fun. It isn't turning into us being together. He knows I'm leaving and neither of us is looking for a relationship. It was what it was and now I need to concentrate on selling that house." Kinsley's phone buzzed, interrupting their conversation.

532 Hazelwood Way.

It was from Bastian.

30 minutes.

Kinsley stared at her phone like it'd grown horns. She texted back, *Huh?*

That's my address and my daughter's countdown to bedtime.

She tried her hardest not to crack a smile. *And I would want this information because?*

When you get here, I'll give you 5 good reasons. I counted them last night.

Kinsley tried to keep her giggle quiet.

"Who is that?" Debbie asked, disrupting Kinsley's dirty thoughts.

"Oh, it's Sharon confirming the walkthrough time tomorrow." Jesus, she was a bad liar.

"Like hell it is." Debbie snagged her phone right out of her hands and stared at the screen.

"Hey! Give that back." Kinsley tried grabbing it from her, but she maneuvered pretty quickly for a woman of sixty-four.

Debbie's eyes widened. "Five times? That man made you have the big-O five times in one night?"

Kinsley made a yucky face and snatched her phone out of Debbie's iron-fisted grip. "I'm not talking about my O's with you. Now if you'll excuse me, I need to take Petunia home. Thank you for dinner and the tea."

"Why don't you leave the dog here? I still have a bag of her food left."

"Now, why would I do that?"

"Just in case you don't make it home this evening…" Aunt Debbie smiled brighter than fireworks on the Fourth. "And so you have to tell me all about it when you come pick her up."

The idea was tempting. Kinsley didn't feel like having to wash the bed linens a second time before the buyer showed up again tomorrow. And lord knows the less she and Petunia were physically in the house, the less it could get messed up. "Alright, but I'm not going to be giving any details tomorrow when I come get her. That's just gross."

Debbie held up her hands in surrender. "Fine by me. I'll just get out my Venus Butterfly: The One Hour Orgasm book and you can point to the pictures of the things you all did."

Kinsley tied Petunia's leash onto the porch to keep her staying put while she tried desperately not to think about why her aunt owned a Venus Butterfly book. Sitting on the porch during a warm summer evening had produced a film of sweat on the inside of her thighs, and quite possibly other places which might be on the menu this evening, so she stopped by her house before driving to Bastian's. She jumped in the shower for a quick rinse and afterwards slipped into a comfortable pair of worn in jeans and a pink tank top.

Her GPS directed her through an isolated subdivision towards 523 Hazelwood Way, and before she knew it, she was angling up his driveway. Bastian's rental was a quaint one-story brick home, which was secluded from the main road by a large front yard and a barrier of trees. A grassy area lay in the middle of the u-shaped driveway where Kinsley parked her car at the end. Not knowing how heavy of a sleeper his daughter might be, she lightly closed her car door and avoided walking on the gravel as much as possible.

Kinsley didn't even need to knock. Bastian flung open the door as soon as her foot hit the first step on the porch. "Hey," she whispered, "I wasn't sure if I should park in the driveway because I didn't want—"

She didn't have a chance to finish her sentence. Bastian grabbed the back of her head while embracing her ass with his free hand and yanked her to him. His tongue invaded her mouth with eagerness. Kinsley drowned in the intensity and dropped her purse on the porch to reciprocate his touches. It wasn't until she wrapped her legs around him that she realized how sore she was from their escapades last night.

He carried her inside, closing the door behind him. "What about my purse?" she whispered quietly in between kisses.

"I live out in the middle of nowhere. It's fine...I'll let you get it in between."

"In between?" She murmured against his lips.

"The first round and the second."

Kinsley didn't have time to take in the layout of Bastian's home. On their walk through the house he was either kissing her or sucking on the top part of her breasts so hard she couldn't help but close her eyes. She was pretty sure she was being carried through the living room and off to a bedroom. He opened the door to a dimly lit room with a massive king-sized bed in the center. He closed and locked the door behind him before laying her down on top of the comforter.

Straddling her waist, he tugged her shirt over her head. His assault on her nipples from the outside of her bra caused them to perk at the cooler temperatures of the fabric. She ran her hands through his hair in search of an anchor as sensation swept her away. "What about your daughter?" She asked, partially incoherent from the pleasure. "What if we wake her?"

Bastian removed his mouth and found the clasp of her bra, conveniently located in the front this time. He pulled apart the black lace, revealing her breasts. "Jodi's bedroom is on the other side of the house and she sleeps like the dead. I've spent the last four hours watching some fairy princess movie and listening to all the shit Martin Jenkins has been up to. The only thing that's gonna stop my head from spinning is fucking you every way imaginable in my bed."

Eager as ever, she reached for the top of his pants to begin working on his buckle. "Well, I wouldn't feel right if I didn't do my part to help stop your vertigo."

He drew her forward to peel her bra off the rest of the way. Before she even got his pants' zipper halfway down, he stood up from the bed and began yanking at her jeans.

"Aren't you going to take your clothes off?" she asked as he hooked his thumbs in her panties and dragged them down her legs.

"Not yet. I only want you to be naked while I go down on you." Bastian knelt down in between Kinsley's knees, grabbing her hips and positioning her at edge of the bed. "Put your feet on my shoulders."

Kinsley gently placed one heel of each foot on the front of Bastian's shoulders. She was completely naked but he remained clothed. She felt like a submissive doll he could do whatever he pleased with. He had the clothes, so he had the power. The whole scenario had her totally aroused.

Bastian took two fingers on his left hand and spread apart her lips. The cool air of the room mixed with the warm heat from his breathing, sending a flurry of sensation through her. Using his pointer finger from his other hand, he slowly drew circles on and around her clitoris. The slight sting from being sore mixed deliciously with the pleasure of his caress. She hitched and shuddered as he dipped a fingertip inside of her, only to pull it out and spread her moisture around her opening. He continued the motion several times, causing her to let out a whimper.

"Shhhh. If you start getting loud I'm going to have to cover your mouth." He dipped his finger in fully this time and circled it around, unwillingly forcing a moan from her mouth. "I'm not going to have to find a way to keep you quiet, am I?"

She couldn't speak. If she tried she wasn't going to be able to control what words came out or how loud they'd be so she just shook her head no.

"You won't make any noise even if I do this?" Bastian began simultaneously rubbing her clit in the same rhythm and speed as he massaged her G-spot. Kinsley fisted the blankets underneath her, accidentally letting out a moan of such sweet pleasure that she didn't recognize it as her own.

"Now, what did I say? You're already making a commotion and I haven't even gotten started yet. I can't get you the way I want to if I can't trust that you'll be quiet."

"Please," she begged in a hushed voice. "I promise I'll be quiet." It was so difficult for her to talk while Bastian continued to torture her with his fingers. Out of nowhere, he increased the speed. Kinsley let free a desperate yelp. She was already so close to coming apart.

He slowed his hands down again. "See, that's what I was afraid of. I need you to convince me." His fingers increased in speed by a fraction.

"How can I convince you?" Her breathing was labored and the blood drained from her hands with her tight grip.

"Maybe if you tell me how badly you need it, I'll take my chances." His pace increased again ever so slightly.

"Please, Bastian. I need you." Kinsley could feel sweat forming in the crease of her pelvis and propped up thighs. Her knees shook. She was a bomb ready to explode.

"Tell me what you need me to do, Kinsley. Tell me how bad you want me to do it. How bad you want me."

"Please, put your mouth on me," she sucked in much needed air. "I want you to."

"Do you need me to?"

"Yes, I need you to. I need you. I just need you. Please." Bastian lifted his finger from her clit and replaced it with his tongue, but kept his other finger inside of her, and expertly moved his tongue from side to side.

Kinsley was biting hard on her bottom lip, trying to let out soft whimpers, but there was only so much a woman could take. Feeling herself build higher, knowing her climax was close, her eyes darted around frantically. There was no way in hell she was going to be able to keep quiet on this one. She was too turned on from his dominance. The minor discomfort from her soreness brought the sensual touches to a whole new level.

Fortunately, a pillow was in reach. She needed to hold on long enough to grab it and shove it over her face. She was going to have to moan; there was no way around it. She released the blanket and reached for the pillow. Throwing it over her lips at the last possible second, she felt herself shatter in his mouth.

She screamed into the pillow while he stayed with her through her release. She could tell from the creases around his eyes that he was amused with the impact he had on her.

Bastard.

He crawled slowly on top of her, smiling. "Had to gag yourself, huh?"

"I was afraid I would wake your daughter," she said, tossing the pillow to the side.

"Don't worry, there's no way you could wake her. I was just giving you a hard time. I promise she can't hear you." He leaned up, pulling his shirt over his head and discreetly wiping his mouth with his sleeve. Bastian slipped off the bed and stood in between her sprawled legs. "Take off my pants."

Kinsley sat up and did as she was told. When he stepped out of his jeans, however, she decided to take advantage of his erection and wrapped her lips around him. She could hear his breathing intensify as he rested his hands on her shoulders. She tortured him for several minutes before he growled, "I need you now."

He slid onto the mattress and opened the top drawer of a small nightstand next to the bed. Drawing out a condom in record time, he handed it to her and lay down.

"Are we not doing tit for tat?" she asked, ripping open the packet with her fingers.

"As much as my tat loves being in your mouth, right now I need to get it inside of you." He helped her roll the condom down to the base and drew her on top of him. Even though she didn't want to admit it, she was so sore from last night's debauchery that her nerve endings inside shot out in mild retaliation at the thought of being provoked again. But she couldn't help it. She was like an addict in a sea of opiates and needed to get her fix. She wanted this man again regardless of the rawness she could already feel between her thighs.

She lowered herself onto him slowly so she could savor

every luxurious sting. He placed his hands behind his head and watched as she slid further down. Friction wasn't the problem here, she was already very wet. The sensation reminded her of being in college and the first time she started having sex with a steady boyfriend. It didn't matter how sore they were or how many times they had already done the deed, they needed to do it again...and again...and again. Bastian wasn't her boyfriend. Hell, she didn't know if she'd even see him again after she left, but she needed to have him again...and again...and again.

Once he was inside of her to the hilt, she guided his arms out from underneath his head and interlocked her hands with his to steady herself. She maintained an easy rhythm, circling her hips in one direction while gliding up and down on his shaft. The mixture of pain and pleasure was exquisite.

"Does it hurt?" he asked through labored breath. He was so hard and she was so tender that it bordered on the verge of uncomfortable.

"Yes, but I need to fuck you anyway." She was about to close her eyes to help absorb the mixture of sensation, but then he tilted his head up to watch the show. The fact that he was so into watching himself enter her repeatedly turned her on even more, causing her to increase her speed. His response was intoxicating.

"Jesus Christ," he said through clenched teeth. The discomfort inside her made her climax stall, but it built higher with each gyration. It was as if she was dangling on the edge of a cliff using only her fingertips to avoid the plummet and she was losing her grip one finger at a time. She was on the cusp of frustration because she wanted to come so badly, but her body wouldn't allow it. Suspended between a high peak and release, she wasn't sure how much longer she could take the feeling.

Reading her body like an open book, Bastian grabbed her ankles and instructed her to prop up on her feet. With her knees bent and her ass slightly elevated, Bastian began to drive into her. She was paralyzed, unable even to return his thrusts from her squatting position. The only way to brace for what was getting ready to happen was to grip his hands even harder.

"Oh my God," she moaned as he pounded her relentlessly, trying to force her beyond her hang up. A warm pooling started inside of her, born as a dimly lit match before growing into a fireball and engulfing her body. "Don't stop, please don't ever stop," she cried as her climax continued endlessly.

"I'm never going to stop. Keep coming for me baby, feel me in you." The flames that had taken over her body exploded into a frenzy of embers.

Although she was exhausted, when the smoke cleared she realized Bastian had not found his own release yet. Despite the tightness in her knees and the ache in her thighs from squatting for so long, she fought through it and pumped her body as fast as she could. It was only a moment from the time his face began to tense until he called out her name as she rode him through his orgasm.

When they released each other's grasp, she rolled off him onto her side of the bed. After catching her breath, she stared at the man who had given her the best orgasm of her life. Although he was sweaty from the workout along his forehead, she noticed his hips, groin, and sheets were also fairly wet. She propped up and pointed, "What's that?"

Bastian kept his arm draped over his eyes while trying to catch his breath. "You came."

"I know I did, but why are you so wet? It's on the sheets too," Kinsley said, running her hand along the beige bedding.

Bastian laughed. "No, Kinsley. I mean you really came. That fluid is from you."

She tried to bottle her embarrassment, but it had to show on her face. "I don't think so. I've had lots of orgasms and I've never done that before."

He raised a brow. "Have you ever come that hard before?"

She squinted at him. "Asking for compliments isn't becoming."

"I'm not asking for compliments. I'm asking you a genuine question. Have you ever come that hard before?"

She could lie to him and tell him that she had more orgasms like that than she could count. That was probably the best option, since telling him he had ravaged her in a way that would ruin her for any other men would only inflate his ego. But, then again, why wouldn't you give a horse that placed first in a race the trophy? "No, Bastian. I've never come that hard before. That was incredible. I thought I was going to pass out." It was the most sincere answer she could give. A man whom she had dreamed about for years had lived up to the fantasy she had built in her head. He was wonderful to be around, hotter than Joe Manganiello—werewolves eat your heart out—and a genius in bed. A girl could get her heart broken by a man like that.

He flipped onto his side and threaded his fingers through her hair. "Women ejaculate too; it just doesn't happen that often unless you find the right guy."

"I suppose you think you're the right guy for me then?" Kinsley wished she hadn't asked. She didn't intend for it to come out the way it sounded and she didn't know which way he would interpret her question.

He smiled and kissed her softly. "I guess we'll see."

What does that mean?

"I'm gonna get rid of this rubber and get your purse off the porch. Don't put your clothes on and we'll see if I can make you do it again."

Oh...

He tapped her on the nose before getting off the bed and slipping into his pants. As he left the bedroom, Kinsley debated getting her clothes too and getting the hell out of there. She could use the worry about the dog as an excuse to leave. He didn't know Petunia was at her aunt's house, so she could say she needed to get home to her. If she stayed, she'd be treading a field of landmines. If she wasn't careful about where she stepped, she could lose a limb...or worse, her heart. She sat up and started to scan the floor for her clothes when the bedroom door opened. Bastian stood in the doorway with a beautiful bare chest and his jeans partially open at the fly. In one hand, he carried her purse. In the other, he was carrying a bowl.

"What's that?" He locked the door behind him and put her purse on the nightstand.

"Ice cream." He smiled. "I thought you might be hungry." He sat on the bed, scooped out a small spoonful of strawberry ice cream, and fed it to her. It was cold, creamy, and delicious. "I also had an idea about what I'd like to do with it," he said, eyeing her wickedly.

Kinsley let the ice cream melt in her mouth and contemplated her dilemma. Should she get up and leave, ensuring that she protected her heart or participate in whatever fantasy it was Bastian had preplanned in his mind? He leaned forward and kissed her, letting the ice cream slip from his mouth to hers. He tasted like strawberries. Kinsley made her decision.

"I'm always in the mood for dessert." Yep. She was screwed.

Chapter Nineteen

K insley reached up to move her hair away from her face, but the sticky residue from the ice cream only made the strands stick to her fingers. She cocked one eye open and realized the room was lit up a lot more than it should be. *Had Bastian turned on the ceiling light?* She lifted her head. *No, he hadn't.* Her eyes shifted over to the window and saw the light streaming in from the outside.

"Shit!" She shot up from the bed and glanced over at Bastian who was curled up and asleep next to her. Somehow, after the dessert fiasco—and his decision she should find a comfortable seat on his face—they had fallen asleep. She remembered lying in bed, talking about the house deal and some punk kid named Martin Jenkins, and thinking she was just going to close her eyes for a second. Apparently, they both closed their eyes and for a lot longer than they should have.

She smacked Bastian on the arm, making his eyes snap open. "We fell asleep," she yelled as quietly as she could. "Do you think your daughter's up yet?" She jumped out of bed and yanked her shirt over her head.

Bastian grabbed his cell phone off the nightstand. "It's only six-thirty so I don't think so."

Kinsley hadn't dressed so quickly since the time she and

Patrick were almost caught fooling around in the food pantry in Africa. She snatched her purse and dug through it for her keys.

"Okay, I'm going to sneak out before she gets up."

"Are you even gonna give me a kiss goodbye or was this like hooker sex?" he asked, mocking her panic. She rolled her eyes before diving onto the bed and giving him a quick kiss on the cheek. She leapt up and cracked open the door to the hallway. She didn't see anybody or hear anything, so she quietly tiptoed into the living room.

She made it all the way to the front door and thought she was in the clear before she heard, "Hey, who are you?" Kinsley turned to see a little blonde-haired girl in the kitchen nook with a bowl of cereal. She was still in her pajamas and her hair was all askew.

"Oh, uh. Hi." Kinsley didn't know what to say. She was leaving this little girl's father's house at an ungodly hour in the morning. She didn't want Bastian coming out of the bedroom and making it anymore awkward. "I'm Kinsley. Just keep it quiet, okay?"

The little girl's eyes widened. "Daddy! The robbers are in the house! Quick, get the gun!" Leaping up from behind the table, the girl ran past Kinsley towards Bastian's room. Kinsley squinted and put her hand on her forehead. She could feel a major migraine coming on. Bastian's door opened before his daughter had a chance to make it across the living room. He was dressed in gym shorts and a white under shirt.

"Morning, Jodi girl. What are you doing up this early?" She jumped into his arms.

"That lady's here to steal your TV! I told you, Daddy. Get your gun!" Bastian laughed it off as cool as a cucumber while Kinsley felt like she was getting ready to have a stroke.

"That isn't a robber, sweetie. She's my friend. She came over this morning to meet you and have breakfast with us." Bastian and his daughter looked over at Kinsley. He discreetly winked at her, letting her know she needed to play along.

"Yes, breakfast. Your daddy said cereal and I came running. I love cereal." She held her hands out in defeat. It was the best she could do before seven a.m. and no coffee.

"See," he said smiling at her. "Kinsley, this is my daughter, Jodi. Jodi, this is one of Daddy's friends, Kinsley. Now, why are you up so early on your own? I thought I'd need to wake you for breakfast."

"Nature camp finished last week and I had to be there super early. I still get up at six in the morning cause of it." Jodi pushed away from her father so he would put her back on her feet. The little girl in Hello Kitty pajamas walked up to Kinsley, eyeing her suspiciously. There were so many holes in her father's story you could drive his jeep through it.

Kinsley let the questions she saw in the little girl's eye run rampant through her mind. *Why does your hair look messy? Why were you coming from my daddy's bedroom? Are you trying to be my new mommy?* She braced herself, ready for the inquisition to begin.

"Do you want Cheerios or Cinnamon Toast Crunch?"

Kinsley glanced between the little girl and Bastian. His arms were crossed over his chest and a shit-eating grin plastered on his face. She wanted to slap him. "Uh, Cheerios please."

"Okay, come on. I'll get you a bowl and a spoon." Jodi ran into the kitchen, snagging the cereal box and putting it on the table. Kinsley glanced over her shoulder at Bastian and shrugged. They both headed to the kitchen.

If Kinsley learned anything from her breakfast date with Jodi Harris, it's that the girl could talk. A lot. It took Jodi forty-five minutes to eat a bowl of cereal because between each bite she had to give an exposition on her different camps, her fish Mr. Bubbles, and the Dennis the Menace behavior of a one Mr. Martin Jenkins. Although Jodi dominated the conversation, Kinsley found she was enjoying it. The only children she usually talked with were preteens and teenagers, so a child wanting to tell you what was going on in their life and not looking at you as if you were a loser felt pretty damn good.

Once the bowls contained nothing but a small pool of milk, Kinsley decided she needed to make an exit. "Jodi. Thank you very much for the delicious cereal. I have never had anyone prepare it as deliciously as you did, but I have to get going. I need to check on Petunia."

"Is Petunia your daughter?" Jodi asked before tipping her bowl to finish off the rest of the milk.

"No, Petunia is my dog." Kinsley nearly swallowed her tongue, surprised by the comment. She didn't say Petunia was a dog she inherited or a dog she was watching for a little bit...simply *her* dog.

"You have a dog?" Jodi smiled so large that milk seeped out of the corners of her mouth.

"Yep. My Aunt is babysitting her while I...came over here for breakfast. So, I need to go and pick her up."

"Can I meet her? I want a dog, but Mama and Mark won't let me have one yet. Maybe if you let me babysit your dog, I can prove to them I can take care of something too big to flush down the toilet!"

"Jodi, honey, we'll have to see about that later. We're pretty busy this week so you may not get a chance to even meet Petunia." That stung Kinsley a little. She didn't expect them to go and pack a picnic in the freaking park just because she got caught doing the walk of shame by his kid and had to stay for a bowl of cereal, but still.

"Your daddy's right. I know he has a lot of fun things planned for you this week. You're a wonderful hostess, Jodi. Enjoy your time together." Kinsley rose from the table and picked her purse off the floor. Bastian began to stand, but Kinsley held her hand up to stop him. "Don't worry, Bastian. I can see myself out. Bye, Jodi."

"Bye Kinsley. Give Petunia a hug for me."

"Will do." Kinsley turned around and headed towards the door. She started down the driveway for her BMW, but heard gravel shuffling behind her. She spun to see Bastian jogging towards her.

"Hey, I wanted to say thank for playing along."

"With what exactly? Your strawberry shenanigans or you telling your kid she won't be seeing me again?"

"No, I meant the whole coming over for breakfast thing. I didn't tell her she wouldn't be seeing you again." He wrinkled his forehead. "And as far as I can recall, you didn't mind my strawberry shenanigans too much last night." He stepped closer to her and grabbed her chin. "In fact, I seem to remember a certain someone begging me for more...shenanigans."

Kinsley smacked his hand away. "If you say shenanigans one more time I'm gonna deck you." He started smiling and she almost did too. "Don't you dare make me laugh."

"I didn't say she wasn't going to see you again," he reiterated. "I was giving you an out in case you didn't want to do the whole single father with a kid thing the last few days you're here." He shrugged. "I don't want you to feel like you have to come around and play friend to my kid if you don't want. That doesn't mean I'm not going to try my hardest to see you privately before you go. You know...for more shenanigans."

"Hopefully, after today at four, me and my shenanigans will have an offer on the house and I'll be hitting the road." She shooed him with a flick of her wrist. "Go spend time with your daughter. I'll let you know how the walkthrough goes, and if I want any shenanigans, I'll text you when I'm good and ready."

"Then I'm sure I'll talk with you this evening." He winked at her before turning around and going back inside.

"Conceited asshole," she said underneath her breath. As much as she tried to fight it, she smiled the whole drive to Aunt Debbie's house.

Kinsley arrived at Aunt Debbie's around eight-thirty in the morning. As soon as Petunia saw her red BMW park, she came bounding off the front porch like a lunatic. When she opened the door, the sixty-pound pooch dove into her car on top of her lap.

"Okay, Okay. I'm back. Did you miss me or something?" Petunia laid a big wet kiss on Kinsley's face before racing back for the porch. Debbie came out of the front screened door with a gigantic smile on her face.

"Well, well, well. Looks like someone had an interesting night. Would you like a cup of coffee or some Advil perhaps?"

"Debbie, I'm not hung-over."

"Maybe not, but those dark circles and the fact you ain't wearing a bra indicate a pretty interesting night. Can I at least get you some breakfast?"

Kinsley glanced down at her shirt and sure enough, she was braless. The excitement of getting caught by Bastian's daughter must have had her brain swimming so much that she didn't notice. Had she really sat through an entire bowl of Cheerios without noticing her lady friends were free and uninhibited? And why didn't that jerk-face, Bastian, say anything? "No thanks. I already had a bowl of cereal."

"Oh come on, surely that isn't enough to recoup the energy you must have lost."

Truth be told, she was still ravenous from her rendezvous. "Yes, something to eat would be nice."

Debbie stuffed Kinsley with a stack of pancakes, real maple syrup, and enough bacon to give a horse a heart attack. After she was sufficiently full and had smacked that damned Venus Butterfly book away about four times, she leashed up Petunia and headed home. She spent the afternoon getting the house ready for the final buyer visit and washing the smell of Bastian off her body. Around three-thirty in the afternoon, she harnessed up Petunia and decided a walk in the park was more doable than spending another afternoon at her aunt's house. The woman was a bloodhound for information about her previous evening's escapades.

It turned out to be a lovely, cool afternoon—not at all typical for the time of year. A steady breeze wisped through her hair while she and Petunia walked the trails of Gypsy Park. A massive oak tree next to the walking trail marked a wonderfully shady site. The exhaustion of cleaning and not sleeping well the night before was getting to her. Her muscles ached. She needed to take a breather, so she veered Petunia off the sidewalk and sat under a tree. Allowing her thoughts to drift, she sent up a hopeful plea that at the same moment she rested her body in the shade, the buyer was making plans with Sharon to write up an offer on the place. She needed to hurry up and get home before any other shenanigans got in the way of her mission and tempted her to stay longer than absolutely necessary.

"Kinsley!" called an excited, high-pitched voice. She turned her head to see Jodi riding a bicycle in her direction. Her blonde pigtails stuck out underneath her bright pink helmet and flapped in the wind similar to Petunia's ears when she ran through the yard. She came to an abrupt halt in front of Kinsley under the tree.

"Hey there, Jodi. You and your dad having a bike ride?"

Jodi braced herself on the concrete with her feet. "Just me. Daddy's walking behind me. Is that Petunia?"

"Yes, ma'am," she said, patting the dog on top of her head.

"Can I pet her?"

"Sure, she's very friendly." Jodi jumped off her bike, letting it crash to the ground, and plopped down next to Petunia and began petting her back.

"She's so sweet...and flabby!"

"Yeah, she's a basset hound. They're pretty flabby dogs." Kinsley smiled.

Jodi reached around the dog and snuggled on her, which

Petunia was more than happy to oblige. She lifted her head up with her arms still wrapped around the dog. "Daddy! Look, it's Petunia and Kinsley."

Bastian was climbing the small hill leading towards the tree. Of course he appeared well rested and fantastic in his faded blue t-shirt and khaki shorts while Kinsley wore yoga Capri pants and sported bags underneath her eyes.

"I can see that. What are you two doing here?" he asked, slipping his hands in his pockets.

"Taking a walk while the realtor works her magic with the buyer."

"Are you moving?" asked Jodi.

"Sort of. It's not my house, but it was left to me by my father when he passed away. He left me the little bag of flab you're petting right now too."

"Did he die a long time ago?"

"A little over a week ago."

A frown crossed Jodi's face. "I'm sorry your daddy died. Don't you want to keep the house?"

"Well," Kinsley searched for the right words, "I don't live here, Jodi. I live about four hours away. It doesn't make sense to have a house here when I have to go back home."

"Not even for visits? What about Petunia? Are you going to sell her too?" Jodi flung her body in front of the dog like a protestor trying to block a customer from entering a fur coat store.

"Nope, I'm not selling her. I decided to go ahead and keep her." She pointed a stern finger at Bastian. "And not one word from you."

He put up his hands and smiled. "I'm not going to say anything. I don't need to."

She turned her attention to Jodi. "So are you guys having fun?"

"Yep. We went and saw Uncle Tommy at the shop for

lunch and then came to the park so I could ride my bike. I like this bike better than my bike at my mom's house because this one is pink with sparkles and has a basket on the front. The one at my mom's house has Dora the Explorer on it. It's such a baby bike. We're having a cookout tonight, you want to come? You can bring Petunia." If there were a contest for people who could switch topics the fastest, Jodi would be champion of the world.

"Oh no, that's okay Jodi. You and your daddy should spend some time together."

Jodi waved her off. "We've been spending time together all day. Plus, I'm still a bit sore at him for not teaching me how to shoot a gun. Do you know how to shoot a gun?"

"I'm learning now, but I never knew how to before. I'm sure he'll teach you when you're a bit older."

Petunia rolled over displaying her belly for Jodi to rub. "That's what he says, but I think I'm old enough now. So are you coming to our cookout then? We're having hot dogs!"

Kinsley raised an imploring brow at Bastian, but he wasn't offering any help. "It's impolite to refuse a dinner invitation from an eight-year-old."

"I'm almost nine. My birthday is this Thursday!" she protested.

"I know! I heard our birthdays are only a week apart. Mine is next Thursday."

"So you have to come. If you sell your house and leave, then Daddy won't be able to get you a cake. We're having cake tonight," she leaned over to whisper in Kinsley's ear, "but Mrs. Ida Robinson made it, so there's probably something yucky in it like peas or Diet Coke." This little girl had already learned the ropes of living in Staunton.

"Okay, Petunia and I would love to come to your cookout." She inclined her head at Bastian. "Do you need me to bring anything?"

"Only yourself. We've got the rest covered. Want to come over around five-thirty?"

"Yeah, I think Petunia and I can manage that. We'll see you all then."

Jodi planted a kiss on top of Petunia's head and jumped up to get her bike. "You ready, Daddy?"

"Sure, baby girl. Stay where I can see you this time, please."

"Then quit being so slow!" With that, she sped down the trail.

"She's beautiful...and spunky. You're gonna have your hands full when she gets older, you know that right?" Kinsley stood up and wiped the dirt from the back of her pants.

"Yep, I'm going to have to stand on the porch with my shotgun twenty-four seven." He walked over and reached down to pet Petunia. "We'll see you two lovely ladies in about an hour." His eyes glimmered with a mischievous sparkle.

"Just so you know, shenanigans are not on the menu this evening."

Bastian shrugged. "My grill, my rules."

"And I expect my bra to be returned to me in the same condition that I left it in."

"Baby, I was with the army for several years doing shit you can't imagine. Don't try using pressure tactics on me. You'll lose." He rose, nodded at her, and headed down the trail to try and catch up with his daughter.

Kinsley eyed Petunia. "I think we might be in a bit of trouble, what do you think?" Petunia responded by wagging her tail. Kinsley sucked her teeth. "Traitor," she hissed before heading in the opposite direction of the aforementioned trouble. When she got to the parking lot, her cell phone rang. She smirked at the screen display. *Stick Figure Succubus.* It was her contact name for Sharon Wilson.

"Hello?" she answered, loading Petunia up in the car.

"Hey, Kinsley. It's Sharon. Mr. Harper asked for another

day to think about it, but I am almost one-hundred percent positive you're going to have an offer some time tomorrow morning. Go ahead and make an appointment to have the junk haul people on standby. I don't think he wants it furnished. You okay with waiting until tomorrow before we move forward?"

"Yes, tomorrow is fine. But if there isn't an offer by tomorrow morning, I want it posted on your website to push for other buyers. I can't keep waiting around on the hopes that this guy, who is supposedly in a hurry, makes up his mind."

"Understandable. Frank Goldman and I are taking him out to dinner tonight at Sammy's Steak House. It's a small town so might not be a bad coincidence if you show up there."

"Thanks, but I already have plans." Should Kinsley tell her about where her dinner plans were or more importantly, whom they were with? Yes, she should. "I'm going over to Bastian Harris's house for a cookout."

Blessed silence echoed over the line for a few seconds.

"Oh, that's nice. At the Fourth of July picnic this year he offered to grill for me. It was fantastic." Was she trying to bait her and make her jealous? Two could play at that game.

"Yes, he's grilled for me a few times before. Tonight he's giving me a hot dog. I know I won't be disappointed." Set. Match. Point.

"Enjoy. I'll talk to you tomorrow."

"Until tomorrow." Kinsley hung up the phone and debated whether or not she had chosen wisely in returning this woman's innuendos. She did need her to sell the house, but on the other hand, if she viewed Kinsley as a possible threat that might make her work even harder to sell the place and get her the hell out of town. It was most likely a good idea that she piss her off about Bastian as much as possible to speed up the sale process. It was unfortunate, but a sacrifice she could live with.

Chapter Twenty

The drive over to Bastian's house was not easy. Kinsley decided it best to stop at Martha's Cake and Candy to buy a half dozen cupcakes in case Ida Robinson decided to get creative with the dessert she delivered to Bastian and his daughter. When Petunia wasn't shoving her head out the window next to the passenger seat, she was trying to open the box of cupcakes and gobble them up. After a couple of sternly worded "bad girls" and an empty threat of taking her to the shelter, Petunia settled down in the front seat for the rest of the ride.

She pulled into Bastian's driveway at 5:25 and parked in front of the house. A stainless steel grill fit for a king was already heating up on the front porch. Off to the side of the house, a picnic table was being set by a wet haired Jodi in a blue and white sundress. At the sound of the car settling in the gravel, Jodi came running.

"Hi, Petunia!" Jodi apparently thought the dog was the guest of honor. She opened the passenger door and grabbed her leash, helping the dog jump down. "Hi, Kinsley. Can Petunia come with me to set the table?"

"Sure she can. Your dad's house is pretty far from the road, so I don't think we need to worry about keeping her on the leash too much. Did you just finish swimming?"

"Nah, Daddy made me take a shower as soon as we got home. Said he didn't want me to have to stay up late to take a bath."

Mmm-hmm.

Kinsley reached in the backseat for the pink bakery box. She walked around to where Jodi was kneeling next to the dog and whispered, "I stopped by the bakery and brought some cupcakes...just in case." She lifted the lid so Jodi could see the assortment of chocolate and vanilla with a solitary strawberry cupcake in the center.

"Dibs on the strawberry," said Bastian from behind her, peering over her shoulder.

"Daddy loves strawberry. It's his favorite."

"You know something, I thought that it might be." Kinsley stood up, closing the box while Jodi and Petunia took off towards the picnic table.

Bastian ran his eyes up and down the length of Kinsley's body. "You didn't have to get all dressed up on our account, but I can't say I'm disappointed." She guessed the decision to change into a teal green sundress was a good one. Her judgment in showing up at his house, however, was still in question.

"Can I put these in the kitchen? They're buttercream so they need to be refrigerated."

"Yeah, let me help you." Bastian led her inside. This time she was able to take a look around. His living room was fairly large. Oversized beige furniture encompassed the room with pictures of his daughter during every year of her life hung in simple frames. A counter on top of a half-wall separated the eat-in kitchen from the living room. Decorative paper with small yellow daisy flowers lined the walls of the kitchen with a rack of stainless steel pots and pans next to the stove.

"Nice wallpaper. Never figured you for a daisy man," she joked.

"It's a rental. Can't change the wallpaper. I was only allowed to paint. You didn't notice it this morning?"

"As if I could! I was too busy trying not to have a heart attack when I was discovered sneaking out of your house by your eight-year-old daughter and her yelling that you needed to get your gun!"

He laughed as he reached for the box of cupcakes to put them in the refrigerator. "Your face was priceless. Reminded me of the time in eighth grade when Mr. Felcher caught Chris Bishop passing you that note and you had to read it in front of the entire class."

"What? Are you an idiot savant or something? Have an eidentic memory about all of Kinsley Bailey's mortifying moments?"

Bastian cleared his throat. "I believe it was something like 'Kinsley, I really like you and want you to go to the Spring Fling with me. I promise we don't have to fast dance and I won't use my inhaler. Will you go with me? Circle yes or no.' You don't forget romantic sentiments like that. Your face turned a shade of red I didn't know existed."

He closed the refrigerator and turned to glance out the front door. Must have been all clear because he grabbed Kinsley's wrist and wrapped his arms around her. "You know your face turns a lighter version of that red when you are getting ready to come." He ran his hands up the bottom of her dress and sprawled his fingers over he thighs.

The fact that he apparently stared at her face when she was pre-orgasm should have probably made her feel embarrassed. She'd slept with one man before whose face contorted like he was having an epileptic seizure when he climaxed. But she didn't feel ashamed or self-conscious. His index finger running along the inside edge of her panty and his soft lips grazing her ear made it obvious he wanted to make her face turn that color again. She would have gotten lost in the moment if the sound of shuffling rocks and Petunia barking hadn't given her a violent shove back into reality.

She spun away just in time for Jodi to come running in the front door. "Are we ready to cook the dogs yet, Daddy?"

"Getting them now, peanut." He opened the refrigerator and began handing Kinsley the ketchup, mustard, and a bowl of chopped onions. "Kinsley and Jodi, you two can put the fixin's on the table. The bags of chips are in the pantry and the slaw needs to be put out right when the dogs come off the grill."

Jodi walked into the kitchen and opened the pantry door. "Doritos! Yes! Come on, Kinsley. We can do it together and then you can show me all the tricks Petunia can do while Daddy cooks the food."

Kinsley wasn't sure what tricks Petunia was capable of other than snarfing down a bowl full of Pedigree in under a minute, but she figured it was worth a try. As it turned out, Petunia knew a lot of tricks when bits of hot dog were used as an incentive. She knew how to sit, stay, speak, shake, and even roll over.

Bastian watched them intently as she and Jodi played with Petunia in the front yard. It made goose bumps trail over her skin. The contentment apparent in that stare of his sent butterflies winging through her insides.

Right about the time Petunia had eaten her fill of Ball Parks, the cooked dogs were ready to come off the grill, and it was time to eat. Just like it had been at breakfast, dinner took almost an hour for Jodi to finish. Between every bite was a story about "one time when" and "hey, do you know what." Kinsley nodded with every tale she told, but every once in a while, she would get distracted by Bastian running his foot up her bare calf under the table. It wasn't until he got up to get the cupcakes that she could concentrate enough to listen to Jodi ramble on.

"...and I wanted to come to the parade, but mom said she needed Mark to help with the drive. So I asked Mark if we could leave a day early and they could come to the parade too, but then I remembered that Mark doesn't get out of the car when Daddy's around."

That got Kinsley's attention. "Oh? Are they not friends?"

"They used to be. Mark was over all the time…even when Daddy was away at wars."

Uh-oh.

"And then the last time Daddy was gone, Mama said he left so that she and I could move away to be with Mark. Then they got a divorce and Mark and Mama got married. Now Mark doesn't get out of the car and we can't have holidays or birthdays together."

"I'm sorry to hear about that. That must be hard for you. Have you talked to your mom or dad about how that makes you feel?"

"Nope. Last time Daddy and Mark were around each other, Daddy hit Mark in the nose and made it bleed. Mama and Mark tried to tell me he did it on accident, but I watched the whole thing from my bedroom window last summer when Daddy dropped me off at my house. It sure didn't look like an accident and he never said he was sorry either, but Mama said I should forget about it. I don't want him to hurt Mark again, so I pretend like I didn't see it. Was your dad that died your real dad or your stepdad?"

Now that was a million dollar question right there. By no means was she going to give an eight-year-old the sordid details of her parental circumstances, but she did want Jodi to know parents can be tricky situations for lots of people. "The man that died and left me the house wasn't my father by blood, like your father is to you, but he did what he needed to in order to protect me and take care of me the best way he could. I think those things are what real fathers do for their daughters, even if they don't share the same DNA. So, I just say he's my dad." She shrugged.

"Yep, both Daddy and Mark do that for me. I think I'd like it better if they liked each other though. I love 'em both."

Bastian came bounding off the front porch with the cupcakes on a gigantic white platter. "Okay, who wants what? Remember the strawberry is mine."

Jodi chose the chocolate on chocolate cupcake with the biggest mound of frosting in the half-dozen. Kinsley selected the vanilla cake with lemon buttercream icing. After dessert, they all pitched in to clean up the table. In the disappearing summer sun, Jodi and Petunia headed outside to try and catch lightening bugs while Kinsley and Bastian worked on the dishes.

"You better be careful, I think Jodi might try and hide that dog in her bedroom before I leave." Kinsley loaded the last plate into the dishwasher. "Where are your tabs?"

"Pantry," he gestured towards the closet. She opened the door and walked into the small closet-sized pantry.

"I don't see any cleaning things in here," she called. She didn't need to turn around because she knew Bastian was right behind her. She could feel his breath on the back of her neck and his mouth next to her ear. He put his hands on her shoulders and slid them down the front, resting on her breasts.

"I lied, they're under the sink. I wanted to get you in here so I could cop a quick feel." He kissed the side of her neck and massaged her breasts on the outside of her dress.

Kinsley hesitated. "Bastian, I don't think this is a good idea right now."

"I know," he whispered in her ear. "Jodi will be going to bed soon." His hands continued their dance, slipping underneath the top of her dress, but Kinsley stepped forward and his hands lost their place.

"No, I mean tonight in general. I'm gonna take off and get the dog home."

Bastian's eyes scrunched together in confusion. "Why? Are you worried? She didn't wake up at all last night and with how she's running around like a maniac with your dog I'm pretty sure she'll pass out in the next forty-five minutes or so."

"No, it's not that."

"Okay, what is it then?"

Kinsley pushed passed Bastian to get back in the kitchen. The pantry was so small and he was so massive, it started to feel suffocating. "I just don't think it would be a good thing for your daughter to wake up this morning and see that I'm here and go to bed tonight with me here too. It might complicate things for her." And possibly Kinsley too.

He followed her out of the pantry and leaned against the sink. "She's so wrapped up in that dog I'm pretty sure she wouldn't notice if you spent the whole damn week here."

She could tell by the tone of his voice that he was starting to become a bit agitated. "I don't want to add to your daughter's confusion, that's all."

"Hold on a minute, what other confusions do you think she has?"

And here we go... Kinsley had heard variations of this question for several years during parent-teacher conferences. Middle school seemed to be the most popular timeframe in children's lives for their parents to get divorced. Philandering fathers or emotionally distraught mothers thought their behaviors had no effect on their children because they might not shove it in their faces. However, its impact was always easily seen by teachers. There were a few times Kinsley had about enough of a child morphing into a depressed mess because their father decided he didn't get to live life enough in his twenties. Parents didn't take it too well when you let them know their selfish choices were negatively impacting their children, so his defensive demeanor didn't surprise her.

"Who's Mark?" she asked point blank. His face hardened and his arms tensed. She had definitely struck a nerve.

"He's Jodi's stepfather."

"No, I'm asking you. Who is Mark to you?"

"Not a goddamn thing." He reached into the refrigerator and pulled out a Sam Adams Pale Ale. He twisted off the top with his bare hand and threw the cap in the sink.

"If he isn't anything, then why can't he get out of the car?"

Bastian paused with his beer bottle halfway to his mouth. The question had definitely caught him off guard. "Excuse me?"

"Jodi told me that he can't get out of the car. That you all can't have birthdays and holidays together because last summer you broke his nose when you dropped her off at her house."

"She told you that? Did she say her mother told her about me hitting Mark?"

"No, she saw it from her bedroom window. Her mother tried telling her you did it on accident, but she's too smart for that. Jodi wants her family to be unified, but she's afraid to talk to anyone about it because she doesn't want you beating up her stepdad." She tucked a strand of loose hair behind her ear. "I know blended families don't get along some of the time, but usually they can be around one another without coming to blows, especially when it's been over two years. So I want to ask you again, who is Mark to you?"

He set his beer down on the counter and put his hands in his pockets. His face was cold, unreadable. "I'm not sure exactly why you think you can go asking so many questions."

Kinsley's eyes widened a fraction. Did he really just say that to her? "I'm asking because your daughter reached out to me about it. You were inside getting the cupcakes. She knows something has been going on and she's hurting about it."

"I never talk about any of that with her and neither does her mother. That's one thing she and I can still agree on. My refusing to be around that son of a bitch isn't going to put my daughter in therapy." He grabbed a dishrag and swiped at the counters although they had already been cleaned minutes before.

"I'm not saying what you're doing or not is going to make your child end up in a group home for runaway teens. What I am telling you is she wants to talk about it because she loves you both so much, but she's afraid to." She wrapped her arms around her midsection to stop from reaching for him. He wouldn't stop scrubbing the counter so he could avoid being face to face with her and it was starting to piss her off. "And if you act like this much of an asshole when people try to talk to you about sensitive subjects, I think I can understand why she wouldn't."

Bastian threw the rag into the sink and spun around to face her. "And what makes you think you have some sort of clout to come in *my* home and tell me how to conduct things with *my* daughter? Do you think because we've been fucking like rabbits the past few days you have the authority to tell me what to do about my family?" His arms crossed defensively over his chest. "Hooking up does not give you relationship rights. Thought you would have figured that out about twenty years ago."

Her nostrils flared as she inhaled in order to avoid screaming at him. It was like she had been sucker punched in the gut. Not only did he tell her their actions in the bedroom and the moments they shared over the past few days meant nothing, but he also berated her thirteen-year-old self. The girl that hid in the bathroom and cried over this same jackass. The girl who asked herself for months what she had done wrong while he went and dated any other girl with a size B bra. To hell with that! That girl may not have been able to stand up for herself then, but this woman would go to bat for her any day.

She squeezed her sides. If she held onto something, she was less likely to haul off and slap him. She stepped towards him and concentrated on speaking as evenly as possible. "What I've learned in the past twenty years is that zebras don't change their stripes. You give the guise of being forthcoming and upfront, but then your actions and words weave a web of bullshit so convoluted it alters reality for anyone you're around." Heat surfaced under her breastbone. "Then, you have the audacity to make me feel like a fool for misunderstanding. I did learn that lesson twenty years ago, and I never forgot it."

Her breath hitched ever so slightly as she sucked in much needed air.

"As much as you might like to believe I deluded myself into thinking we were in some sort of relationship, don't kid yourself. We were fucking, plain and simple. And it wasn't the sex that made me think I could try and have an open discussion with you about your daughter, who again reached out to me first." She thumbed her chest. "The only delusion I'm guilty of is thinking we had some sort of friendship with a mutual respect and concern for one another. Somehow twenty years later, you got me on that again."

She stepped backwards and released the fabric of her dress. Standing there, she waited two breaths for some sort of smartass remark, but he said nothing. A silent staring contest in the middle of his kitchen ensued for several seconds, but he shifted his gaze away first. "Nothing to say? Avoiding the situation? I guess you have some old habits that die hard too." She sighed. "Please be sure to let Tommy know he will be my point of contact from here on out regarding the consignment."

Grabbing Petunia's leash and her purse from the kitchen table, she headed out. In the cooler evening air, she found Jodi with the dog in the front yard. She needed to smile and pretend to be happy. This little girl didn't need any more drama in her life. "Jodi! Petunia! It's time for us to go."

"Oh, do you have to?" she whined following the dog.

"Yes, sweetie. I'm sorry. It's getting late." She clipped the leash on Petunia.

"Will you be coming over tomorrow? Daddy has the whole day off so we're going fishing at Blue Hole Lake. I asked him before you got here and he said that was fine with him." Jodi's eyes twinkled.

Kinsley didn't have the heart to tell Jodi the invitation had been revoked by her father. "No, sweetheart. I can't go. But good luck catching all those fish. We'll see you later."

"Daddy, Kinsley is leaving...and she said she can't go fishing with us tomorrow." Jodi ran up the porch, calling to her father.

Kinsley focused on maintaining a tall, confident posture while all but sprinting to her car. The empowerment from walking away without remorse would keep the tears and second guessing at bay and maybe show that ass once and for all that she was stronger than her desire to be around him. But the fact that each step created more distance between her and Bastian crept in, convincing her to glance out the rear window of her BMW before she wouldn't have the option. He stood at the front door watching her and giving no indication that he was going to try and stop her...or that he even wanted to.

Chapter Twenty-One

Close to midnight Kinsley had as much chance at sleep as Kristen Stewart did at winning an Oscar. Instead of tossing, turning, and analyzing her falling out with Bastian, she decided to make better use of the insomnia and get cracking on the basement. She planned on calling the junk haulers tomorrow and didn't want any nostalgic personal effects to become decorations for the landfill.

Petunia stayed buried under the covers while Kinsley put on her slippers and headed downstairs. Before opening the basement door, she grabbed a broom from the hallway closet in case she needed to whack any vermin or defend against a bug. Armed with her weapon, she went down the stairs and began to dig through the other two boxes that had her name on them. It was mostly items from her bedroom: posters, scrapbooks, her honor roll awards her mother insisted she keep.

Evidence of her growing up in the late eighties and early nineties made her wonder where the hell time had gone. Finding her lava lamp lightened her heart a little, even more so when she plugged it in and found it still worked. A black magic eight ball was tucked in next to her see through telephone, all the rage back then. She picked it from box and figured what the hell.

"Will I sell this house tomorrow?" She shook the ball upside down and flipped it over to reveal its answer.

Better Not Tell You Now.

Typical. "Will Bastian Harris be crowned king douche bag at next year's Founder's Day Parade?"

Better Not Tell You Now.

"Worthless piece of junk. Now I remember why I used you to prop my door open." Behind her, she heard the faint sound of a squeak and froze. She waited on baited breath for the sound to happen again. Maybe it was all in her head. But then in the pale blue glow of the lava lamp, she saw something scurry across the floor. She jumped up with her broom in one hand and her box in the other and hauled ass upstairs. Realizing she had left her lava lamp on, she psyched herself up for ten minutes in order to go back down there...but not without her broom and a can of furniture polish for defense. Deciding the wee hours of the morning were probably not best to clean out dark places, she decided she needed to try and rest.

Her restlessness subsided around four in the morning as she slipped into a light sleep. Unfortunately, it didn't last too long because her cell phone started ringing at nine a.m. on the dot. Hopefully, it was the "Stick Figure Succubus" telling her to pack up her shit cause the house was sold. She rolled over to see the screen displaying a number she didn't recognize with a Staunton area code. "Hello?"

"Yes, may I speak with a Mrs. Kinsley Bailey, please?"

"Speaking. And it's Miss."

"My apologies, ma'am. This is Paul Wheeler from the Wilbur and Wilcox Funeral Home. I wanted to notify you that your father's remains are ready to be picked up."

"Oh...um, okay. When can I come by?" She had forgotten all about having to pick up his ashes.

"Anytime today before five o'clock will be fine. We have gone ahead and placed the ashes in the urn a Mrs. Debra Bailey selected, so everything is prepared."

"Okay, I'll be by later this morning. Thank you." After hanging up the phone, she flopped back down on her bed. Petunia peeked her head from under the covers and yawned. "Well this is a strange situation, Petunia."

Kinsley wasn't sure exactly what to do. Although her father had explained everything that happened, she still hadn't completely accepted it. Changing your entire outlook on a person wasn't as simple as flipping a light switch. She had months of hammering this out ahead of her before she could discern how she felt. Maybe even a session or two with Dr. Haverty, her therapist from when her mother passed. Remains were meant to be kept by loved ones, not by people with conflicting emotions.

Kinsley took Petunia outside to get her business done and ready for the day. Worried that shaving her legs while she was this tired might cause an incident in need of stitches, she opted for her navy blue linen pants and a white tank top. She continually checked her phone every twenty minutes to see if the succubus had tried to get in touch with her, but she had no missed calls. Not from her with an offer on the house and not from a certain butt wad offering an apology. Kinsley would have been a little worried about running into him since the funeral home was right across the street from Five Points, but she remembered Jodi said he had taken the day off to go fishing. If he wasn't going to say he was sorry, she would rather slip out of town without seeing him again. Even though the thought of it bothered her more than she would like to admit.

The drive to the funeral home was uneventful, thank god. She had about had enough of the crap this town was offering on a silver platter, so a boring drive helped tip the scales. She was ready to make the left hand turn to the funeral home when her eyes darted across the street at Five Points. The store was open and Bastian's jeep was nowhere to be found. She switched her turn signal to indicate a right hand turn and pulled into the parking lot. After ringing the doorbell, Tommy greeted her at the front door and let her in.

"Hey, Kinsley. Bastian isn't here right now. He took the day off to be with Jodi."

"I know. I'm not here to see him. I was in town and decided I'd like to get one last round of shooting before I leave. Is the range open for people to use right now?"

"Sure is. Did you bring your own gun?"

"I don't have one." Then, she remembered the gun in her father's dresser drawer. "Well, actually I do, but I forgot to bring it. May I rent one of yours?"

"You can borrow one, but not rent it. Bass would kick my ass if he discovered I charged you for something." Tommy walked behind the counter that held the ammunition and safe with the rental equipment.

"I'm guessing you haven't spoken with him since yesterday afternoon then?"

"Nope. He's not supposed to be into work until tomorrow. And he's off again for Jodi's birthday."

"Okay, then I insist on paying for the rental and everything else I use today."

Tommy paused with a box of shells in his hand. "Why's that?"

"I'm an independent woman and that's how I roll." She didn't want to discuss anything with Tommy about what had happened. If she said anything, then he would talk to Bass and he might think she stopped by the shop hoping to see him. In no way, shape, or form did she want to appear needy.

"Okay, woman's lib. I get it. Let's get you set up."

Kinsley spent the next hour working on her aim. She had improved some, but three targets later, she still couldn't hit the damn bulls eye. She kept making bets with herself that if she hit the target in the middle, it was a sign she would be out of this town by the end of the week. Unfortunately, it didn't amp up her ability. Regardless, after she finished handling her father's house, there wasn't one thing that was going to bring her back to this place. Well, except Aunt Debbie. Despite everything, she was thankful that she got to know her better. Since her mother's sister and her cousins moved out to the west coast ten years ago, Debbie was the only family she had around.

After returning her equipment, she drove across the street to the funeral home and collected her father's remains. The urn Debbie picked out for him was beautiful. It was a deep mahogany box with a golden lock and key. The lid doubled as a picture frame holding a photo of him and Petunia on the porch at Aunt Debbie's house. On the front, a quote was burned into the wood.

Fatherhood is putting your own life on hold to fulfill the promises for your child's tomorrow.

With her father's urn in her passenger seat, she started to drive to her aunt's house. She knew exactly where the urn belonged.

***

It was four in the afternoon before Kinsley made it back to the house. Petunia was about to explode and must have peed for a solid three minutes by the time she got let out and made it to her favorite tree. Once the dog was back inside and devouring a raw hide on the kitchen floor, Kinsley went into the bathroom to check her appearance. She looked like a gothic teen because of how much her mascara had run from her sob fest with Aunt Debbie. Kinsley wasn't a crier, at least not as an adult, but when Debbie got choked up at Kinsley's request for her to keep the urn until she was in a place where she could love her father again, the waterworks started.

She was concentrating so hard to wipe the make-up away with toilet paper that her cell phone ringing startled her. She picked up the phone to see it was the succubus. "Please, Sharon.

Tell me we have some good news."

"Well, I do, but it's not what you're expecting."

Her shoulders dropped in defeat. "He lowballed, didn't he?"

"Sort of. He wants to offer twenty grand less than the appraised value." Kinsley started to shake her head. Maybe she should take it and run. She didn't need the money from the sale. "But I do have better news. I went ahead and listed the house online this morning when I felt like Mr. Harper was dragging his feet and you received a full price offer."

"What? From someone else? They haven't even come by to see the place. What's the catch?"

"No catch. He said the pictures were on point and the house is what they've been searching for. I wanted to call you and allow you to choose which offer to accept. I know it's a no brainer, but I have to present you with both."

"The full price offer, of course. Do they want the furniture?"

"Unfortunately, no. So you may have to stick around an extra day or two to oversee that the stuff gets hauled away. Can you spare that time?"

"Yes, of course. This is unbelievable. I had no idea people bought houses without seeing them in person. So what's the next step?"

"You arrange for the movers and I'll get started on the formal offer. I should have the paperwork done by tonight and we can go to closing at the end of the week."

"We're going to close that soon? I won't have to come back?"

"Nope, that's the next best part. It's a cash offer. We don't have to mess with any banks or contingencies of mortgage approval. They provide a cashier's check and viola. You're heading home."

"Okay, I'll make a few calls now to see if I can schedule something for tomorrow. Thank you again, Sharon. I was beginning to lose hope."

"No problem. I'll call you when the paperwork is ready to be signed."

Kinsley punched a search into her cell and began calling moving and junk hauling companies. After dialing three different companies that couldn't accommodate her until two weeks later, she sucked it up and decided to give You Toss It, We Trash It a call. She didn't much care to see Chuck again, but she was desperate.

"You Toss It, We Trash It. Chuck speaking, how can I help you?"

She pictured him sitting on the other end digging in his ears with his keys. "Hey, Chuck. It's Kinsley Bailey. We met at your Aunt Ida's house a few days ago."

"Hey there, Kinsley! What can I do for you? Doesn't have anything to do with bird turds, does it?" At least he found his own joke funny. Kinsley wanted to smack him through the phone.

"No, not at all. I've sold the house and the buyer wants all the furniture out of here. I know its short notice, but I was hoping you all could be here on Wednesday. We go to closing on Friday and I am hoping to make my final trip out of town right afterwards."

"We had a cancellation this week for Thursday. After that, we're booked up all next week." Having it done Thursday would be pushing it, but it was the lesser of two evils when compared with having to come back in town.

"Thursday will have to work. I'm not interested in keeping any of the items, but there are some good things here that would be useful to a Good Will or Salvation Army. Do you all donate anything or just trash it all?"

"We pick out the items we're able to donate and take them over to Shelly Michael's Halfway House for Battered Women. What kind of things should we be on the lookout to donate?"

"There's a stereo, some furniture that's in good condition, a flat screen television, lots of housewares. I don't have time to go through it all so use your discretion. I've already gotten everything I want to take with me, so anything not fit for the halfway house can be tossed. What time can I expect you Thursday?"

"Crew starts at nine. Is the number that came up on the screen a good number in case I need to contact you?"

"Yes, it's my cell. Do you need the address?"

"No, ma'am. I know exactly where the house is."

"Okay, Chuck. Thank you again for your help and I'll see your guys Thursday morning."

"Bye, Kinsley."

One step closer to getting home.

***

Bastian's jeep turned from the dirt road that led to Blue Hole Lake onto Cherry Creek Way at around five p.m. The drive home from the lake was quiet except for the squeaking of the Styrofoam cooler that held their fish. This was the first time in a long time Jodi had nothing to say. She sat with her arms crossed and her little nose, tinted pink from the sun, held up high in the air. She was pissed at her father, which didn't happen often.

Their day had started out on the right foot. Although Bastian was in kind of a pissy mood from his argument with Kinsley last night, he was looking forward to taking Jodi out on the lake and spending the day with her. Tommy even let him borrow his boat so they didn't have to fish off one of the docks. He needed a distraction from last night's incident with Kinsley, and if anything could bring him out of a bad mood, it was his daughter. At least it was that way until she accidentally dropped her fishing rod in the lake.

Under usual circumstances, accidents and mishaps didn't

upset Bastian too much. However, being on edge from arguing with a certain auburn haired woman without getting any sort of release afterwards may have pushed him to lose his shit a bit. "Damn it, Jodi! How many times did I tell you to quit jumping around the boat and watch what you're doing? Now you've lost the rod!"

Jodi stood there in the boat with her little life preserver synched tight around her chest and her mouth agape in shock. She stood that way for several moments as he waited for the crocodile tears to flow. Instead, her little face scrunched up and she exploded. "I didn't do it on purpose! I tripped and it slipped out of my hand!"

"Sweetie, if you would have sat still like I asked you to do at least five times then you wouldn't have tripped, would you?"

"It doesn't matter. You don't yell at people for what they do on accident. That's what Mama and Mark always say and they don't yell at me unless I do something on purpose!"

"That's nice, but I'm not especially interested in what your mom and Mark say. I handle things my way." He started packing up the fishing gear and was ready to bring the boat in to dock. He'd had enough fishing for one day. Then, her eyes started watering up.

"You should be interested! That's what they told me about you when you hit Mark last summer. They say you did it on accident and that's why they didn't want you getting in trouble for it. But I saw it for myself and I know you did it on purpose. Mama didn't yell at you, I didn't yell at you, and neither did Mark!"

He was over Mark being considered a martyr. "Honey, one day you'll understand I could hit Mark five times in a row, and he still wouldn't have any justification to yell at me."

She stomped her foot. "I don't care what you're mad at him about! He's my stepdad and I love him! I'm tired of having to do everything separate. I'm tired of having to go back to the car to say goodbye. I want all three of you at my parties! I want everyone there when I do my dance recitals."

"I...I...," he sucked in air through clenched teeth, "you're sounding pretty selfish right now, Jodi."

"When you won't be around him, aren't you thinking about you? Isn't that selfish too?"

The question caught him off guard. How was he supposed to explain to his eight-year-old daughter that he had the right to be selfish in this situation? That he was the one that got dicked over by his best friend and now couldn't go to any birthday parties or dance recitals? "I'm done talking about this, Jodi. Sit down and put on your seat belt."

She stomped over to one of the white benches on the side of the boat and strapped in. She crossed her legs and even her arms to get the point across that she was ticked off. Loading up the jeep was done in silence as was the ride home. He looked over at his daughter and her angry, hurt little face, anticipating her to say she wanted to go home early. Then, she would be celebrating another birthday without him. Just like all the other special events, he always had to wait until later to share with her because he wouldn't let go of his anger with Mark.

Bastian reached the end of his driveway and put the car in park. After turning off the ignition, Jodi unbuckled her seatbelt, but she didn't hurry to get out of the car. Bastian shifted in his chair towards his daughter. "I suppose you're going to want to go home now, huh?"

She sat twisting her fingers in her lap. "I don't know. I just got here and I don't get to see you that much."

He slightly smiled. "And you'd get to see me more if Mark could get out of the car...or come out of the house...or show up at the same parade."

With a trembling chin and big, wet eyes, she squeaked, "Yes, that's exactly it."

Bastian had a decision to make. He could continue in his

current direction, refusing to see or be around Mark and making his daughter miserable, or he could try and do what was right for his child and let go of the resentment that was making it impossible to share so many things with her. He took a deep breath, "Okay, Jodi. I'll try. I need you to understand I can't be Mark's friend, but I can let him get out of the car without me acting stupid. I want to be around more for your parties and special things and if that means I have to behave around Mark, then so be it. It won't be easy for me, but I love you and if you love him, then I will try. Okay?"

Her sunburned nose wrinkled up as a grin grew on her face. She reached over and threw her arms around him. "Deal!"

"I'm sorry I lost my temper with you earlier."

"Me too. Mama says we're cut from the same cloth...whatever that means."

He laughed at the thought that he helped make a beautiful, blonde-haired, blue eyed girl with his temperamental issues. Sort of reminded him of another lady with a similar disposition, but she had darker hair and the nature of a bull shark.

"Come on, let's go inside and gut some fish." Jodi nodded in agreement and eagerly jumped out of the car. Yep, she was his daughter alright.

As her pigtails bounced up to the front porch, Bastian thought about his discussion with Kinsley the night before. It really wasn't a discussion, more of him being a jackass and not wanting to listen to a word she said. But thankfully, his hard head must have taken in some of the conversation because it led to him and Jodi coming to a solution about Mark. Bastian knew he could contribute his earlier foul mood as result of realizing he wasn't going to be seeing Kinsley anymore...naked or otherwise. The strange thing was, the longing for the 'otherwise' far outweighed the naked...although the naked was pretty damn spectacular.

Bastian came to a turning point today with Jodi. He

recognized her need to have him cut his bullshit so he could be more of a father to her. He owed that to Kinsley. At least when he was hurting Jodi, it wasn't intentional, it was done out of blind anger and bitterness. But with Kinsley, he had been a deliberate bastard and pushed away the sexiest woman he could stand to be around both in and out of the bedroom since his wife Linda left him. He knew he needed to make amends. Even if he didn't get to see her naked ever again, her forgiveness would be worth the 'otherwise' she may be willing to stick around for.

Chapter Twenty-Two

Wednesday morning, Kinsley once again found herself in a dilemma. Petunia must have had a sixth sense and predicted her opportunities to take a swim in Middle River behind the house were coming to an end. She had been trying for thirty minutes to get her up on dry land. It was hotter than usual and since the water level only came up to Kinsley's calf, the dip proved more of a pain in the ass than a cool frolic in the water. "Come on Petunia, I don't have time for this today! We're supposed to go to Debbie's for a goodbye lunch before we have to pack up all our shit so it doesn't get mixed in with the junk haul."

A sharp whistle came from behind Kinsley's right shoulder and Petunia booked it out of the river and onto the bank. She turned to see the whistle coming from a certain tight t-shirt wearing a-hole who was walking down the hill. Petunia scrambled towards Bastian, weaving in and out between his legs and whoring out to his petting. Kinsley blew the hair from her eyes and headed to land.

"What are you doing here, Bastian?"

"I dropped Jodi off at Ida Robinson's house. She watches her for me when I have to go into work."

She crossed her arms. "I'm not on the way to Five Points

from Ida Robinson's house. So what can I do for you?"

"Can we go inside and talk please?"

"Why? Afraid your insults will be heard by my neighbors?" She didn't wait for him to answer; she just started walking uphill towards the house and didn't care too much if he followed her.

He hurried behind her. "Your neighbors on either side are almost a football field's distance away."

"So you better talk loud then if you want to get the full humiliation factor taken care of." They both stepped onto the porch and entered the house through the sliding glass door. She sat on the couch while he remained standing in front of her. "Okay, say what you came to say."

"I'm sorry."

"Yes, you are pretty pathetic, but I already knew that. What new news did you bring?"

He sucked his teeth and shook his head. "See, it's that mouth that gets me every time."

"I hope you didn't drive all the way over here to talk to me about my mouth."

He rubbed his face with both hands before walking around the coffee table to sit next to her. "Your mouth does kind of have something to do with it."

She put up her hand. "Let me stop you right there, buddy. If you think you can speak to me the way you did and then come over for a blow job on your way to work, you've got another thing coming."

"No, no, no. Not what I meant." He laughed. "What I meant was I'm here to say I'm sorry. And the bit about your mouth is because you were right about what you said."

"Of course I was..." She blinked. "Which part are we talking about?"

"You were right to try to talk to me about Jodi. You were trying to be a good friend and tell me what she confided in you. I was an asshole. I shouldn't have told you to mind your own business or that because we had slept together a few times you didn't have the right to talk to me about something so personal." He rubbed the back of his neck. "I hit below the belt on that one and rather than walk away and avoid it, I wanted to come and straighten it out with you."

She waved a hand for him to continue. "I'm listening."

"Mark was my best friend. He was even my best man and in the waiting room when Jodi was born. I trusted him completely. So much that I asked him to help my wife out with things around the house and to check in from time to time when I was away with the Army." His brow furrowed and his face hardened. "I don't know how it started or why, but they had an affair. It was more than a fling, because when I came back from my last deployment I found out she had left me to be with him. They took Jodi too."

Hell. Her insides rolled at his confession. "Do you still love your wife? Is that why you can't be around him without wanting to hit him?"

His eyes widened. "No, I don't love Linda anymore. To be honest, I was more hurt about losing my best friend than losing my wife. She and I were on the rocks for a while before that all happened. If I would have come home and found her gone, he was the person I would have gone to for clarity. But suddenly both of them were out of my life. It was the ultimate betrayal and as much as you might want to laugh about me saying this, loyalty is very important to me."

She sucked on her bottom lip, thinking it over. "Okay, that answers the question of who Mark is. Now, what are you planning to do differently?"

"I promised Jodi that I'd try being around him for her, because I love her. And that she didn't need to worry about making sure Mark stayed in the car anymore."

Kinsley smiled. "Good for you. I can tell you firsthand that someday she'll appreciate the sacrifice you're making for her. A father puts his own life on hold in order to fulfill the promises of his child's tomorrow, or so I've read. And who knows, maybe one day you can be friends again."

"Nope, that'll never happen. But I can be civil if it means I get to see my little girl more and she isn't worried every time Mark and I get around each other. Besides, I have a new friend that does way more fun things with me that I never wanted to do with Mark." He put his hand on top of hers and she quickly slipped it away.

"Bastian, I forgive you. But I'm thinking there's some cosmic sign the universe is trying to tell me about you since you've managed to burn me twice in one lifetime. I'll be your friend, but I don't think it would be wise for us to be anything more than that...casually or not." She put some more distance between them. "I'm leaving on Friday."

"This Friday? The house sold to that guy already? Doesn't it take a few weeks to close on a house?"

"A new buyer stepped in to offer full asking price. It's a cash offer. We close Friday and I'm free and clear. Whatever is left to be taken care of can happen by phone or email."

He put his head in his hands. "Not everything, Kinsley."

"Bastian, I'm not going to drive into town on weekends to be your booty call. Putting all my eggs in one basket that you'll somehow change eternally considering me just a friend is not a chance I'm willing to take. I sat around waiting for you to change your mind once before, I'm not doing it again. I deserve more than that."

Bastian lifted his head from his hands and reached for her. "I'm not talking casually, Kinsley. You don't have to sit around and wait for me to change my mind because I've already made my mind up. I want to be with you."

Kinsley could have sworn her heart stopped beating. This couldn't be reality. Situations didn't work out this way for her. "What about me leaving?"

"I know you have a house and a job on the peninsula. I don't care how we figure it all out as long as we give it a try." He squeezed her hand. "I need to be with you. I'm sorry it took me over twenty years to finally get it."

Kinsley climbed into his lap and straddled him. She wrapped her arms around his neck and gave him a long soft kiss. Without her consent, her eyes filled up with water. "What took you so damn long?"

"There's that mouth," he teased before lifting her up and carrying her into her father's old bedroom.

An hour and a half later, Kinsley dragged her body from bed with Bastian doing everything in his power to pull her back in. "I have to be at Debbie's house in thirty minutes! I need to wash the sex off me and get over there."

Bastian continued to lie in bed as if there were nowhere else he needed to go. "Why are you in such a hurry to get over there?"

"She planned a goodbye lunch for me. I'm gonna be too busy tomorrow with the junk people, Friday I go to closing, and after that I leave. It's the only time I have to say goodbye to her."

"Oh, so that's why Ida was carrying on about making apple fritters with the Red Hots."

Kinsley stopped dressing with only one leg in her shorts. "Red Hots? The cinnamon candies? Inside apple fritters?"

"Jodi didn't seem too pleased about them either."

Kinsley rolled her eyes before shoving her other leg inside her shorts and running out of the bedroom. She bolted up the stairs and showered faster than she used to when there was a water shortage in Africa. She put on a coral colored sundress and twisted her wet hair on top of her head.

Upon returning downstairs, she found Bastian going through one of the boxes that managed to make it up from the basement the night before. He picked up the Magic Eight Ball and tossed it in the air.

"Don't even bother, that thing never works." Kinsley sat on the couch and laced her sandals.

"Maybe it doesn't like you. Oh Magic Eight Ball, will I be able to give Kinsley another four orgasms today?" He shook the ball and turned it right side up to view the window. "Without a Doubt. Hot damn."

Kinsley jumped from the couch to see. "Son of a Bitch! I can't tell you how many times I asked that damn thing questions growing up and I always got 'Better Not Tell You Now'." She shook her head and started searching for her purse.

Bastian tossed the ball between his hands. "Did you ever ask it questions about me? And don't say you better not tell me now."

"Maybe one or two, but I never got anything good from it. I also asked a fortune teller at a fair about us once and she said we were never going to be boyfriend and girlfriend. Who's laughing now old lady?" she called at the ceiling.

Bastian plopped the ball in the box. "Maybe her crystal ball only saw so far into the future."

"No crystal ball, she did it with cards. And that couldn't be it cause she also told me I was going to be murdered one week before I turned thirty-four." Kinsley let Petunia outside for a quick tinkle before they left for Debbie's.

"One week before?" he asked, his voice dropping an octave. "As in tomorrow?"

Kinsley had almost completely forgotten her birthday was right around the corner. "Yeah, I guess so." She shrugged off the realization and Bastian, Kinsley, and Petunia walked to their cars in the driveway. "I never believed in any of that crap anyways. I stopped when I found my cousin using a magnet to move the thing on the Ouija board."

"Glad you aren't superstitious. I might be treading more carefully if I got a fortune like that." He shrugged. "I better get to work. Tommy is gonna have a shit fit." He grabbed her by the waist and gave her one last goodbye kiss to hold her over until he could make good on those four predicted orgasms he said. At the end of Eagle Rock Lane, he turned left to go to Five Points and she turned right to go to Red Hots apple fritter hell.

***

Bastian walked in to Five Points with a rather pissed off Tommy standing behind the register. "Well, well, well. Look who decided to show up," he paused looking at his wrist watch, "almost three hours late."

"Sorry, Jodi didn't feel well this morning."

Tommy pointed at him. "Liar! Ida Robinson called here two hours ago to tell *me* to tell *you* that she was taking Jodi over to Debbie Bailey's house for lunch!"

Bastian sucked his teeth. "Can't take a leak in this town without it getting in the papers, can you?"

"Spill it. Where were you?"

"Kinsley's house."

Tommy pounded the counter. "That's what I thought. You two kiss and make up?"

"Not that it's any of your damn..." He cocked a finger, "Wait a minute. How'd you know we got in a fight?"

"I'm not at liberty to reveal my sources," Tommy said, staring at his fingers as he stretched them across the counter.

"Tommy!"

Tommy held up his hands. "Okay, fine. Jodi told me."

Bastian froze. "Jodi?"

"Yep. Yesterday before you stopped by on your way to the lake, Kinsley came in to shoot and insisted on paying for everything. She was acting funny, but I figured, she could be a feminist. That Emma Watson chick is supposedly a feminist and she is real ladylike, so I figured it was just a trend."

"Who the hell is Emma Watson?"

"That chick from the Harry Potter movies...that Hymen girl."

"It's Hermione, you dumb bastard!" Bastian had to harness every ounce of self-restraint he had not to choke his Hogwarts fan of a cousin.

"Anyways, when you and Jodi came by for lunch and you went to grab the pizza, she told me that you, she, and Kinsley spent the day together yesterday and she came over for dinner. She also said she watched you two get into an argument from outside the window and then Kinsley left."

Bastian ran his hands through his hair. "Damn it! That kid needs to quit spying through windows."

"So, you guys make up or what? You going to ask her to forgive your dipshit ways and stay with you or should I tell her myself why I bought that house?"

"You did what?" Bastian headed straight for his cousin and Tommy ran around to the other side of the counter. "You bought her house? It was you? You're the full price cash offer? Why?"

"To give the house to you. I didn't know if she needed the money and those guns are gonna take a while to sell. I figured if I bought the house, it would stop her worrying about it. Then if I gave the house to you, she might stick around and stay with your sorry ass cause you all would have a....I don't know...connection, I guess."

Bastian threw his hands in the air. "Why the hell would that thought even cross your mind? Do you know how stalker it's going to look when she finds out you bought the house to give it to me to keep her in town?"

"I don't care if it looks psycho or not, you belong with that girl."

Bastian put both his hands on the counter and stared at the floor. He couldn't believe the shit storm his life was turning into. First, he was going to have to play nice with Mark, to save his relationship with Jodi, and now he was going to have to find a way to explain his future ownership of a certain woman's property. He suddenly regretted teaching her how to shoot a gun.

Tommy returned to the register. "Look man, since you came here two years ago I have seen woman after woman, some gorgeous some unfortunate, come on to you. Quite frankly, it made me sick. No single man should have that much ass being thrown at him, but you never showed any interest in a single one until that girl walked through the door and back in your life."

The silence strung a beat between them.

Tommy sighed. "You may be my cousin, my business associate, and a royal pain in the ass most the time, but I also consider you my best friend. If I have to shell out some cash in order to try and keep a woman around who is the only female that made you smile like that in two years, then that's just the kind of guy I am. Call it psycho if you will."

Bastian tilted his head up and stared at Tommy who was busily counting the money in the register. He had spent so many years angry about losing Mark as his best friend that he forgot to open his eyes and see the man right in front of him. One that would do whatever he could to make sure he stayed happy and wouldn't run off with his woman. "So where'd you get the cash?"

"This business was around long before you showed up my friend. Don't you worry about that."

Bastian pushed off the counter and headed for the workshop. He stopped behind Tommy. "I know this hair-brained scheme made sense to you, and only you, so thanks." Tommy didn't turn around. He just nodded. Bastian continued to the steel door and punched in the security code.

"By the way, if she does stick around you all better knock off screwing in the store, the workshop, and the classroom. This is a business for Christ's sakes."

Goddamn security cameras.

Chapter Twenty-Three

The clock showed almost eleven at night before Kinsley had finished packing up everything she wanted to keep. Since Petunia tried darting past the front door every time she tried to carry out a box, she parked her BMW in the garage. Aunt Debbie's goodbye luncheon ended up taking a lot longer than she had anticipated, but at least it was enjoyable. The one less than pleasant aspect was Ida's Red Hots fritters. The woman insisted on watching everyone's faces when they took the first bite and it took everything Kinsley had to make yummy sounds while her gag reflexes rebelled.

Luckily, she had managed to toss the rest of the fritter in one of Debbie's potted plants when Ida got up to refill her iced tea. The fern was sure to be dead by morning. Unfortunately, Jodi used Petunia as her scapegoat and now the dog had gas that could choke a maggot. She even had to open up some of the windows to let the toxic fumes out of the house. At least it was a cool breezy evening. She much preferred the sounds of crickets and cicadas to the usual sirens and traffic she heard back home.

After texting a very disappointed Bastian that she would not be making an appearance at his house that evening to fulfill the four orgasm prophecy, Kinsley decided it was time to hit the sack so she could be up and lucid by the time the junk haulers showed up. She locked all the doors, but kept a few of the windows cracked to keep fresh air flowing in. The last thing she needed was a house full of sweaty men when it already smelled like rotten cabbage. She carried Petunia up the stairs and slipped into a pair of white cotton shorts and a green t-shirt. She opened her bedroom window in case Petunia continued to pollute the air and slipped in between the cool sheets. Sleep would not elude her tonight. Her exhaustion acted like a Lunesta pill she would happily swallow. Plus, now that Bastian and she had made up and cemented a commitment at least to try the long distance relationship, she was certain her dreams would be more enjoyable.

As Kinsley dozed off, her dream consisted of her and Bastian on a beach somewhere sipping Mai Tai's. They sunbathed naked and played in the ocean surf until the swarm of jellyfish elevated to the top and shot out of the water like fireworks. Sometimes her dreams didn't make too much sense. Bastian grabbed her and guided her to the white sandy shore while smacking the tops of the jellyfish to keep them from flying and exploding in their faces.

Smack. He got one. *Smack. Smack.* Two more down. *Smack...Huh?*

Kinsley's eyes fluttered open, aware that the smacking she heard wasn't happening in her dream. It wasn't even really a smacking sound, but more of a rustling. She sat up in bed and glanced over to make sure Petunia was still there. The dog had dug herself under the blankets and snored. Was that the noise she was hearing? Doubting her own lethargic senses, she was getting ready to lay back down when the sound of the sliding glass door opening gave her a violent shove into consciousness.

Jesus, someone's in the house! Could it be Bastian? Would he have snuck over after Jodi went to bed? He wouldn't leave his kid alone, would he?

She grabbed her cell. It was almost one in the morning. She switched the ringer to silent and texted Bastian.

Are you in my house?

She waited a few heartbeats while the soft sounds of someone downstairs pounded through her ears. Her phone vibrated.

No. Why?

"Shit!" With her phone in hand, she slipped her feet from between the covers and tiptoed towards the stairs. She stood on the top platform for several seconds, waiting to prove the noise was all in her head. When she heard something shuffle, her heart sank. It wasn't in her head. Something or someone was down there. Her phone vibrated again, indicating another text message, but she was too focused on walking as silently as possible down the steps to check it.

She reached the landing at the base of the stairs and saw the silhouette of someone moving through her father's living room. The figure was slender so it couldn't have been Aunt Debbie. She froze, concentrating as hard as she could not to make any noise or even breathe. Her eyes darted to the left at her father's bedroom. The gun she had found in the Five Points box still rested in his nightstand.

The shadowed figure carried something large through the sliding glass door. This was it, now or never. She could run unnoticed from the stairs to her father's bedroom before he came back in the house. As she willed her right foot onto the floor, her cell started vibrating madly. Somebody was calling her. She'd been concentrating so hard on getting to her father's room that the vibration startled her and the phone plummeted to the ground. At the sound of it hitting the floor, another figure appeared from inside the kitchen. There were two of them…maybe more.

The intruder sprinted in her direction and slammed her into the door before she had any time to react. The force from her head smacking against the metal disoriented her focus. A large hand covered her mouth and the faint smell of Old Spice filled her nostrils. She tried in vain to scream, but his calloused hand made her desperate efforts come out muffled and small. He grabbed the sides of her head and banged it against the door again, attempting to knock her out. She slid to the floor, consciousness fading as she fell. Dark spots invaded her vision, but she could still spot another person coming into the house.

The sound of a giant thud sounded from upstairs. "There's someone else upstairs," the heavy voice of a long time smoker yelled to the other intruder. The man released his hands and Kinsley slid the rest of the way to the floor while he darted upstairs.

Oh shit. Petunia! He's gonna kill my dog.

With a thunderous pain in her head worse than any she had ever known, she staggered off the floor. The person at the porch slid the door closed and charged for her. She dove at her father's bedroom and onto the bed. While pulling at the drawer to get to the gun, the person pounced on her from behind, flattening her on the mattress. He was so heavy she couldn't move. Already having difficulty breathing, her struggle was infantile. The black spots grew bigger and unconsciousness threatened. But through the haze overtaking her and beyond the foul smelling breath of the person panting into her ear, she heard barking and the scampering feet of a dog running down the stairs.

The person pushed the upper half of his body off Kinsley, ready to defend against a possible dog attack. The absence of his weight was enough to let air slip into her lungs and will her body to move. She reached into the drawer, grabbed the entire wooden box, and swung it around to smash him on the temple. He groaned, grabbing his head and rolled off the edge of the bed. Kinsley flipped the lid of the box and yanked at the gun. Leaping off the bed as adrenaline raced through her, she jumped up and reached for the light switch next to the door. When a yellow glow filled the room, she saw Petunia running towards her with a large man in a grey t-shirt following behind. He had a large metal rod lifted above his head, readying it to come down on the dog's back. Without hesitation, Kinsley lifted the gun and pulled the trigger.

The shot struck the intruder next to his left armpit. The jolt of pain caused him to drop the rod and fall to his knees. Petunia ran in between Kinsley's legs and latched onto the ankle of the second man trying in vain to hide under the bed. The man started yelping as the dog's teeth latched on. "Get this damn dog off me!"

Kinsley looked at the wounded man in the hallway as he was trying to get up. "Don't you fucking move a muscle or I'll blow a hole right through your god damn head! Lay face down on the ground with your arms spread out," she barked.

"Alright, alright," he grunted on his way to the carpet. "We weren't gonna hurt anybody." Turning sideways and with her gun still pointed on the man in the hallway, Kinsley grabbed intruder number two's other ankle that Petunia wasn't gnawing on and yanked. When only his face was still under the bed, she took turns pointing the gun at him and the man in the hall.

"Slide out slowly or I'll shoot you right in the fucking face!" Kinsley didn't recognize the sound of her own voice. Full of adrenaline and fear, her commands were coming from a darker more authoritative place than she had ever been. The man braced his hands on the mattress and pushed free the rest of the way. Kinsley almost toppled over at the sight of him.

"Chuck Writtle? Are you shitting me right now!"

Chuck let his head rest on the floor as the sound of sirens in the far off distance got closer.

"I didn't see your car. I didn't think you'd be home." She hauled off and kicked him in the ribs. He bent over on his side in pain.

"It's in the garage you asshole!"

"I didn't think you were home. You and your dog surprised us, that's all." Blue flashing lights filtered in through the windows. Three loud bangs could be heard at the front door.

"Mrs. Bailey? Are you alright?" a man yelled through the door.

"I'm in here! I have the two intruders!" The police came barreling into the house with Chief Gregory Whitman leading the parade. The officer next to him knelt down, placing his knee on the back of the man lying in the hallway. The pressure must have hurt his gunshot wound because he screamed out in pain.

Chief Whitman walked calmly in her direction with his hands up to show he wasn't going to hurt her. "Mrs. Bailey...are you okay?" Kinsley's hands began to tremble, evident by the unsteadiness of the gun. "Mrs. Bailey, I need you to give me the gun. It's all okay now. We've got it from here." Chief Whitman reached out and slowly took the gun from her hand.

The pain in her head suddenly became too excruciating and she started losing the ability to focus. "It's Miss," was all she could sputter out before the black blobs took over.

***

Kinsley's dry mouth and the jackhammer some little man was pounding on the front of her head brought her out of sleep. Her eyes started to flicker open and she moved her head slowly to the right. The first thing she could comprehend was her Aunt Debbie asleep on a sofa next to a window. She slept sitting up, her head tilted back, and her mouth open like a Venus flytrap waiting for lunch. Gazing downward, she noticed her Aunt had put on knee high panty hose but wore a pair of shorts. Kinsley would have laughed if her head didn't hurt so much.

The sound of a door opening willed her to swivel her head in the other direction. It was Bastian holding a carrier with two coffees. Although it was difficult for a man naturally as beautiful as he to be anything but majestic, the bags under his eyes told a story of worry and lack of sleep. Seeing her eyes open, a mixture of joy and relief spread across his face.

"Hey there," he said placing the coffee on a tray next to the bed. "How are you feeling?" He put his elbows on the bed and threaded his fingers through hers.

"My head hurts like hell and I feel sort of nauseous. Can I have something to drink, please?" Bastian handed her a cup of ice water sitting next to her bed. She drank the whole thing in three gulps.

"Doctors said you have a concussion and might feel some after effects from the 'fight or flight' rush, but you don't have any major injuries so you should be able to leave soon. Do you want me to get a nurse to get you something for your headache?"

"No, not until you tell me what happened."

"Apparently Chuck Writtle and his friend Scott Roach are the ones who have been breaking into people's houses. When the cops looked into it further, they found that all the places getting ripped off were on You Toss It, We Trash It's schedule over the next few months. Chuck would get the customers to work in details about the items for donation and such, and then he and Scott would go rob the place. When Chuck didn't see your car in the driveway, he thought you weren't home. You scared them as much as they scared you."

A horrific thought rushed into Kinsley's mind. "What about Petunia? They didn't hurt my dog, did they?"

"No, but Petunia did a number on Chuck. He had to get about twenty stitches before they hauled his ass off to county."

"Where is she now?" Kinsley blinked, willing the headache to dissipate.

"With Jodi at Tommy's house." He took a strand of her hair and tucked it behind her ear.

"Why did the cops show up? I didn't call them."

"Do you remember texting me and asking if I was in the house?"

She nodded.

"After I told you it wasn't me, I texted you back to ask if you were okay." He touched her chin. "You didn't answer. So I tried calling you. It was ringing and then all of a sudden I heard a loud crash and a man screaming. I called the cops and sent them over there. Then, I got off the phone with them, piled Jodi in the car and took her to Ida's house. After what felt like an eternity, I got to your house…you were unconscious and being lifted into the ambulance. I about lost my fucking mind." He roughly ran his hands over his face, trying to keep it together.

Kinsley lightly touched his wrist. "It's okay, Bastian. I'm fine."

"Are you sure?" he asked, his eyes bloodshot. "They didn't do anything else to you, did they?"

She reached up and caressed the side of his face. "No, they didn't. I really do think they were only trying to rob me. I had left the windows open because your daughter fed Petunia some of those Red Hots fritters, so I guess that's how they got in. It wasn't until I was downstairs trying to figure out what was going on that I remembered the gun in my father's nightstand in a Five Points Box." Kinsley stopped and her eyes widened.

"What is it?"

"Don't listen to the sound of cicadas and run towards the star! Holy shit!" Her mouth dropped open. The old gypsy woman was right. Then again, she hadn't been entirely correct about the future…she and Bastian were together now.

Debbie let out a loud snort and her head shot up. "Oh, honey. Thank goodness, you're alright! I could ring that Chuck Writtle's neck for what he did. Ida Robinson is gonna get a strongly worded letter from me about her nephew!" Debbie scooted off the sofa and walked to the hospital bed. She wrapped her arm around Kinsley and kissed her on the forehead.

"Debbie, I'm okay. Don't let this sour your friendship with Ida. I doubt she knew what her nephew was up to."

Debbie harrumphed. "Well, one thing is for certain. If I find Sylvia Nickel's stuffed dead dog, Trixie, over at her house...her invitation to ride with me to Bingo on Fridays is revoked."

Kinsley sat up a little too quickly and got a head rush. "Damn it," she said, rubbing her temples.

"You need something for the pain?" Bastian asked while pushing the nurse call button.

"It isn't Friday now, is it? I wasn't unconscious for the whole day?" she asked, pinching the bridge of her nose.

"No, Sleeping Beauty. It's still Thursday." Bastian grabbed a washcloth from the bathroom and dipped it in the pitcher of ice water. He folded it up and held it to Kinsley's forehead. "Why?"

"I'm supposed to close on Friday. I wanted to make sure I didn't miss it. I don't want to make the buyer mad." Kinsley noticed Debbie and Bastian staring at one another as if urging the other one to spill the info. "Oh, no. The buyer backed out, didn't he?"

"I think I'll take a walk down to the cafeteria and get a muffin to go with that coffee," said Debbie. After grabbing her purse from the couch, she hurried out the door.

"Ah, crap. She only runs like that when she's hiding something. What's wrong? Did something happen with the sale?"

"Sort of, but not what you're thinking." Bastian's jaw tightened. She could feel the blood drain from her face. The nurse picked that exact moment to check in on her patient.

"We doing okay in here? You need something?" she asked Kinsley.

"Something for the pain and make it a double. I have a

feeling I'm gonna need it." She didn't take her eyes off Bastian the entire time.

"Sure thing. I'll have the doctor sign off on something for you. Be back in a jiff."

Kinsley didn't speak again until the nurse had closed the door behind her. "What's going on?"

Bastian sighed. "I don't want you to worry about closing tomorrow. I don't think the buyer will mind waiting a few days."

She eyed him wearily. "How do you know?"

His face scrunched up. "Because right now he's too busy watching Jodi play with your dog to care."

Her head throbbing delayed her catching on as quickly as she should have, but when she did... "Tommy?"

He nodded.

"Tommy is the full price cash offer? But why?"

"Because he wanted to give the house to me."

Her mouth gaped open. "To you? Why would he want to give the house to you?"

Bastian scrubbed at his face. "Because Tommy's IQ lies somewhere in between a mountain goat and a toaster oven and he thought buying the house would alleviate your financial troubles."

"But I don't have any financial troubles. I could stop working today and still pay to have my ass powdered by hot young men up until I'm old and senile. That doesn't explain why he wanted to give it to you."

Bastian reached down and put her hand in his. He rubbed across the top with his thumb. "To try and keep you here...for me. He thought if he gave me the house that you'd be inclined to stick around a little longer. He said we belong together." He looked up at her like a lost dog in need of a home and waiting for some kind of signal to express how she felt.

The nurse came into the room with a syringe and injected

the contents into the IV portal attached to her arm. "There you go. That should help. You need anything else, you be sure to let me know. The doctor will be in shortly to speak with you."

Kinsley waited until the nurse was out of the room. "Do you think we belong together, Bastian? Like having a permanent structure you have to pay property taxes on together? That seems pretty rushed for a man who just said a few hours ago he would like to 'give it a shot'."

He bit his lower lip. "That few hours ago happened before I heard you being attacked on your cell and couldn't do anything to help you but call the police. I thought I'd lost you. The drive to your house was unbearable because I didn't know if I was ever going to see you again. Then I saw you being put in the ambulance and it all became clear."

"What became clear?"

"I don't need to 'give it a shot.' This isn't rushed. I've known you for over twenty years. You were one of my best friends then and I consider you one of them now. I may have been thirteen and did some stupid shit, but that isn't happening this time. I love you, Kinsley. If you don't want Tommy to buy the house, I'll tell him to pull the offer."

"I want Tommy to pull the offer," she said on a breath. Bastian stared at the floor. She could see his thoughts churning, despite his downcast face. She interrupted those thoughts. "I'm keeping the house."

His head shot up. "What?"

"I want Tommy to pull the offer. I'm keeping the house. Not for you, but for me. I have some things I need to resolve about my family. You can't face your demons if you refuse to stay at the gates of hell, which is what I used to call Staunton coincidentally enough. On my time off from teaching I'll work on the house, work on myself, and work on my relationship with you. I love you too, Bastian. You're all I ever wanted. Whether or not we make it might be a mystery, but life's a mystery. Everyone must stand alone. I hear you call my name and it feels like home."

Bastian tilted his head and cocked up half his mouth. "Did you just quote Madonna?"

Whew…the pain meds must be kicking in.

Epilogue

Balloons coated in pink and silver glitter were tied off to anything anchored in the ground. The whole landscape reminded Kinsley of the scene in *Finding Nemo* with the underwater naval mines. The matching ribbons and tablecloths made the yard look like they had been coated in Pepto Bismol. Even Petunia had put on a pink bow for the festivities, which Jodi was currently fussing over.

"Kinsley, the man with Jodi's birthday cake is here!" Debbie called from the porch. Kinsley had finished taping down the tablecloths so the river breeze wouldn't pick them up and carry them away. She walked up the hill, past the back porch, where Bastian was busy getting the coals ready for the hot dogs. As she strolled past, he winked at her and held up four fingers...a quiet bragging right for his performance that morning.

The white van with Martha's Cakery and Candy logo painted in pink on the sides parked behind her beamer. Jodi had specifically asked for a princess themed cake with giant glitter candles shaped in the number '10' on top. She had also asked if they could hire a fairy godmother that told people's fortunes, but Kinsley told her it would be a waste of money since it was all a bunch of hokum. Mark and Linda parked their car next to her mailbox and waved. The party would be starting in thirty minutes so she was glad they arrived early. She could use the help.

The delivery driver, a skinny redhead with more freckles than Lindsay Lohan, got out of the van. "Excuse me are you Miss Harris?"

Kinsley smiled and felt a wave of content wash over her. "It's Mrs., actually."

The End

Thank you for reading! Find book two of the Summer Love Novels coming in 2017.

Please sign up for the City Owl Press newsletter for chances to win special subscriber-only contests and giveaways as well as receiving information on upcoming releases and special excerpts.

www.facebook.com/katrinamillsfanpage/

@ KatrinaM_Mills

All reviews are welcome and appreciated. Please consider leaving one on your favorite social media and book buying sites.

For books in the world of romance and speculative fiction that embody Innovation, Creativity, and Affordability, check out City Owl Press at www.cityowlpress.com.

Acknowledgements

I must start this acknowledgement by thanking all the individuals, who despite seeing that little paperclip icon indicating another handful of chapters anxiously awaiting their critiques, still opened my emails and didn't put me on a blocked senders list. Laurie, Wenda, and Kelly, I apologize and strongly suggest upping your email storage space.

To my husband and daughter, the countless hours you allowed me to lock myself in my bedroom with my laptop and disappear into my book is one of the greatest gifts you have ever given me. You supported my escape because you knew that it made me more than just a wife or a mother, it made me complete. And we all know…happy wife equals happy life.

For my family and friends, you are the rock on which I stood while trying to find the right publisher to represent my work. Your cheering and support from the sidelines gave me the determination to hold on until destiny brought me to City Owl Press and the most amazing editor, Tina Moss.

A special thank you to all of my fellow teachers out there in the educational trenches. Endless hours of planning and grading, that child who somehow obtained a doctor's note for unlimited restroom breaks (even though we see them eternally roaming the hallways), and the mornings where we can't remember if we even put on deodorant bind us together. This book is in honor of you and the wild experiences I hope you have on your well-deserved summer breaks.

And finally, for all of you…the readers. Words cannot adequately express my gratitude to you for taking a chance on reading my first novel. It is my greatest hope that you enjoyed the story I have shared with you and that our paths cross again with future stories. Hope to see you next summer!

About the Author

KATRINA MILLS resides on the Hampton Roads Peninsula of Virginia with her husband, daughter, and three fur-babies that spend their day wreaking havoc on the household. When the voices in her head aren't demanding she stop everything and write, she spends her time advocating for bully breed dogs and educating the community on animal welfare. After twenty years of dreaming about

becoming a published author, she is a firm believer that goals can be achieved with determination, passion, and belief in your desires.

www.facebook.com/katrinamillsfanpage/

About the Publisher

CITY OWL PRESS is a cutting edge indie publishing company, bringing the world of romance and speculative fiction to discerning readers.

www.cityowlpress.com

CPSIA information can be obtained at www.ICGtesting.com
Printed in the USA
LVOW11s1217130616

492378LV00001B/98/P